Kin or Country | Paul Alster

Producer & International Distributor
eBookPro Publishing
www.ebook-pro.com

Kin or Country
Paul Alster

Contact: paulealster@gmail.com
ISBN 9798663898102

Kin or Country

PAUL ALSTER

PROLOGUE

Israel, 2048 - Christianity. Islam. Judaism?

Following the death of the prophet Mohammed in 632, Islam split into the Sunni and Shia factions. Saudi Arabia is the Sunni powerhouse, while Iran is overwhelmingly the dominant force in Shia Muslim society. Sunni and Shia have fought countless, brutal wars against each other for dominance of the Islamic world. It's an ongoing, impossibly complicated conflict that to this day has a major impact on the Middle East, in particular, as well as Europe, Asia and Africa.

The Christian world split in the early 16th century as a result of the Protestant Reformation, a change that challenged the long-standing doctrine and domination of Catholicism, the Church of Rome. Catholics and Protestants fought bloody wars for dominance of the religion on a pan-European scale for nearly 400 years, viciously persecuting and killing one another. That violent hatred is more or less a thing of the past as epitomized in Northern Ireland half a century ago in the late-1990s where the terrorist bloodletting was ended by mutual agreement with the Good Friday declaration.

The Jewish people had been without a home of their own for

nearly 2000 years, until 1948. They invariably stood together, regardless of their ethnic varieties or degree of religious observance, continually facing persecution and even genocide for being different to the majority populations of the countries in which they made their homes and built communities. Now, 100 years into modern nationhood, the long-standing tensions between religious and secular, democracy and theocracy, have driven a possibly irreparable wedge between the two manifestations of Judaism in the ancient Holy Land.

Will they succeed via their own ballot box in doing to each other what the Romans, the medieval Catholic states, the Nazis and, most recently, the Arab world have failed to do; tear the Jewish nation apart - tear it apart from the inside with devastating, potentially nation-ending consequences?

One hundred years after its establishment, after surviving countless wars and becoming the predominant military power in the Middle East, having turned itself from a rural, socialist economy to a capitalist hi-tech powerhouse, Israel has seen its population grow more than fifteen-fold in just ten decades and faces its biggest and most lethal challenge yet.

Jerusalem has become a bastion of Ultra-Orthodox (Haredi) Judaism; few secular Jews remain. Seven out of ten of its adult male residents do not have full-time work, most dedicating their life, to varying degrees, to day-long religious studies. Yet the Israeli capital flourishes, shored up by massive donations from the international Jewish community, and from Evangelical Christian Zionists, many of whom hail from the United States "Bible Belt."

Together, Jerusalem and the adjacent Israeli-run West Bank, itself an area increasingly heavily populated by over a million right-wing national religious Zionist settlers, have effectively become a state within a state, dancing to a different tune to the vast majority of the rest of the country.

Tel Aviv, on the Mediterranean coast, is the polar opposite of the traditional, conservative Israeli capital. It is the de facto capital of a mainly secular Jewish population, standing at the center of Israel's hi-tech boom, flourishing with sky-high buildings and equally sky-high property prices. The cafe society of the Middle East, the majority of its high-school graduates, both male and female, still serve up to three years of often traumatic, compulsory military service in the Israel Defense Force (IDF), service from which, controversially, the Haredim have almost always been exempt.

Despite numerous attempts to bring the religious community into the mainstream fold, all efforts to change this military exemption have been resisted, sometimes violently. The Haredim justify their status by insisting that the power of prayer is more important and more powerful than any military might. Crucially, they also hold the balance of political power. Neither Israel's left- nor right-wing parties are able to form a majority coalition government without them. It is an issue that is literally tearing Israeli society apart; an issue that lies at the core of growing calls on both sides to separate from one another.

The "two Israels" are as different as could possibly be imagined, but thus far have been united under one flag for a century. Whether that unity can last another century, another decade, or indeed another year is now very much in the balance. A once-in-a-lifetime referendum has been called to decide whether or not to split the Jewish nation into two; a new Haredi-run religious State of Judea, and a slimmed-down, secular State of Israel.

And if they do separate, will it be a peaceful parting of the ways, or an all-out, bloody, Jewish civil war?

CHAPTER 1

**Holyland Television Studios, Jerusalem, Israel -
Sunday, May 3, 2048**

"Just eleven days to go to the most important decision ever made
by the Jewish people."

Quite a statement, but the country's most respected political talk
show host, Tal Barda, a man famed for his witty asides and long,
doubting looks into the camera when encountering questionable
statements made by his studio guests, wasn't joking this time. He
was deadly serious. He knew that in an era when the vast majority
of people chose to watch streaming media on a mobile device at a
time of their choosing - not when it was originally broadcast - this
event was bucking the trend.

Research published online that very morning had indicated most
Israeli adults would be watching live, such was the fevered interest
in the arguments and how the four studio guests would perform.
Another poll published that morning indicated that while 71% of
the public had already made up their mind on which way to vote,
the remaining 29% were still undecided, more than enough to

swing the decision one way or the other.

Under a law passed a few months earlier by Israel's parliament, the Knesset, a successful vote for separation required more than a simple majority. A winning margin of a single vote, or just a few thousand votes wouldn't be enough for the Yes campaign to succeed. There had to be a clear 5% margin, at least, in favor. In other words, the winning post for the separation campaign could only be reached if they achieved 52.5% of the votes cast, producing the magical 5% winning margin.

This change to the referendum law, initiated by Prime Minister Doron Gal, leader of the No campaign, only just passed a Knesset vote by 61-59. Time would tell whether that act of political foresight would prove to be the difference between success and failure for those seeking to divide Israel into two nations.

For the first time in two generations it had been decided there would be no commercial breaks in this one-hour broadcast debate, in order to ensure the best possible use of the time on offer.

This was a referendum that would change lives forever. What until recently was quite unthinkable was now a distinct possibility. This studio debate had, for the first time, brought the key figures on both sides of the argument together in one room. It had taken weeks of delicate negotiations that would have tested the patience of a saint to persuade all four to face each other in a live debate. Only when the original plan to present the program in front of a studio audience had reluctantly been shelved did the last of the four finally accede to take part. He had been uncomfortable at the thought of it turning into a slanging match of shouting, jeering and cheering in the manner of those despicable game shows, or the mind-numbing plethora of vulgar, lowest common denominator reality TV series. He wanted reasoned debate where his points would be clearly heard.

He didn't do "gladiatorial-style" politics.

"Ladies and gentlemen," Barda began, "'we are joined this evening by arguably the four most important figures in the arguments for and against the proposal for the State of Israel to separate into two nations. Placed before you in a week's time will be a decision on whether or not a new, independent state of Judea should be created."

"Judea would be a new nation governed by Talmudic religious law that adheres to the word of God. It would be ruled by a Supreme Chief Rabbi, chosen by an electoral college of rabbis, supported by all the Haredi sects as well as those religious groups falling outside of the variety of Ultra-Orthodox traditions, such as those representing the majority of settlers in the current Judea and Samaria regions, the area also known as the West Bank. It would encompass the greater Jerusalem area, with the holy city of Jerusalem - with the exception of Palestinian East Jerusalem - as its capital. It would stretch as far as Beit Shemesh in the south and include the current Judea and Samaria regions stretching across to the River Jordan. Full citizenship of Judea would be granted only to Jews. Those currently living in the new Judea hailing from other religious minorities would be welcome to stay, on the understanding they adhere to the new societal rules."

"The rest of the country would remain as the State of Israel, with Tel Aviv as its new capital. It would be governed broadly as it has been for the last 100 years. It would enshrine secular, democratic, Jewish values and continue to be home to its Jewish majority while also welcoming Christian and Muslim, Druze, Baha'i and other citizens. The new State of Israel, however, would immediately adopt a different version of proportional representation as its electoral process. The threshold for parties entering parliament would be raised from the current 3% to 8%, in a bid to ensure coalitions of large blocks and, argue its advocates, to provide government less exposed to disproportionate influence from minority, fringe parties. Any Haredim staying in this new State of Israel, or other Ultra-Orthodox Jews, would be liable to compulsory military service.

"This, essentially, is the choice before the people of Israel."

Barda looked hard and straight into the camera lens, speaking directly to all his viewers.

"A separation of states into one religious, one secular. Two states with separate passports, separate legal systems, separate tax authorities, different rules on *kashrut* (kosher observance), separate foreign policies, etcetera, etcetera. This referendum is asking one simple, but seismic question: After 100 years, is it now better for religious and secular Jews to live apart from one another, for citizens of the current State of Israel, established in 1948 in the aftermath of the Holocaust, to choose to divide their land and go their separate ways?"

Barda introduced his four studio guests:

"Prime Minister Doron Gal of the right-wing Likud Party, wishes to maintain the status quo, arguing more effort should be made to accommodate the needs of the religious majority community into the current state, and that the Jewish people would be better standing together, not splitting into two nations. He believes that, if divided, the two new countries will both be more vulnerable to attack and potential annihilation from regional enemies. 'Together we stand, divided we fall' is Gal's campaign slogan."

"Ilana Shwartz, former head of the Mossad intelligence agency, now leader of the centrist Hofshi Party. She'll argue that enough is enough, that no longer can the minority of secular and mainstream Israeli Jews afford to pay the bills of the religious majority. That no longer should only their children be drafted into an army to defend the Haredim in Jerusalem and the national religious settlers in the West Bank and its surrounds. Her party believes it would be better for all concerned to make a clean break and that the simple reality of the current Jewish demographics within the present State of Israel make it impossible for the prevailing status quo to continue."

"Chief Rabbi Akiva Bermann, leader of the largest Ashkenazi Haredi sect in Jerusalem, is the man tipped by many to be Supreme Leader of the new State of Judea, should the Yes camp win the referendum. He argues in favor of separation, of a return to the word of the Torah, of the sanctity of Jerusalem as the home of the Jewish people, against what he sees as the sordid status quo in current Israeli society. He opposes the right of women to be involved in politics; he opposes secular Judaism which he referred to recently as 'a rapidly progressing cancer of the Jewish people'; he opposes modern electronic communication, is against divorce, believes the LGBTQ community are an 'abomination', and believes strict religious observance will be the only salvation of the Jewish people."

"Our fourth speaker is Rabbi Zvi Tenenbaum. Rabbi Tenenbaum has emerged during the referendum campaign as a renegade voice on the Haredi side, arguing against separation. He argues: is it essential to bring secular Jews back to the fold? Won't Israel's enemies be licking their lips at seeing Jew pitched against Jew, sometimes within the same family? Tenenbaum argues that separation would weaken both sides, that the survival of the Jewish people through millennia has been because they have always stuck together; that there is a middle way. He insists he represents a large but until now silent minority in the Haredi world who feel that, if parted, all Jews might soon be in jeopardy. Despite his relative youth, Rabbi Tenenbaum is regarded as a world-leading Talmudic scholar."

Families across the nation gathered to view the debate. At every coffee shop, falafel stall, religious institution, police station, surf club, retiree society, and youth organization, groups of people assembled to hear the arguments for and against the division of the State of Israel. All channels were carrying the broadcast live; no other TV content was on offer.

The first twenty minutes were set aside for each of the four speakers to make their case before the nation, five minutes each, no more. They all stayed within their allotted slot. Indeed, Rabbi Bermann spoke for less than two minutes, making no other point than stating that the choice was to separate now and retain their individual ways of life, much as he regretted the fact that many Jews would remain secular. The alternative, said Bermann, was simply to stay together and wait a few more years for the Haredi majority to continue to grow at the current rate, at which point they would numerically overwhelm the rest of the country and everyone would soon have to conform to their way of life.

"As the Americans say, 'You'd only be kicking the can down the road,'" concluded Bermann.

The debate only really began to take off once they'd passed the half-hour mark. Things began to liven up when Ilana Shwartz accused Prime Minister Gal of corruption.

Shwartz said that Gal's determination "to be prime minister at all costs" had resulted in him cutting deals with coalition partners that were nothing short of bare-faced bribes. She suggested that the only reason Rabbi Bermann's right-wing Haredi political party had joined Gal's coalition was because Gal had promised, and delivered, on a pledge to transfer half of the secular education budget to religious colleges and yeshivas.

"You have raped Israel's state education system in order to

satisfy the main condition insisted upon by Bermann for shoring up your coalition," insisted the dark haired, immaculately presented Shwartz, her voice raised, her finger wagging.

"The very people who pay the taxes that keep the country afloat - namely the secular and modern Orthodox, moderately observant Jews and Arabs - are the very ones whose children now have to go without schoolbooks, whose class sizes have jumped from 30 to 50 children per teacher, and whose schools are falling into disrepair while your black and white army contribute nothing and get everything. This is only one example, among many, of how Gal has sold everything except his own mother in order to hold on to power. Israel won't stand for this corruption any longer!" she roared.

Prime Minister Gal was a smart politician, but not the best of debaters when put on the spot. His chubby face began to flush red and his forehead shone as Shwartz launched her very personal attack on Israel's embattled leader. Gal was known for his short temper. His advisors had impressed upon him the need to keep calm and appear more statesmanlike than Shwartz, a woman renowned for her powers of debate, her ready wit, and persuasive manner.

"Ilana Shwartz is trotting out her usual lines," said Gal, with a half-grin. "We've heard it all before. Left to her the entire state education budget would go solely to mainstream state schools. She would deny any funding at all of religious schools and yeshivas. To do such a thing is to deny the existence of a huge section of Israeli society, and to deny them the education that most suits their way of life. Shwartz, essentially, is peddling a racist agenda; discriminating against religious schoolchildren and students, in favor of those from a non-religious background."

"He calls me racist!" said Shwartz, voiced rising in both tone and volume. "What could be more racist than to leave behind the major part of the tax-paying public in favor of the side that is now melded to his own morally bankrupt government? He should be thoroughly ashamed of himself!"

"Gal paints himself as a man for all the people," continued Shwartz. "He has three high-profile corruption investigations pending against him, not just in relation to potential misappropriation of state funds, but also the case regarding his allegedly undisclosed foreign bank account, and the case involving the disappearance of a chunk of our Golan oil resources, mysteriously sold with an incomplete electronic trail or any definitive record of exactly who has been the beneficiary. If there were any justice or proper rule of law under this crony-ridden administration," added Shwartz, "he wouldn't even be allowed to continue as prime minister while these incredibly serious cases are being investigated. He's guilty as sin. The honest, tax-paying, army-serving public of this country want rid of his him and his ilk, and his religious paymasters."

At this, the prime minister lost his cool, forgetting all his advisors had impressed upon him about appearing more statesmanlike than his rivals.

"Shame on you! Liar!" he shouted into the face of the former spy chief. "You are in no position to make moral judgments about anyone, Mrs. Shwartz. Yours is a racist, separatist agenda that seeks to demonize religious people. Should we separate, you would force those Haredim remaining in Israel to live under a regime diametrically opposed to everything they believe in.

"Israeli society," continued Gal angrily, "has leaned more toward the religious direction in recent years as they represent the fastest-growing section of our society, but this country has not failed because of this. We have record inward investment, a flourishing hi-tech sector, massively improved tourism figures and low inflation.

These are not the signs of a country on the brink of collapse, as you characterize it!"

"Please, let's calms things down a little," said Tal Barda. "Let's maintain an appropriate tone in this debate. I should add that Mrs. Shwartz's comments are her own opinions and that, as we all know, there have been no charges brought against the prime minister - although investigations are continuing."

"If I was looking to present a case for ridding ourselves of the petty, narcissistic politics of the modern era, then I could do no better than refer the religiously observant public to the statements of the last couple of minutes," smiled Chief Rabbi Bermann. "The State of Israel, this country that has so lost its way, bears no resemblance to the vision of the traditional Jewish state as foreseen by the great rabbis and learned men of so many generations.

"I hold up my hands," said Bermann, raising his palms skyward in line with his bushy gray, slightly nicotine-stained beard. "I'm guilty of believing that the prime minister would genuinely support the religious community and allow us to play a more active role in decision-making. But he has time and again sought to keep my senior rabbis away from key ministerial roles such as welfare, and infrastructure. He might say he wants to support our yeshivas and colleges, but we need much more than he provides.

"Only if we take matters into our own hands, in our own country, with the holy city of Jerusalem as our capital, can true believers have a home to call their own; a country run according to God's laws, abiding by the principles that saw us thrive among all peoples more than 2000 years ago."

"Rabbi Tenenbaum, we haven't heard too much from you so far in this section of the debate," noted Barda. "You must have a view on what you've heard and witnessed in the last few moments?"

"I do," nodded Tenenbaum. "I'm saddened by what I've heard from each of the three previous speakers. Ilana Shwartz is indeed, as the prime minister noted a few moments ago, veering into overt racism in her demonization of both the Haredi and national religious communities. Her incendiary language gives no credit to her argument. Some might say it smacks of desperation."

"Now just a minute," cut in Shwartz, incensed at Tenenbaum's dismissive tone. "I reject everything the young rabbi has just said and resent his characterization of my campaign. I don't believe for a minute the claims he's been putting forward about the alternative, tolerant face of the Haredi world. He's come from nowhere and has more than likely been put into lull voters into thinking everything in the garden will be rosy with such as him involved in the campaign to maintain the status quo. It won't.

"What has he ever done for this country?" continued the Hofshi Party leader. "I ask you, what has he ever done? He hasn't served in the military, and I'd be very surprised if he's ever paid any taxes. I am certain he gets his monthly handouts for child allowance and other social security benefits paid for by the hard-working, mainstream Israeli society. He's a fraud. Nothing more, nothing less. If he and his argument win, the Haredim will completely take control of the agenda and overrun the government. They're outbreeding us. They will turn us into a Jewish Iran. If we don't separate now, peacefully, and by mutual agreement, I fear the only outcome will be an all-out Israeli civil war."

"Mrs. Shwartz," the debate chairman cut in immediately. "Can you clarify your last remark? Are you in any way suggesting that if the vote goes against separation you would condone violence, or even support an armed struggle to achieve the division into two states?"

The camera closed in on Shwartz, who paused for a moment. She wasn't a woman scared to speak her mind. She determined that now was the time to lay her cards slap bang on the table.

"Mr. Barda, what I am saying is this; the hard-working, tax-paying, army-serving, enterprising business community, and honest, secular and moderately religious Israelis of different denominations will not let this country slip through their fingers and become a Jewish theocracy, similar to the abomination that is the People's Republic of Iran. I've spent my adult life in the intelligence services fighting to protect the Israeli people from Iran and its proxies. I, and I believe millions like me, will be damned if we'll let Israel descend down the same slippery slope right in front of our very eyes. If we don't separate peacefully and by mutual agreement, I cannot rule out the possibility that some people might choose to take matters into their own hands and try and achieve separation by other means."

There was an uncomfortable silence.

"Rabbi Tenenbaum, you were making a point before we were diverted by Mrs. Shwartz's notable intervention. Please continue," said Barda.

"Thank you, Tal. Mrs. Shwartz, your threatening and unstatesmanlike response to my observations says so much more about you than it does about me and the Haredi community. The public are not fools," responded Tenenbaum.

"Absolutely right!" exclaimed Prime Minister Gal.

"If I may continue," asked Tenenbaum, nodding deferentially in the direction of the prime minister, "not only do Mrs. Shwartz's arguments and threats fill me with dismay, but it pains me to say my own revered Chief Rabbi's view on this issue is also disappointing. Despite allegations of corruption, of racism against religious Jews within their own country, I believe it is essential for all Jewish people to stick together, be they religious or secular. I have grown up in the Haredi world but have also engaged with mainstream society. I appreciate the value of both sets of ideals, although I believe dedication to learning Torah in the Haredi world is the ultimate commitment to God, the ultimate fulfillment for the individual, and for the soul of Jewish society.

"I call on all Israelis viewing this debate - and that includes those Christian and Muslim Arab Israelis, Druze, Bedouins, and others also taking part in the referendum - to think very carefully about the prospect of separation.

"Look where we are in 2048, one hundred years since the founding of the modern State of Israel, and just 103 years since the end of World War II and the Holocaust. Could anyone have believed in 1945 that from the ashes of the six million there would rise a democratic Jewish nation that would now be a world leader in so many fields? A country that would be able to withstand attempts by so many of its neighbors through its first 80 years to wipe it from the face of the map, but which has now achieved peace with so many of its old enemies, including the Palestinians?

"All this," reasoned Tenenbaum, "you considering jeopardizing at the risk of both potential new states being left genuinely vulnerable to any geo-political changes in this most volatile of regions. Remember, the USA no longer has our back to the extent we once knew. Israel has gone it alone, more or less, for the last twenty years - and survived. In fact, it hasn't just survived, it has thrived; thrived through a combination of hard work and enterprise, and the prayers of the religious community.

"Mr. Barda, I am a religious man. Actually, a very religious man," continued Tenenbaum. "I have my own views on what a Jew should be and how he or she should lead their daily life. But, Chief Rabbi, and with the greatest respect, I am not so conceited as to believe I have all the answers. This argument from our religious leaders that it is "My way or the highway" is against all we have believed in, and all that has held us together for so long. I am not willing to give up on so many millions of Jewish people in Israel and around the world who choose not to be as observant as us.

"I, and many like me in what is a growing, silent minority in our religious community, do not want to close the door on cooperation, education, and enlightenment for those who follow a different strand of our religion. We must stay together and not divide ourselves - for divided, I am absolutely certain, and as the prime minister has so often stated, we will fall."

"Chief Rabbi," asked Barda, "do you have any response to the points made by Rabbi Tenenbaum?"

For a few moments Bermann contemplated whether or not to respond. But eventually he did have a few words for Tenenbaum.

"Conceited? You take it upon yourself to declare that this "growing, silent minority" among Haredi and other religious Jews share your views, a populace from whom barely a word has ever been heard. Could there be anything more conceited or fantastical than your attempt to undermine your own community?

"You are a publicity seeker, Rabbi Tenenbaum, an intelligent young man who has promised so much, I grant you, but who is now reduced to peddling half-truths - some might even say *lies* - in order to further your own agenda, whatever that may be.

"If, and I very much doubt it," concluded the chief rabbi, "the referendum goes against the establishment of separate Jewish states, you will have to look to your own conscience and ask if your fantasies have played a pivotal role in undermining the case for a state of our own. God help you."

CHAPTER 2

Five days later: Jerusalem Hills, Friday, May 8, 2048

Those famous pine-clad hills around the great city of Jerusalem are disappearing fast, the ones that surprise first-time visitors to Israel who envisioned it as a parched desert. Housing projects encroach on the timeless beauty that for millennia has beguiled pilgrims and adventurers encountering this unique spot on the globe. But people have to live somewhere, and with so many people crammed into such a tiny space something has to give.

Roi and Adva Brunner have always loved these hills. Once upon a time they regularly toured this area with their three children, but the kids have grown up now and left the nest. So it's just the two of them these days, and at least once a week they fill a rucksack with salads, quiche, and four liters of water, heading off on foot to combine the physical test of the tough gradients with the inspiring majesty of views that literally take the breath away.

This particular Friday morning, after setting off early and walking for a couple of hours, they journeyed on by car to a spot rarely visited. It's difficult to park close by. Only a narrow sand track allows access to vehicles, but their jeep had no problem coping with the terrain. Guided by its robotic system they relax in the rear of the car, enjoying the scenery without distraction.

A single picnic table set back from the edge of the hill stood in splendid isolation, surrounded by pale gray boulders and pine trees circled at the base of their trunks by crisp, dry, aromatic needles. The silence is deafening in a land where noise is almost impossible to escape. Clear baby blue skies, a golden sun, a light breeze. Despite it all, the world can be a special place when it wants to be.

After a strenuous walk it had been Roi's idea to return to this old haunt, a place known only to the few locals scattered around the area, and those, like them, who take hiking seriously.

They'd been in earnest conversation throughout the morning discussing the referendum in just six days' time. Virtually everyone in the country had strong views one way or the other on the subject. It had dominated the headlines for months. Nothing else really mattered.

Roi decided weeks earlier that he would vote No to separation, but Adva hadn't made up her mind yet. She was more inclined to vote Yes. They argued the points back and forth, then she told him she didn't want to discuss it anymore as she was having a great time on their walk. But then he pointed out they wouldn't be able to walk there any more if the Yes vote won, because this stretch of forest connected Jerusalem with Beit Shemesh, a majority Haredi town; the only major town outside of Jerusalem and the West Bank that was to be included as part of the separation deal for the new Judea.

She hadn't appreciated it would be not only Beit Shemesh that would be handed over to Judea, but the whole swathe of land that linked it to Jerusalem. It included much of the Jerusalem forest and smaller towns such as the modern residential area of Tsur

Hadassah, the ancient Ein Kerem, home of John the Baptist, and all the villages and kibbutzim dotted in between.

She was dismayed at the thought of losing such a beautiful area and the unimaginable upheaval it would cause to the communities there, but insisted it would be a bigger disaster if the status quo remained. To do nothing, she said, would ensure that the whole of Israel would become a Haredi-dominated nation within a decade or so. She stressed the numbers just didn't favor those, like them, who led a mainly non-religious lifestyle.

"Would you want that Chief Rabbi Bermann as our prime minister?" she asked. "I don't think so. And why should we send our sons and daughters into the army to protect them when they don't even recognize us as proper Jews 'cos we don't go around all covered up and breed like rabbits? You're making it out to be a cut and dried decision to stay together, but after watching last week's debate I'm inclined to vote Yes and go our separate ways."

"If we separate, we've all had it," he sighed. "The Arabs will very conveniently forget how much they hate each other to focus on us for a while. They're probably on standby right now, ready to march in and take over the new Judea, then they'll be breathing right down our necks. What a fucking mess!"

She told him not to swear, then began setting out lunch as he headed away into the bushes to take a leak. He was in full flow when he noticed something out of place a few meters ahead in the undergrowth, but couldn't make it out. Zipping himself up, he moved closer. It looked as though something had been dumped there, covered by a dark green overcoat that blended in well among the foliage. Strange.

He reached the pile then stopped abruptly. Birds chirped in the branches overhanging the pile, but flies buzzed around the coat in numbers. Wide-eyed, he pushed the coat and its contents with his foot and gasped as it fell away revealing pale human skin, an adult male body, face down, completely naked.

"Oh my God! Adva, come here!"

She dropped everything on hearing the unbridled horror in his voice, and rushed over.

"What the hell's going on?" she shouted, then, abruptly, she too stopped still as she saw what had so shocked her husband.

An experienced cardiac nurse, she was far less squeamish than him. Grabbing a stout, gnarled stick laying close by, she forced the body over. Now it was her turn to cry out in horror. The blonde young man's face was horrendously disfigured. His teeth had been smashed out; his hands had been hacked off.

It was an awful, stomach-churning sight.

***

The police cordon began at the point where the single-track dirt path left the sealed road. It was around two hundred meters to the picnic bench and lookout point, close to which the body had been found.

CHAPTER 3

The modern world has a dizzying array of labor-saving devices, but unless you want a robot under your feet 24 hours a day most chores remain the same as fifty years earlier. When young kids make a big mess, someone has to tidy it up. Hila Sonfeld has got used to picking up after her boisterous three and six-year-old boys every morning.

That comes after her 'me time', fifteen minutes when she returns to a quiet house, pours herself a cup of coffee, and sits back to listen to the news headlines. "Israel news", she declares, and her voice recognition system (VRS) dutifully reads her the latest headlines. It's rare that anyone actually reads anything themselves anymore. Print media finally turned up its toes around 2030, and even the Internet is old hat these days. Why sit and scan for information or read articles or social media posts when your VRS can read it all to you?

Thirty-three years old, married to Ed, a fairly large cog in the big wheel of the opposition Hofshi Party, hers appears the bog-standard, old fashioned life of housewife and mother. To a great extent it is, and it's everything she dreamed of as she grew up in a very different world.

Wearing jeans, a T-shirt, and open-toed sandals, it's hard to imagine her previous life in the Haredi world, a world where modesty is the only policy. Little has really changed since the 18th and 19th centuries in the Haredi community when the Jewish sect began in Eastern Europe, in the area for many years known as the Baltic States. It's a region that for more than 20 years has been just another part of the resurrected and overwhelmingly powerful Russian Union.

One of fourteen children born to Baruch and Yoheved Tenenbaum, Hila was 13th on the scene. Contrary to Christian superstition, many Jews consider 13 a lucky number; she still hasn't decided one way or the other. Only Zvi, her youngest brother, came after her. By the time Zvi was born, her oldest sister, Ruth, was married and already mother to a newborn baby boy when her own final sibling arrived. Another blessing from God.

Hila's father, like most of his contemporaries, spent long days studying at the yeshiva seminary, trying to understand and passionately debate the intricate messages of the Torah and Talmud; the ancient Jewish scriptures that have guided the world's oldest major religion for thousands of years.

With fourteen children, Hila's mother rarely had a moment to herself. As was usual for the majority of wives of Haredi scholars and students, for many years she also went to work each day - having a part-time, six-hour job as a bookkeeper - to help support the bursary provided by the state to her husband. Hila had been in awe of her mother's ability to manage the house, care for her horde of children, and hold down a job at the same time. Her father left home before six o'clock each morning for dawn prayers, and would often return only after sunset, which in the summer months would be around nine o'clock in the evening.

By that point, those children still living at home - Ruth was married, and some of the older boys had been sent off to board at yeshivas around Jerusalem, others as far away as the ancient city of Tzfat in the north - were already in bed. They lived on, or near the edge of poverty, in perpetuity. Her father insisted they were following God's will so this, their often-dire financial state, was meant to be.

"When we become the majority in this land - which won't be too much longer," her father would often say, "we'll return this country to what it should be; a place where the word of God rules, and not the word of the US dollar, the cannabis cookies, corrupt politicians, or gung-ho army generals. It's the only way we Jews will ever return to our truth path."

His statements were a legitimate point of view but hid the fact that Hila's father overlooked major flaws in his own society, and in particular, in his own behavior. For as long as she could remember he would come to her bedroom in the middle of the night, a room she shared with four of her sisters. He would move from bed to bed to cuddle, then caress them, telling them how beautiful they were, and how much he loved them. In her case it went no further than that; she was uncertain that was the case with some of the other girls. They never spoke about it.

The girls hated him but had nowhere to turn. When on one occasion one of her older sisters tried to discuss her father's actions with their mother, she received a firm slap to the face and was told she "had a filthy mind and must never talk like that again."

Their community was a closed society. They rarely went outside the confines of their enclave. It was a world within a world. The men dressed in the black suits and large black hats that served them so well in the harsh Lithuanian climate hundreds of years earlier. Some still wore heavy coats and fur-trimmed hats even though temperatures could hit 100 degrees and more in high summer.

Women above the age of 17 had to wear a wig to hide their hair for modesty reasons, even those that were not married. Until a few years earlier hair covering had been demanded only of married women, but that had changed as the community battened down the hatches and became increasingly zealous in its determination not to allow anything to distract its followers from serving God. No flesh could be shown. Not an ankle, not an elbow. They wore skirts of at least knee-length, under which thick woolen stockings were obligatory, even in the summer heat.

Despite the paucity of fully employed Haredi men - religious study was considered far more worthy - the community managed to provide for almost all the basic needs of its members. There were many good, decent people among this secretive sect, people who were loving and caring, selfless, witty, and generous. Somehow there were always sufficient funds to ensure life went on without having to live in unmanageable debt, but it wasn't easy, particularly for the women.

No one starved though. There were clothes banks that distributed garments to those in need, and they shared Sabbath dinners on Friday evenings, enjoying one another's company. Few, if any old people were lonely. Old timers would always be invited to dine with one family or another if they had none of their own around them. And on the festivals there was a feverish buzz of excitement as the community came together as one to celebrate days like Rosh Hashanah (Jewish New Year), or Chanukah (the Festival of Lights), or to mourn on days like Yom Kippur (the Day of Atonement).

The sect answers to their reclusive leader, Rabbi Mintz, a man in his eighties whose word, for his followers, is the closest thing to that of God himself. All issues are decided by him and his circle of advisors, who include the Chief Rabbi, be they legal, moral, political, or anything else. If the rabbi says you must vote for a specific political party, then that was what all 100,000 or more followers must do. And invariably they did, without question.

When there were crimes in the community, the police or civilian authorities were rarely, if ever informed. To go outside of the community was a bigger crime than the crime itself - even if you had been raped. You couldn't trust the civilian authorities; the Haredi masses had always been told. The secular Israeli media would report the incident on their television and social media channels, painting all Haredim as criminal or perverted. The Haredi authorities would deal with miscreants themselves, in their own way.

Anyone who questioned the word of the rabbi and his teachings was given intensive "re-education" to purify their mind, expelling any thoughts of stepping outside the circle into the wider world. Those rare few who decided to leave the fold were never heard of again. Families would say the kaddish prayer (the prayer for the dead), and that person's name was henceforth never mentioned. It was as if they had never existed.

The year was 2032, Hila Tenenbaum was 17, and conversations were already at an advanced stage for her arranged marriage to an older man in his late 20s who she had met only once - a Talmudic scholar, of course. Only a couple of years earlier the Haredi block in the Knesset had forced through legislation lowering the legal age of marriage to 17, from 18, a move designed to further expedite the growth in their community.

When she pleaded with her mother to intervene and stop the marriage her cries fell on deaf ears. Her objection to this age-old tradition - one to which her older siblings had not objected, and that resulted in a host of apparently happy and fruitful unions - only served to anger her parents. 15-year-old Zvi was the only one to quietly support Hila in her quest to have the arranged marriage taken off the table.

He suggested that a postponement would be of no harm to either party, his own family, or the family of his sister's selected suitor. He also proposed that the two be allowed to meet a few more times prior to the agreement in order to "settle his sister's nerves." Already looked upon as a young guru figure whose words were worthy of great consideration, on this occasion his father ordered him away from the discussion.

Baruch, father of Zvi, Hila, and the other twelve, was the brooding head of the household but worshiped the ground on which his youngest son walked. He wasn't ready yet though to be guided on family matters by his baby boy. Compromise wasn't an option.

Despite the overwhelming impact of digital communication and artificial intelligence in the world of 2048, this powerful Haredi sect had decades earlier been ordered to never use any kind of mobile communication device, the Internet, or any voice activated technology. Anyone caught with such devices was brought in for questioning and robustly persuaded not to use such a thing again. They risked potential expulsion from the community.

The day before the arranged marriage was to be finalized (and a month before the wedding itself), Hila confided in Zvi that she wasn't going to allow this to happen. He was shocked, but not totally surprised. He appreciated his sister's trauma. He'd noticed how depressed and anxious she had appeared of late and empathized with her opposition to the marriage. He offered to help. His intellect had brought him to the attention of Rabbi Mintz himself, who agreed some months earlier that the boy's talent would be further developed if he studied under another great rabbi with whom the community had good relations.

Rabbi Nusbaum lived just outside the walled community, and twice a week Zvi would go, with the blessing of Mintz and his advisors, to discuss Torah and Talmud and questions of religious significance with the venerable sage.

Zvi agreed with Hila that, regrettably, the only way to stop the marriage would be for her to leave the community. The pair secretly and seriously discussed the option. Fearful though she was of the outside world, shocked at the thought of leaving behind everything she knew, her girlfriends, her mother, and her many siblings, Hila had no doubt she would be better served outside, rather than inside the community. She could not go through with this marriage.

With no time to spare, her young brother suggested he could find a contact outside who would help her start anew. Later that day, on his way to Rabbi Nusbaum's, he diverted into one of the main thoroughfares adjacent to Jerusalem's King George Street. Walking into a synagogue frequented by mainstream religious Jews rather than the Haredim, he encountered curious looks from worshippers as he asked one of the elders if he could make a private call using their VRS.

Welcomed by the synagogue secretary, he was discreetly ushered into an office, without question. The secretary appreciated that seeing a young man from such a sect in these unfamiliar surroundings meant he needed some kind of help.

"Because it won't recognize your voice, you need to override the system by punching in this access code," the secretary explained.

He handed Zvi a piece of paper and pointed to a set of numbered keys on the side of the VRS, not unlike the now defunct credit card PIN machines. When the secretary left the room, he entered the code, said a prayer that he would be granted the strength to succeed in this mission, and proceeded with the task in hand. The clean-cut teenage boy in the wide brimmed black hat knew enough about VRS to operate the system and more-or-less understood how it worked. He asked it to place a call to an organization called Ahutza (the Hebrew word for "outside"), a charity that helped religious Jews leave their communities and make a fresh start in the secular world.

"Ahutza. How can we help?"

"I'm a Haredi from Jerusalem and my older sister is in big trouble. She needs help very fast."

"Is she injured?" asked a clear-spoken, deep male voice.

"No."

"Is her life in danger?"

"Well, it might be," whispered Zvi. "She's being forced into a marriage she doesn't want, and the engagement is planned for tomorrow night. She prefers to leave the community rather than go through with it."

"OK. And you say you are her younger brother? How old are you, and how old is she?"

"I'm 15. She is 17."

"So, if you're helping her, do you also want assistance to leave the community?"

"Oh no, I don't. I've no intention of leaving. This is about my sister, not me."

"OK. Does she understand that if she leaves, let's say tomorrow morning, she'll be cutting herself off completely from you and the rest of the family? It's very important she understands this. It can be hugely traumatic to lose all contact with family and community. It's not dissimilar to bereavement."

"I love my sister. It will be hard for me and the others not having her here, but I can't bear to see her so desperate."

"Do you understand it will be very difficult for you to see her for the foreseeable future? It's not impossible you may never see each other again."

Those words hit him where it hurts.

"Young man, are you still with me?"

"Yes," came the faint response, soon repeated more forcefully, "yes."

"OK, just tell me your sister's first name only?"

"Hila."

"OK, this is what we'll do. I assume this is not your VRS, am I right?"

"Yes."

"And am I correct in assuming you have no audio recording facility?"

"That's correct."

"OK. You must not write this down, do you understand? You must not write this down. We can't afford these details falling into the wrong hands."

The man instructed Zvi to tell Hila to make her way to the corner of Geller and Jabotinsky Streets in Jerusalem at 12 noon the following day where a young woman, wearing a red headscarf would be waiting for her in the doorway of the Zenith hardware store. She would then be driven to a safe house where she'd receive all the support needed to start a new life outside the community.

"One final thing," he concluded. "If she changes her mind, will you try and let us know. If we don't hear from you or her then we'll expect to see her at 12 noon tomorrow outside Zenith."

In other circumstances, in other organizations, in other parts of the world, the man from Ahutza would probably have taken time to verify the situation and check there was nothing untoward about the request, but experience told him time was absolutely of the essence and this case had to be dealt with as a matter of urgency.

The following day, as instructed, and without saying goodbye or giving even a hint of what she was about to do to anyone other than her younger brother, Hila was ready to go.

She took a small handbag with her in which she had a corn dolly her mother had given her as a small child, some photos of the family, and a prayer book. She handed Zvi a letter to pass on to their parents and suggested he tell them he found it on his bed after she had gone. She and Zvi had always been closest among the fourteen. She hugged him, something usually deemed inappropriate in their community for siblings of their age. She would miss him so much. He gave her a letter of his own to read at another time.

With no personal belongings other than the clothes on her back and the contents of her small handbag, Hila Tenenbaum strode purposefully through the streets of Mea Shearim close to her home that had been her whole world. Acting as if this was just another day, she acknowledged a couple of former school friends coming the other way, then simply turned the corner of the main street of the enclave, walked the two hundred yards or so to the corner of Geller and Jabotinsky, and saw, as promised, a young woman with a red headscarf standing in the Zenith shop doorway.

Thirty meters from her target she stopped, wracked with second thoughts. How could she leave her mother behind? What about Zvi, her other lovely sisters and brothers, and her friends? How would she manage in the outside world with no money, no friends, no home?

But then again, she couldn't allow herself to be married off to a man she barely knew, a man that her father, "that awful man," had personally chosen for her. There had to be more to life than being a teenage mother, going on to have ten or more children, even if it was God's work.

She took a deep breath. Outwardly calm, but churning furiously inside, she approached the young woman in the headscarf, a woman just a few years older than herself.

"Shalom. I'm Hila," she said.

"Shalom Hila," smiled the stranger. "It's going to be OK. I promise."

She nodded towards a white car parked a few meters away. The engine was running. The two hurried inside and the car moved quickly away into the flow of traffic heading out of Jerusalem in the direction of Tel Aviv on the Mediterranean coast, just over 40 miles away. She'd done it. She was away and gone, but now she had to take further courage and try to build a whole new life for herself without the family and friends that had always been the mainstay of her existence.

Back in Jerusalem, after reading the letter she left with Zvi, a furious Baruch Tenenbaum swiftly arranged for the kaddish prayer for the dead to be said that very evening for his daughter - the same evening she had been due to become engaged. It was attended by hundreds of mourners offering their sincere sympathies to her parents at the sudden loss of their fine young girl.

Hila's mother, Yoheved, was inconsolable.

CHAPTER 4

Just over forty miles from home, but she was seeing the Mediterranean for the very first time.

They arrived at a non-descript apartment close to Hayarkon Street in central Tel Aviv and stepped out of the car. Her senses were so utterly confused. On one hand she was already mourning her lost family and the only way of life she had ever known; and on the other she experienced a wave of excitement at having made the break, escaping a fate that would surely have stifled her and made life thoroughly miserable. This was the start of a new and completely different existence.

Across the main road the beach shimmered in the summer heat and the vast expanse of ocean glistened a piercing blue. Gentle waves rolled toward the shore capped by small, frothy white peaks. It was mesmerizing and seemed to go on forever, and the air so close to the sea smelled quite different to the city air of Jerusalem. Tel Aviv's haphazard buildings were less appealing though, and the high-rise hotels far less attractive than the famously beautiful Jerusalem stone facades of the acclaimed architecture in the Holy City. Not that she had seen much of that either. Her enclave had been run down, unkempt, and, in hindsight, somewhat depressing. Yet it was something that hadn't dawned on her for the 17 years she called it home.

She marveled at people, young and old, in short trousers. Some of the men closer to the beach were bare-chested, and some of the girls accompanying them wore skimpy swimming costumes. She could hardly believe what she was seeing. So much flesh! It was overwhelming, trying to take it all in, to understand that she too was now free to enter this completely new, uninhibited world. Where do you begin?

A simple but comfortable room at the apartment had been prepared for her, along with some money to get started and new clothes, including a first pair of jeans. Ahutza was funded by Israelis who understood how hard it could be to begin a completely new life in a world full of strangers, amid what at first would inevitably feel an alien society.

She had never worn trousers before; they felt inhibiting when compared to her flee-flowing skirts. She had never worn a patterned T-shirt before but adjusted surprisingly quickly to her new look in the days following her flight from Jerusalem. Other aspects of her new life would take much longer to come to terms with.

Sivan, the young woman in the red headscarf who met and rescued her, was a fun-loving, gentle person. She too had made the daunting move from Haredi society to the outside world, some four years earlier. She knew exactly what Hila was going through during those first astonishing days in Tel Aviv.

Sivan recognized the young woman's incredulity at this very different existence. She remembered how she had been unable, and indeed unwilling to give up her prayers for a long time after leaving her past behind, despite all she had been through. The guilt at deserting her family; the fear of the unknown; the wondering, "What happens next?"

***

Two years later, Hila graduated from basic training in the army. She had been drafted as a lone soldier; a soldier without a family to support her, much admired by her female colleagues, all of whom were serving their own compulsory two-year terms. The Israeli army draft, established at the foundation of the state and now more than 86 years old, was still restricted to mainly secular or moderately religious young men and women. Some religious girls, not Haredi though, did enlist nowadays, but mainly in national service, commendably working within their own communities in hospitals, old age homes, youth centers, specialist schools and the like.

Unrecognizable as the teenage Haredi girl who fled her home and close-knit society in 2032, Hila was selected after basic training for a job in military intelligence. A bright young woman, she had soon grasped the advanced technology that accompanied her new life and melded it with study skills learned during her formative years of religious application. She was tasked with monitoring movements of potential radical Islamic infiltrators (mainly connected to Iran) on Israel's northern border.

A year later, at her army camp in the Upper Galilee, a young American-born soldier raised in Israel from the age of four, arrived at the base. Ed Sonfeld was a 20-year-old lieutenant in the intelligence corps. He and Hila struck up a friendship that soon blossomed during their time in the north.

Discharged from the military within a couple of weeks of each other, Ed and Hila went traveling for six months with a group of friends, spending most of their time, as so many Israeli ex-soldiers do, in India, the destination of choice for young twenty-somethings looking to leave behind all they had experienced, good and bad, in the previous years of military service.

He proposed to her during their last week there, on the balcony of a hotel in Dharamshala that had a view of the Himalayas as a backdrop. They were married a few years later at the kibbutz, not far from Tel Aviv, where he had grown up.

In the age-old tradition of kibbutz weddings, an ancient 1970s tractor was used to convey them at sunset through the guests to the chuppah, the canopy under which a clean-shaven rabbi married Hila and Ed. The year was 2038. His family and friends traveled from different corners of the globe to be there for the big occasion. There were, of course, no relatives from Hila's side at the celebration. Sivan, she of the red headscarf, had become Hila's closest friend and gave away the blue-eyed, blonde bride.

Two kids and ten years later, Hila worked part-time from home for a cyber security company. Ed worked long days at the Hofshi Party headquarters. Times were exciting and challenging in equal proportions. The May 14, 2048 referendum was closing in fast. Ed had been tasked along with another three senior colleagues, with preparing all materials promoting his party and its vision for two separate states in what had until now been the unified State of Israel.

***

When David Ben Gurion, the founding father of modern Israel, made his famous declaration in late-1947, announcing the arrival of the new nation, it caused shockwaves around the world. Ben Gurion offered to share the country with its Arab inhabitants, but local Arabs in what was then the British Mandate of Palestine were encouraged by adjacent Arab nations to reject the offer, which many did.

It was a different world, a time when there was immense sympathy for the Jewish people and collective guilt on the part of the European and North American governments that had done precious little to save the Jewish communities of Europe from the Holocaust during which some six million Jews were brutally murdered.

The State of Israel, a return home for the Jewish people whose forefathers had inhabited, developed and thrived in the ancient Land of Israel so many years before, was officially recognized by the United Nations on May 14, 1948.

Just 24 hours later, surrounding Arab countries, including Egypt, Syria, Jordan and Iraq, declared war on the new nation. That Israel won this first fight for its survival was seen by many as a modern-day miracle, but not those Arabs who, in order to let the massed Arab armies move in and in anticipation of the annihilation of the Jews and their new nation, had "temporarily" vacated their homes on the advice of neighboring Arab governments. They had absolutely been assured of victory.

The local Arabs expected to return and carry on where they left off after the job of wiping out the Jews had been done, but for hundreds of thousands that simply didn't happen. They had been handed false hope of an Arab victory, and while the armies of the neighboring Arab nations returned defeated across the borders to their respective homes, the Arabs of the now former mandated Palestine were left with nowhere to call their own.

Temporary refugee camps became permanent homes in Lebanon, Syria and Jordan. The very countries that urged them to get out of the new State of Israel, leave the way clear while they wiped out the Jews, perversely and steadfastly refused to acknowledge that the Palestinian predicament was a result of their own inept military and false promises in what became known by the Arabs as the Nakba (the disaster).

Adding insult to injury, with the exception of Jordan, many Palestinians were refused full citizenship by their Arab brethren after seeking sanctuary in these neighboring Arab lands. They were left to live in squalor and without hope for more than 80 years.

Used as political pawns, incited to commit terrorist acts, misled, abused and ripped off by their own Palestinian leadership, the Arab world eventually caved in to international pressure in 2037, finally granting citizenship to all Palestinians and their descendants who had been kept in what were called "Palestinian refugee camps," but which were, in reality, seething cement cities of poverty and deprivation.

It was no coincidence that this offer of citizenship only came *after* Israel and the Palestinians reached a peace agreement the previous year that included dividing the West Bank and Jerusalem; East Jerusalem, always a hotbed of anti-Israeli feeling and still overwhelmingly Arab, became the capital of the new State of Palestine, a decision that caused uproar among many Jewish Israelis and some Jews around the world. The rest of Jerusalem remained the capital of Israel.

The Palestinians in Gaza, whose terrorist leadership had for so long ruled out any chance of peace with Israel, also signed the peace deal. Within days Gazans were offered a new life in other Arab nations, many moving to the conservative Muslim state of Turkey in the post-Erdogan era. Almost all took up the offer, packed their bags and moved out of the hellhole that was the Gaza Strip. Those that stayed behind did so in the knowledge that the coastal enclave would no longer be governed by Hamas but would be a "special administrative region of the United Nations, assisted logistically by the State of Israel and Egypt."

With the Israeli-Palestinian issue more or less resolved, Israeli society should have been able to breathe a sigh of relief and build an easier, more prosperous future. But instead of grasping the opportunity, it turned inward on itself as the simmering fissures between the rapidly growing Ultra-Orthodox community and the rest of the nation burst to the fore at the 2040 elections. At those elections the Haredi parties took 36% of the seats in the Knesset - made up of Haredim from both the Ashkenazi (European) and Sephardic (Middle East and African) traditions. They overwhelmingly held the balance of power.

Producing an average of more than eight children per family, as opposed to the 3.2 of the modern religiously observant Jews, and the 2.6 average of the secular Jewish Israelis, Israeli Arabs, and Druze, the demographic game was rapidly being won by the Haredi religious block.

Doron Gal, of the right-wing Likud Party became prime minister despite his party receiving just 20% of the votes. The Haredi parties wanted power to bring their vision of an Ultra-Orthodox Israeli society into being, but at this stage they hadn't wanted to be the figurehead. They persuaded Gal to take the premiership, but held most of the levers of power: the finance ministry, social security, transport, education, and communications ministries, among others.

Gal's government passed draconian measures that took Israel on a rapid route toward theocracy. The rabbinical council definitively decided who could be married as Jews and who didn't meet their strict religious criteria - it meant a great many non-religious Jews wishing to marry in Israel, their own country, in a traditional Jewish ceremony, often had insurmountable obstacles placed in their path.

There was no public transport anywhere in the country from two hours before the Sabbath began at Friday sunset, to one hour after it ended on Saturday night; in all areas more than half a kilometer from the beach there were modesty laws in which women had to be covered up or face prosecution.

The arts became heavily censored and many films or productions that would a decade earlier have been presented without a thought were banned on the grounds of "decency and morality." It had been declared illegal for Israeli radio stations to broadcast female vocal performances as these were prohibited within the religious Jewish community; the education curriculum had been drastically changed with religious studies now making up nearly half the lessons at the expense of mathematics, English, and science. Darwin's Theory of Evolution, amid huge uproar, was banned from the school curriculum, the Haredi education minister arguing it contradicted the Torah's account of how man was created by God.

Yet the very institutions that ensured the survival of Israel - its army and security services - were still primarily staffed by secular or moderately religious Jews, and Druze, along with national religious settlers from the West Bank.

A law forced through the Knesset made it illegal for Haredim to serve in the military or security forces, even though there had been intermittent spells from the turn of the century through to the 2020s when a relatively small number had answered the draft and become highly competent soldiers and officers. These male Haredi soldiers were often taunted in the street when they returned to their communities. Some were spat on and, in some cases, were beaten up. Eventually, the situation became so polarized that one 19-year-old Haredi soldier returning on weekend leave was set upon by a Haredi crowd and beaten so badly he died in hospital of his wounds the following day.

This furious and ultimately violent opposition to the relative few who chose to serve came as a result of the rabbinical council's growing concern that Haredi soldiers were leaving the community after experiencing something of life outside of the Haredi bubble. The rabbinical council considered the loss of around 10% of the small number drafted to be absolutely unacceptable. Using incendiary language to fuel the crowds into intimidating the Haredi soldiers, they succeeded in making the situation untenable for most. Using their fast-growing political power, they soon ensured it was made illegal to draft any more Haredim to military service.

The Haredi draft exemption had first been instituted by David Ben Gurion in 1949, but that amounted to just a few hundred post-Holocaust Haredi yeshiva seminary students. They were granted the exemption after their religious leaders reasoned that their numbers had been so decimated that to lose any more might place these keepers of the religion in jeopardy.

Ben Gurion had expected the Haredim to find their place in mainstream modern Israeli society, but that never came to pass. He could never have foreseen that the initial tiny exemption of 400 or so would grow into millions just one hundred years later.

The biggest gripe on the part of mainstream citizens who worked long hours and paid high taxes was that the Haredim cut a deal in order to shore up the Gal government that saw funds for those studying at yeshivas double overnight. Payments for child allowance were increased by 50%, meaning a much larger share of the nation's finances was going towards funding religious studies for people who didn't work and who had vastly larger families than their non-religious counterparts.

Prior to the 2044 general election, the Hofshi Party was founded on a platform of no longer funding the religious communities. Even more radically, it sought to break away from them and form separate states within Israel's current borders, something that until a few years before had been considered sheer lunacy. Hofshi proposed that Jerusalem and the Israeli-controlled area of the West Bank, already overwhelmingly populated with Haredi and national religious Zionists - not always the most comfortable of partners - become one religious state and run its own affairs. The rest of the country, still majority secular or moderately religious, would continue as the State of Israel.

This platform, at first mocked by the governing Likud Party and Haredi politicians, began to gain serious traction during the bitter election campaign in the spring of 2044. When two center parties and one left-wing party agreed to stand on the same ticket as Hofshi (endorsing the idea of a split from the religious communities that was proving increasingly popular with the secular electorate), alarm bells began to ring at the top of Israel's political echelons.

But even the parties who supported Hofshi had massive reservations about conceding the great city of Jerusalem and declaring Tel Aviv as the capital of a new, honed-down Israeli state. So many Israelis over the last nine decades and more had fought and died to first liberate, then protect Jerusalem. Now they were going to give it away? That was a discussion that would take place further down the line.

The 2044 elections saw the Haredi parties gain a massive 42% of the Jewish vote, a six percent increase that more or less mirrored their growth in voter numbers since 2040. Doron Gal was again installed as prime minister. Hofshi polled 29%, an astonishing mandate for a completely new party. The Likud slumped to 9% as the electorate viewed them as merely a plaything of the Haredim and a party without a clear view on the Jewish two-state debate. The remaining votes were divided among a variety of smaller parties from both the left and right. Arab parties took 10% of the overall vote.

There was never a chance that Hofshi would sit with the Haredi parties in a coalition, so once again Likud proved the savior of the religious parties. Together they formed a right-wing government, creating a slim but workable majority despite a number within Likud's own ranks suggesting it was unwise to do so. They suggested the party should instead consider joining forces with Hofshi.

In the four years leading up to 2048, income tax rates were raised a crippling 5%, more religious legislation made its way onto the statute books, and a Haredi rabbi had been elected as head of Israel's supreme court. The situation was becoming untenable. When a number of his own Likud parliamentarians ignored the prime minister's urgings and decided to support a bill proposed by Hofshi that called for a referendum on separating into two states, the ground was laid for a bitter campaign that would ultimately lead to a referendum. Decision day would be May 14, 2048 - the 100th anniversary of the establishment of the State of Israel.

With a month of campaigning left, Hofshi reached out to smaller parties to join forces. The old Labor Party that governed Israel for the first thirty years of its existence was now a shadow of its former self but still had four MKs; Haderech, a centrist party, held three seats, while the One Israel party, a moderate right-wing entity also had three seats and signaled that its supporters may reluctantly be prepared to adopt the Hofshi idea of two states for two Jewish peoples.

Shas, the Haredi Party that represented Middle Eastern Jews whose great-grandparents hailed primarily from North African countries and from Iraq and Iran prior to being driven out of their homes in the late 1940s and 1950s, was the one party whose direction on separation was hard to predict.

Shas had been formed in the 1980s by the Sephardic Chief Rabbi, reflecting a feeling that Haredi politics of the time was run and dominated by Ashkenazi Jews (of mainly Eastern European origins) who tailored Haredi politics to suit their particular needs. Like the Ashkenazi Haredim, the Sephardic Haredim had their own yeshivas. There was little love lost between the two Haredi communities.

Against this background of searing religious and social turmoil combined with a lack of trust in most politicians and a deterioration in societal cohesion, the ultimate irony was not lost on the Israeli electorate; what the Arabs had failed to do in the previous hundred years, the Jews now appeared to be on the threshold of willingly doing to themselves via their own ballot box.

CHAPTER 5

Montana, USA - A cloud of dust swirled high into the air as the six horsemen cantered across the parched land. You could easily be mistaken for thinking this was an opening scene from a 1950s John Wayne movie, but the bond between man and horse would always be unbreakable.

Cowboy hats and boots were still obligatory, along with colorful denim shirts, jeans, and spurs. They rode against a backdrop of panoramic plains fringed by high, jagged mountains. It was as if time had stood still. There were no signs of any human settlement across this grand vista.

Reverend Larry Turner always took time out to ride and clear his mind when the dual pressures of his ministry and political career began to get to him. He never went anywhere without his security detail, so those assigned to the Republican presidential candidate had to be capable horsemen. They also needed to know how to handle a weapon to secure a man loved by many in America and hated with an equal passion by others.

The United States of 2048 was a country of massive racial and religious diversity. It was a country that despite losing some of its international clout following the Trump years of the late 2010s and early 2020s remained, along with the reunited Russian Union and China, one of the three great superpowers. Now, there was a real prospect of a religious preacher ascending to the highest office of state. Turner, like so many of the great American Christian preachers had powerful friends, a devoted fan base, and great charisma; he had charisma in spades.

As a young boy Turner watched his father preaching to their Evangelist congregation and filled with pride and admiration as he watched him inspire his followers with soaring speeches proclaiming the values of human decency, hard work, and the love of God. All Larry Turner ever wanted to be was a preacher in his father's image. He took up his own ministry as early as his mid-20s, having shone at university where he graduated in law and international relations.

He marveled at how President Donald Trump had been able to speak to the common man, the Midwest Americans left behind in previous decades who felt excluded from the political debate. He saw how the controversial billionaire had persuaded factory workers, farmers, and so many more across America's vast "Bible Belt" and beyond that he was one of them and stood for their values. Nothing, of course, could have been further from the truth, but Trump, the great communicator, mocked and lauded in equal measure as he polarized his nation, had ascended to the most powerful seat in the world.

Trump's presidency and the Democratic and Republican presidencies that followed, left the American public despondent and disillusioned with traditional US politics; only 47% bothered to vote at the last election. They'd been let down by them all, both on the right and the left of the political scene. Established as the rising young star of the Christian Evangelical world, Turner had already become rich through the flood of donations to his ministry and commanded almost fanatical support from his followers.

The preacher's appeal even crossed over to Democrats and Republicans living on both the east and west coasts who did not believe in God. He was careful not to ram religion down the throat of the electorate, saving his preaching of the love of Jesus Christ and the prospect of the return to Zion for the pulpit. Many believed him capable of taking the United States back to basics; respect for authority, family values, restoring healthcare for the masses, reaching out around the world to help those less fortunate, and pleading tolerance for those holding different political opinions.

The boom and bust of Trump and his successors had left the masses searching for something new. To many Turner seemed to offer that new way forward, ironically by turning back the clock to the "good old days."

He was no stranger to the corridors of power. The fifty-four-year-old had long since found doors opening for him around the globe, especially in Christian countries. There were far less invitations from the Arab and Muslim world where his dedication to Christ was viewed with suspicion, despite Jesus being a significant prophet in Islam.

But it was in Israel that Turner was especially well received. His foundations donated vast sums of money to projects there, both in the secular and religious communities, and the Turner name, along with that of his principal Christian Zionist organization, was always greeted with much affection.

In Tel Aviv, to great plaudits, he funded the remodeling of the once ugly city hall that overlooked Rabin Square, transforming it into a stunning piece of modern architecture. And in Jerusalem his name was writ large on the building directly opposite the Western

Wall itself, the holiest place on earth for the Jewish people; the people he believed were the key to the return of the Messiah and the teachings of Jesus Christ, "the first reform rabbi," as Turner often joked on visits to Israel.

Somehow Turner always managed to rise above the vitriol of the Israeli political and religious scene, carefully ensuring he publicly favored neither one side nor the other. It was a fine balancing act, but one he performed with impressive alacrity. He refused time and again to be drawn into the debate about the future of the State of Israel once calls were made by the increasingly popular Hofshi Party to split the country in two.

"Israel always was, and always will be home to all the Jewish people," Turner would repeatedly tell reporters when asked for his views on the apparent breakdown of relations in Israeli society.

It was on a visit to one of the increasing number of Haredi enclaves in Jerusalem in the early 2040s that Turner had been introduced to a rising star of the Talmudic world by the name of Rabbi Zvi Tenenbaum. From that initial meeting blossomed a friendship that saw Turner increasingly seek the council of Tenenbaum whose wisdom, the reverend soon determined, applied equally well to the gentile world as it did to that of Israel, and indeed the Jewish Diaspora's religious Jews.

Tenenbaum, married with three children - far fewer than most of his contemporaries as his wife was unable to bear any more children after a traumatic third pregnancy - was also seen as someone the mainstream Israeli population could just about relate to. He was less zealous in his criticism of those Jews who weren't as religious as himself, spoke in measured tones, but nonetheless made clear his disappointment at what he saw as much of Israel losing its grip on decency.

He supported those calling to impose stricter religious laws on Israeli society and railed against the overwhelming influence of modern technology on everyday life in Israel, and in so many other countries across the globe.

On his increasingly frequent visits to the Middle East, Turner always found time to meet Tenenbaum, while at the same time becoming increasingly aware of the growing popularity of the Hofshi movement whose calls for separate states for religious and secular Jews were finding great favor among much of the electorate. Mindful that Hofshi might well challenge the status quo and the balance of power held by the Haredi parties, the American cultivated a growing friendship with Hofshi's feisty leader, Ilana Shwartz, a former special operations operative who rose through the ranks to become head of the famed Mossad.

Shwartz was relatively new to frontline politics but came with a background well suited to the wheeler-dealer merry-go-round of the Israeli scene. She usually knew when to show her hand and when to fix a poker face. She looked the part; tall and slim, dark haired, attractive, she was obsessive about personal fitness, and it was not lost on her (or her husband, Avi) that there was a certain sex appeal that helped gain admirers among male voters.

Rumors abounded that Shwartz was a serial adulterer, but no evidence had ever been produced to prove this. If it was true, then the former top spy was still very good at covering her tracks.

Turner, whose relationship with second-term prime minister Doron Gal was also rock solid, knew he had to maintain the best of relations across the political spectrum. It was essential he ensure that whichever way the political winds blew he would be in a genuine position of influence.

It was two decades since the US had ceased its blanket financial support of Israel, a move that proved popular with much of the American electorate, but not the Christian right. This vacuum though allowed Turner and other Christian supporters of the Jewish state to use a combination of their own money and a belief in the path to Zion to have more direct personal influence in Israeli corridors of power.

For the American Christian preacher now tipped by many to win the next presidential election, his main focus was on guaranteeing the survival of Israel, securing unfettered access to Christian holy sites, especially in Jerusalem, and working with those who maintained access to a path he was certain would lead Christians the world over to redemption when Jesus Christ returned, resurrected, to lead his people back to Zion in the Holy Land.

After years of hard work, Turner was sure that at this point in time the Haredim, the right-wing conservatives, and the center-left Israeli parties were all onside on that issue. He felt confident he could adapt to all scenarios being suggested by those on both sides of the debate raging on the potential division of the State of Israel into two independent Jewish states.

Turner's route to the US presidency looked likely, his pathway to Zion was unobstructed, and the ultimate redemption was surely drawing closer.

CHAPTER 6

Despite decades of trying to rein in the activity of key Arab sepa-
ratists and their international sponsors across both the Arab and
Muslim world, Israeli intelligence had, to a great extent, failed to
comprehensively breach the inner sanctums of the main terrorist
player, the Al-Quds Brigades.

Strictly disciplined and with a dedicated, fanatical following, this
Israeli Arab organization worked from within Israeli territory with
the specific goal of removing Jews from the land that had been
known for some years as Palestine during the British mandate after
World War 1 through until 1948. They had been responsible for
terror attacks during the 2020s and 2030s that cost hundreds of
Israeli lives - mostly Jews, but Christians and Muslims were also
victims of their indiscriminate targeting of innocent civilians on
public transport, in supermarkets, and even at a rock concert.

They had "been martyred for the cause and would be forever
blessed", was the stock response from the Al-Quds Brigades, when
asked about the random killing of innocent Arabs.

Like so many terrorist groups they were viewed as "freedom
fighters" by their supporters and were wise enough to present a
political front whose rhetoric was less fiery when its representatives

were questioned by overseas media. What was said behind closed doors to their hard-line followers was a quite different story. They learned well from Hezbollah, the Iranian-backed Shia terror organization that had long proved a thorn in the Israeli side and prompted the 18-year Lebanon War from 1982 - 2000, the brief but bloody 2006 Second Lebanon War, and the awful 2021 three-week war that caused thousands of casualties in Lebanon and Israel alike.

Hezbollah had long since taken over Lebanese politics and commanded a majority in the government of Israel's northern neighbor. For many years it avoided sanctions by arguing that its political wing had little or no connection to its military wing. In Europe, most nations had bought into this lie, with the exception of the British, the Danes, the Baltic states, and others such as Hungary and the Czech Republic.

Many European governments sought to disassociate the political wing with Hezbollah's terror activists, as much as anything else as a self-protection mechanism. They feared they themselves would become targets of such terror if they spoke out too strongly against the Islamist terror group. Germany, France, Spain, Belgium, Sweden and Holland, were among those with a sizeable Muslim minority in their respective populations. They lived in fear of sparking an uprising or violent outburst. Appeasement was seen by many as the most sensible policy, but by others as capitulation to the inevitable creep of Islamic influence on their societies.

The Israeli Arab village of Umm El Fahm had long been a thorn in the side of the Israeli authorities. It lay at the eastern end of the Ara Valley, adjacent to the territory of the Palestinian Authority and the violent, lawless Palestinian city of Jenin. Ironically, with a token, easily overcome wall dividing them, it had always been relatively easy for both people and goods to cross over from the Palestinian

Authority into Israel, and vice versa, avoiding detection, or at least (in the case of non-terrorist goods transfers) with the turning of a blind eye.

It might lie on Israeli territory, but Umm El Fahm resembled so many similar towns in the wider Middle East. Heavily populated and crowded, its narrow streets and alleyways were a maze that only locals could properly fathom. It reflected a completely different age with few signs of the AI culture and influence that dominated modern, mainstream Israeli society.

Its main street appeared stuck in a century-old time warp taking it back to the 1940s. Wooden shop fronts opened onto crumbling sidewalks; the pungent aroma of herbs and spices wafting out of every second or third doorway; merchants sold fabrics for making clothes by hand; Arab women were covered from head to toe to protect their modesty; groups of old men played checkers and smoked cigarettes while passing relaxation beads from one hand to another.

There were eleven mosques in the town, the largest being the silver-domed mosque on the highest ridge of the steep valley. In both the First and Second Intifadas (the Palestinian uprisings of the 1990s and 2000s), Israeli drivers traveling the Route 65 highway from the coastal town of Hadera through the Ara Valley, all the way to Har Megiddo, (the place better known in the New Testament as Armageddon), ran the gamut of Palestinian and occasionally extremist Arab Israeli rioters.

Israeli intelligence knew well enough that radical Islamic elements thrived in Umm El Fahm, but moving in to drive them out could exact a heavy toll and potentially spark another violent uprising among Israeli Arabs who wouldn't normally associate themselves with the terror-inspired views of such as the Al-Quds Brigades.

Instead, Shabak, the Israeli internal security service, would take whatever opportunities presented themselves to pick off operatives of the terror organization when they strayed out of the town. Israeli jails were full to overflowing with captured members of Al-Quds and other splinter groups.

Arab Israelis made up around 18% of the total Israeli population. Most were Muslims, but about one-fifth of Israeli Arabs were Christians, mainly centered around Galilee towns such as Nazareth and the coastal city of Haifa. Arab politicians spanned a similar spectrum of opinion to their Jewish counterparts; some were modernizers and supported Israel's democratic principles; some were borderline Communists and wanted a complete change of political direction; others were Muslim hardliners whose aim was to use Israel's parliament and democracy as a forum to try and bring down the state from within.

The latter group had long been accused of being traitors; a "Fifth Column" was the most common phrase in use. There was strong evidence they acted and were supported both financially and materially by external regional actors such as Iran, Qatar and Turkey. They never condemned terrorist acts perpetrated by the Al-Quds Brigades, whereas other Israeli Arab politicians were quick to distance themselves from such incidents and activities.

The Israeli government, on the eve of the country's 100th anniversary, claimed that Arabs in Israel had "never had it so good", paraphrasing the words of the 1960s British prime minister, Harold McMillan. To a great extent that was true, but not completely so. Israeli Arabs held high office in the judiciary, in academia, and in the field of medicine, there had been a few Arab government ministers, and Israel's Arab population was free to come and go as it pleased, just like its Jewish equivalent.

In the workplace though there was still suspicion, much of it unjustified, on the part of Jewish Israelis who believed it would be hard to work successfully and integrate, so Arab Israelis created their own hi-tech business parks, particularly in the Galilee. These thrived, and a number of their business parks grew into major entities with international Arab investment.

Arab Israelis never had any real say in mainstream Israeli politics though. These were the descendants of those Arabs who didn't flee in 1948 and wait for the Jewish State to be wiped out before it had really begun. They stayed and refused to countenance leaving their homes and businesses - even for a short time. Many resented being a minority in what they viewed as their own land, but they knew well that their lot was among the very best in the whole of the Middle East.

They'd seen the bloodletting of the Iran-Iraq war of the 1980s that cost millions of Arab lives; the 2003 Iraq War with the US-led coalition; the genocide perpetrated by Bashar Al Assad on his own Arab people in Syria in the 2010s; the collapse of Libya into a failed state; the capitulation of Lebanon to Hezbollah, effectively becoming a nation-state satellite of the insatiable Iranian regime; and the disappearance of Yemen as it became a battle ground between Iran and Saudi Arabia during the same period through to the end of the 2020s.

The upheaval in Egypt and the terrorism that flourished there in the 2020s in the Sinai Peninsula on Israel's southern border had caused mayhem. Chaos, death and destruction had also overtaken neighboring Jordan when the Palestinian majority there rose up against their Hashemite rulers in the bloodletting of the mid-2030s.

Being an Israeli Arab wasn't a cakewalk, but most privately felt the relative stability the Jews had brought to this tiny corner of the world had given them a quality of life and personal security that was in short supply in almost all neighboring countries. That said, few would shed tears if the status quo was ever reversed.

And for those extreme elements in Israeli Arab society, such as the Al-Quds Brigades, the cracks that turned into a gigantic chasm between the religious and secular Israeli Jews, were something they felt could easily be exploited to their benefit.

CHAPTER 7

Once host to a large and thriving Jewish community, the ancient Persian city of Isfahan in central Iran was baking in searing summer temperatures reaching into the mid-40 degrees Celsius.

Isfahan international airport was a bustling transport hub serving destinations across the Middle East and, in recent years, a growing number of destinations in Europe. In August 2047, a particularly unusual delegation was noted arriving on a flight from Istanbul. Making their way through the vast main concourse was a group of twelve Haredi Jews, all dressed in black or dark gray shiny coats, some wearing fur brimmed hats that framed their glistening, bearded faces, garter-like stockings, and black-buckled shoes.

Garnering bemused gazes as they walked hurriedly from their arrival gate to a private passport processing area, they cut bizarre figures in a city whose Jewish community had long since disintegrated following the establishment of the State of Israel in 1948. The Jews of Iran, known as Persian Jews, had never been Haredi. Indeed, many were only borderline observant, but they stuck hard and fast to their millennia-old Jewish traditions while at the same time fitting in well to what for centuries had been the broadly tolerant Persian society in which they thrived.

But as one Arab nation after another ordered their Jews to pack up and go in the aftermath of the establishment of the Jewish state, Iran, the nation that officially changed its name from Persia in 1935, eventually followed suit. There followed the mass driving out of hundreds of thousands of Iranian Jews. Most were devastatingly forced to leave their homes, businesses, and most of their possessions, a not unfamiliar scenario played out time and again across the Jewish Diaspora for centuries.

A small number of Jews stayed and weathered the initial storm that Israel's creation engendered and, to a great degree, were able to go on with their lives more or less unhindered until the Islamic Revolution of 1979. But from then on being an Iranian Jew was a dangerous business. They did everything to blend in with their surroundings and not draw undue attention to themselves. The sight therefore of a group of Haredi Jews hurrying through Isfahan airport was quite unique.

Had they come to visit ancient Jewish sites in the region? Or had they come as part of an interfaith dialogue maybe? Not at all. This extreme fringe Haredi sect, the Neturei Karta, had come for a private audience with Rami Samtalan, chief minister in the government of Iran's Supreme Leader, Ayatollah Sanvani. So bizarre were the Neturei Karta that they were viewed in Haredi society as dangerous extremists. Their fanatical opposition to the State of Israel seemed, to most observers on the outside looking in, to be utterly self-defeating.

They had history with Iran. As vehement anti-Zionists they had been in awe of one-time Iranian president Mahmoud Ahmadinejad and forged a close relationship with his administration in the early-2000s. They even sent representatives to the infamous Holocaust denial conference held in Iran during that period, a move that caused outrage in Israel and around the world.

But to these zealots whose dedication to the Messiah surpassed all other reasoned debate on the subject, Israel was an abomination. It allowed Jews to lead a modern life, contravening, in their view, the way Jews should live according to their interpretation of ancient scriptures. The Neturei Karta hated Israel, hated most other Jews, and longed for the destruction of Jewish society, believing only then would the Messiah return to save them and lead them in a new and spiritually correct direction.

A fleet of four vehicles greeted the bizarre party as they exited the main terminal and headed swiftly away in convoy to the main government building in the center of the great city of Isfahan. There were, of course, no women among their number. Neturei Karta, rarely left the confines of their enclaves in either the Jerusalem district of Mea Shearim, or Beit Shemesh, a town close to the capital. Only their men were allowed to travel and make passing contact with the outside world.

Their women dressed in an extremely conservative fashion. Soon after the establishment of the Neturei Karta in 1938, "modesty patrols" were established by the community to ensure no woman dressed in a manner that could be deemed inappropriate. Such "style police" remained active to this very day.

At the Interior Ministry building in Isfahan, Rami Samtalan, one of the top four in the highest echelon of the Iranian government, waited patiently for his guests to arrive. He had instructed his most senior advisors to join him for what was expected to be a highly significant meeting.

The twelve guests filed out of their cars and one by one shook hands with Samtalan who greeted them at the top of a flight of four steps leading into the impressive, 16th century building.

"Shalom *haver* (peace, my friend)," Samtalan said to each one in turn, in Hebrew. They primarily spoke Yiddish but appreciated the sentiment.

The meeting lasted less than thirty minutes and only one of the visitors spoke. The rest watched on without showing even the slightest inclination to contribute to the discussion. Only Rabbi Mordechai Bloch spoke on behalf of the Neturei Karta. He was a man of few words, but what he said almost always caused uproar in mainstream Israeli society.

"Thank you, Mr. Samtalan, for your kind invitation to visit you here," said Bloch. "We could have settled this without journeying this far, but as you know, we prefer not to avail ourselves of modern communications technology wherever possible."

"We're delighted and honored that you made time to visit us here in Isfahan," smiled Samtalan. "We both share a common aim. The people of Iran wish only to support your goal and offer whatever material help we can to ensure a resolution of the current impasse in the Zionist State that benefits both the Neturei Karta and the Iranian people, as well as so many across the Arab world and beyond. Nearly 100 years has been far too long for this abortion of a project to have survived."

"How much are you able to offer us by way of a demonstration of your commitment to our cause?" said Bloch, getting straight to the point.

"There is no limit to the amount of financial support we can offer you," said Samtalan, leaning forward as he lowered his tone. "Billions of dollars can eventually be placed at your disposal. Truly."

Glances were cast from one to another of the Neturei Karta. This was just what they wanted to hear. An atmosphere of solemnity pervaded the room.

"But your people, while great in belief, are relatively small in number," continued Samtalan. "Our commitment to you is dependent on you assuring us of, and proving, the commitment of the majority of the greater Haredi community to our vision. We know this will not be a simple task.

"If you can return here within three months, shall we say, with the leaders of the major Haredi sects, we will commit not less than one billion dollars to support your communities. We wish to assure you of our complete military support for Israel's Haredi Jews in their anticipated battle to separate themselves from the Sodom and Gomorra of the rest of the country."

"Mr. Samtalan," whispered Bloch, the movement of his lips barely perceptible through his face-engulfing full beard. "We don't need the other Haredi sects to come here. You finance us, and we will win them over quickly. We will terrorize the rest of Israel; we will show the Haredim how strong we are. Many will rush to join us even if, at this point, they don't accept or fully understand our view of the way forward. Give us the money now and we'll get things moving right away."

"That's an interesting proposal," responded Samtalan, "but our conditions are clear and non-negotiable. Our financial and military support is dependent on the overwhelming majority of Haredim pledging allegiance to this cause. Your assertion that they will rush to join you once you start the uprising may well be a correct one, but we prefer to know who, and how many are with us *before* we hand over the money, not after."

Bloch looked across to his posse of supporters.

"That will be fine. We'll return home and begin the process of persuasion, but it will take a lot of money to buy the support of these people. We are not the most popular element within Haredi society and doors don't always open automatically for us."

"We anticipated that would be the case," smiled Samtalan. "Each of your party will be handed a briefcase containing two million dollars cash, money to help smooth the way and show our goodwill to the most senior figures in the Haredi community. I hope this will be a sufficient indication to persuade them of our steadfast support for your cause and guarantee their attendance back here in three months' time, *Inshallah*."

"*B'ezrat hashem*," Bloch responded in kind.

The meeting ended with a brief handshake. The Neturei Karta left the room, each man receiving a black briefcase as he headed back to the fleet of cars. The parameters had been set.

CHAPTER 8

Mea Shearim, Jerusalem - May 4, 2048 (10 days to the referendum)

Even in these exceptional times the very private Rabbi Mintz, unlike Chief Rabbi Bermann, was reluctant to personally intervene in mainstream politics, but in light of the previous day's television debate understood that an urgent meeting of the key players from the Haredi community was required. He had granted special permission for his mass of followers to watch the live TV broadcast, and reports already reached him that the morning after the televised debate the impression given of an increasing divide on the Haredi side of the argument was the only subject for discussion.

The differing views expressed openly in front of a nationwide and international audience were not something Mintz felt reflected well on the Haredi world. A united front was required.

Within a day, both Chief Rabbi Akiva Bermann and Rabbi Zvi Tenenbaum, the two Haredi protagonists from the televised debate, had confirmed their attendance. Rabbi Nusbaum, Tenenbaum's one-time tutor and mentor would also be there. So too would Rabbi Menahem Benchimol, the Sephardic Chief Rabbi, a very rare visitor to the HQ of his Ashkenazi opposite number. Rabbi Bloch, leader of the Neturei Karta was also an invitee.

Mintz wanted to do all he could to avoid any antagonism, to find a way to bridge the difference between the parties. Under normal circumstances he would receive visitors in the formal assembly room adjacent to his offices, but this time he took the unprecedented step of holding the gathering in his own private office in the hope this informal setting would make his guests feel more at ease.

All five arrived a few minutes ahead of time and were invited through to Rabbi Mintz's inner sanctum. Nusbaum expressed his surprise that they were gathering there, expressing outwardly the thoughts of the other four. Nusbaum, easy-going and inclined to joviality, was not only a good man to have at any meeting - he invariably found a way to keep even the most testy of matters to a convivial basis - but he was the man who helped shape Zvi Tenenbaum's formative scholastic years, someone Tenenbaum always credited as his guiding light.

Nusbaum also had considerable history with both Mintz and Bermann. They came up together through the Ashkenazi yeshiva ranks at a broadly similar time and had, one way or another, been respected colleagues for well over five, indeed almost six decades.

The invitation extended to 89-year-old Rabbi Benchimol was highly significant, particularly in Tenenbaum's eyes. It strongly indicated to him that the Sephardim were also going to vote for separation.

The presence of the usually ostracized Rabbi Bloch came as an unpleasant surprise to both Nusbaum and Tenenbaum. Bloch and his extremist Neturei Karta were seen as charlatans by most in Haredi society. Their ongoing association with the Iranian regime had been a major source of embarrassment. They were viewed as fanatics.

The six men greeted one another with handshakes and polite conversation. Tenenbaum did not shake Bloch's hand but did engage him momentarily in a few pleasantries.

"Learned colleagues," said Mintz, "I am grateful to you all for finding the time to come here at such short notice. Your attendance is greatly appreciated. If it were not for such an extraordinary situation, I would never have dreamed of imposing on your valuable time in such a way."

"I'm sure we all appreciate the efforts you have made to bring us together," said Bermann. "I am more than hopeful your endeavors will bear fruit."

"I must express my gratitude to Rabbi Mintz for facilitating this extraordinary meeting," added Chief Rabbi Benchimol in hushed, slightly breathless tones. "For too long there has been a lack of sufficient communication between our two branches of the Haredi world. We have our differences on many subjects, but we look forward to working more closely together in the future to benefit both the Ashkenazi and Sephardic Haredi communities."

"Thank you, Chief Rabbi," responded Mintz. "We feel privileged that you are here with us for this gathering."

"Rabbi Mintz, I too am grateful for this opportunity to meet with yourself, Chief Rabbi Bermann, Chief Rabbi Benchimol, and my great friend and mentor Rabbi Nusbaum, but with respect, I don't understand why Rabbi Bloch is present at this meeting?" questioned Tenenbaum.

"Rabbi Tenenbaum, in order that we can move forward with mutual understanding in anticipation of whichever way the vote goes, we have to lay the foundations for cooperation and partnership between all strands of Haredi thought - even those on the very fringes. This is why Rabbi Bloch is here."

"But for years both you and Chief Rabbi Bermann have publicly and repeatedly warned that he is a dangerous man, a rabble rouser with dubious connections to people who are long-standing enemies of the Jewish people. You once even called him 'a traitor.' I have no respect for this man and don't believe it is appropriate for him to be a party to these discussions. I—"

"*I* asked for Rabbi Bloch to join this meeting," interrupted Bermann. "As Rabbi Mintz said, we have to show as united a front as possible, and that includes respecting the views of the Neturei Karta - extreme though they have often been."

"I'm sorry, Chief Rabbi, but on the one hand you sit here talking about the importance of taking into account differing views from within the Haredi world, and on the other hand only last night you refused to properly debate me in front of a nationwide audience when my views failed to fall into line with yours. Something doesn't quite add up here?"

"Gentlemen, enough. Rabbi Bloch is here. He's not going anywhere. Now, let's not beat around the bush," said Mintz, his tone becoming more formal. Tenenbaum seethed at the blunt dismissal of his objection to Bloch's presence.

"I assume that we all saw yesterday's debate, and I am sure we all saw the differing views expressed by both Chief Rabbi Bermann and Rabbi Tenenbaum. It goes without saying that such a schism, exposed in full view of the general public, is not a good thing for any of us. It is important that we reach a common understanding and present a united front to ensure no splitting of the Haredi vote."

"Rabbi Tenenbaum, I'll ask you straight: What would it take for you to endorse the candidature of the chief rabbi for being the first president of Judea?"

"What would it take?" repeated Tenenbaum, taken aback by the directness of Mintz's question. "Well, we could begin by having the Neturei Karta sidelined from any substantive discussions on the subject."

"That's not going to happen, so move on," said a brusque Bermann.

"This is so bizarre!" laughed Tenenbaum ironically. "You know full well I am opposed to the establishment of the State of Judea. I believe it would be a huge mistake. We must not allow our Jewish nation to be divided."

"But surely you must be aware of the polling data presented in the Israeli media that suggests a vote for separation is more than likely?" said Mintz.

"I've seen it, but I'm not convinced by it. You know well enough how inaccurate polling data can be. I truly believe that when people actually go into the polling booths and are forced to vote Yes or No to ending 100 years of the State of Israel, the majority will say No."

"You're wrong," said Chief Rabbi Bermann. "The overwhelming majority of Haredim and the national religious communities in the West Bank will vote to separate. And on the other side of the coin, the left-wingers in Tel Aviv and on the kibbutzim, the wretched homosexuals, and a good percentage of the middle-class who are angry at serving in the army when we don't, and are forever moaning about the high tax burden, will all vote to leave.

"That's going to add up to a majority - a slim majority, I grant you," continued Bermann, "but enough will vote Yes, so it's important for you, Rabbi Tenenbaum, to moderate your language and strike a more conciliatory tone when speaking in public about this matter. Your highly personal attack on me during the debate was unwarranted and did you absolutely no credit."

"I'm sorry, but I stand by every word I said," responded

Tenenbaum. "And please don't try to take the moral high ground. Your attacks on me, calling me a "publicity seeker", and a "peddler of lies", revealed a side to you the public rarely sees. Don't try to demean me. I'm fully aware of your pact with Rabbi Bloch. You didn't think that such an alliance would pass without being noticed, did you?"

"What pact?" asked Rabbi Nusbaum, intervening for the first time.

"Bloch is in the pay of the Iranians. Didn't you know?" explained Tenenbaum. "They've been paying him fortunes to bring the mainstream Haredim onside in return for the Ayatollah offering military assistance to Judea when the new state is created. That is what makes me so concerned that the chief rabbi himself has invited him here. You add two and two together, and the usual answer is four."

"What drivel," scoffed Nusbaum. "Zvi, we know the Neturei Karta have historically had a weird, unconventional association with the Iranians; that's no secret. But being paid by Iran and buying off mainstream Haredim! Where did you come up with such a notion?"

"Notion! Why don't you ask Bloch and the chief rabbi? They're in it together now. And my sources tell me that a huge amount of money is washing around as well, with both standing to benefit greatly if the vote goes in favor of separation."

"Surely, Akiva, this isn't true?" asked Nusbaum, ditching formality and addressing the chief rabbi by his first name. "You and I go back forever, since schooldays. I think I know you as well, if not better than anyone else in this room. I can't believe you'd ever contemplate an alliance with such as Bloch and his *mob*? Surely Zvi has been misinformed. He must have got it wrong?"

"Actually," said Rabbi Bloch, "Tenenbaum is correct in his assertion that there is an understanding between the Neturei Karta and the chief rabbi. As far as his allegation of enrichment from such an arrangement, I resent his tone and his downright lies."

"Iran may have been a sworn enemy of the State of Israel, and has been the main driver behind violence directed at Israelis over the last 70 years or more," added Bermann, "but that is because the Iranians object to a secular Jewish presence in this region. They have never been opposed to a non-Zionist, religious Jewish entity in the ancient Land of Israel. It is the modern State of Israel with its liberal values, its tolerance of intermarriage, and its so-called democracy that offends Tehran - not religious Jewish people."

"That you can even think of aligning yourself with such a regime turns my stomach," lamented Tenenbaum, pointing a finger at both Bloch and Bermann. "They murder and torture their political opponents, engage repeatedly in pointless regional wars that have cost millions of lives, sponsor countless terror organizations around the globe, kill people who are proven or just claimed to be homosexuals, and still have aggressive nuclear ambitions. So, your new state would be run by you and shored up by Iran! Sounds like paradise, doesn't it!"

"With respect to the Neturei Karta," responded Bermann, "they represent a tiny fraction of the Haredi community, as you very well know. We have broad support across the Haredi world, at home and internationally, broad support in the national religious camp, other supporters from the Arab world, and from much further afield. Don't think for a moment that we are isolated."

At that the chief rabbi stood and asked those present to excuse him for a moment. He left the room in stony silence.

Nusbaum, usually so nonchalant and easy-going, threw his hands up in the air in despair.

"This is just ridiculous. I never thought we'd arrive at this moment - not that I'm in favor of the current status quo in the State of Israel. But who knows where this could lead? What's going to happen to the half a million Haredim in Bnei Brak if we split away? They're stuck next to Tel Aviv! Are they simply going to be forced out of Israel, told to pack their belongings on a trolley and be uprooted like in the days of the shtetls in Eastern Europe? And what do we do with the secular and less religious Jews who would find themselves in Judea? What if they refuse to go and refuse to change their ways? Do we arrest them? Expel them? Confiscate their property? Has anyone thought this through? We're going to end up with the unthinkable - Jew fighting Jew!"

The four remaining in Mintz's office fell silent, absorbed in their own thoughts, trying to figure out what should be said and done next.

"Anyway, where's Bermann?" asked Tenenbaum, ending the few moments of individual contemplation.

Right on cue, Bermann's voice could be heard the other side of Mintz's office door, but when he returned to the discussion the chief rabbi entered the room alone.

"Have you all been talking behind my back, by any chance?" he wondered out loud, with a wry smile cracking his gray and yellow beard.

"Only good things, chief rabbi," said Nusbaum. "Only good things."

"Of course," sighed Bermann. "Well, as we're putting our cards on the table and you, Zvi Tenenbaum, given your *exceptional* connections, are seemingly aware of our conversations with the Iranians - something that should never be discussed outside these four walls, by the way, d'you understand? - I feel it appropriate, in view of the seriousness of the situation, to clarify the picture just a little more.

"Zvi, this may come as a shock to you, but I want you to think things through and understand the reality of the political dynamics before you react. You may be of the opinion that we in the Haredi hierarchy are too insulated and have no grasp of international politics and the world outside our community, but that would be a poor interpretation of the situation.

"You think that Doron Gal, Ilana Shwartz, and the rest of those characters have their collective fingers on the pulse of the outside world, don't you? But they just see what they want to see, and any relationship they have with you, any promises they might have made you, are worthless. Believe me. I expect they've told you the international community is on their side - especially Ilana Shwartz. Well, I want you to meet somebody."

The other five men glanced across to one another.

"Would you coming in please!" shouted Chief Rabbi Bermann, in stuttering English.

The moment Tenenbaum heard Bermann call out in English his heart sank. It sank at such a rate he thought he might vomit. He broke out immediately in a cold sweat.

"Distinguished friends," said Bermann, continuing in English, "I have taken the liberty - Rabbi Mintz I do hope you'll forgive me for not telling you in advance - of inviting a special guest to our very special meeting."

Wearing a light gray suit complemented by a purple and lilac tie, immaculately groomed and with a whiter-than-white smile that could have stepped straight out of a toothpaste advert, a middle-aged, clean-shaven, dark-haired man entered the room.

"Good afternoon gentlemen. I can't tell you what a thrill it is to be here, although I do appreciate my presence at this august meeting might come as a surprise to most of you."

He reached out and firmly shook each one by the hand. Tenenbaum all but choked as he tried to summon up a few words but was unable to speak.

"Rabbi Zvi, you know who I am, but for the benefit of you other remarkable gentleman, I should introduce myself. My name is Ray Torrens, and I'm the personal assistant of Reverend Larry Turner, who all right-thinking Americans expect to be the next president of the United States."

"What on earth is going on?" gasped Tenenbaum.

"I'm sorry sir," said Nusbaum, speaking in perfect English to the new arrival. "Forgive me, but I don't understand why you are here at this meeting?"

"I'm with Rabbi Nusbaum," chimed in Rabbi Mintz. "What is this all about?"

"What it's all about," said Bermann, a Cheshire cat-like grin illuminating his aged face, "is that Mr. Torrens is here to inform you that the Reverend Larry Turner - who we very much hope and pray will indeed become the next president of the United States - will be supporting the new State of Judea, both politically and with enhanced financial support, once it is created following the referendum."

"Look, I know Larry Turner very well, and I know that he has financially supported Jewish causes from all sides of the argument," insisted Tenenbaum. "Because of this I know he would not choose one side over the other ahead of the referendum. He's told me that himself, in person, numerous times. In fact, he personally told me that only a few days ago!

"Ray, we've met many times before. You've been present a number of times I've discussed these matters with Larry. I'm sorry, but I simply don't believe what you're saying. This has to be a trick of some kind."

"Rabbi Tenenbaum, we know that you truly believe in the two sides working this one out, but we've come to the view that it's just not going to happen," said Torrens. "As you good Jewish people say, 'You can't have milk and meat together.' I have this letter for you from Reverend Turner explaining our decision. He urges you to come on board as he believes that, down the line, you could be a great leader of the new State of Judea."

Torrens handed Tenenbaum the envelope which he tore open and began reading. His hands shook. The usually composed and clear-thinking young rabbi looked crestfallen as the words on the page sank in.

"You gotta understand," continued Torrens, "the Messiah will only come to this Land when the Jewish people return completely to Zion based solely on the teachings of the Torah and the Talmud, interpreted as they were in the days even before the Romans came to this wondrous place. Across the Christian Evangelical world, we have waited a hundred years during the time of the new State of Israel, but the truth is we see Israel moving further and further in the wrong direction.

"Separation into two states is the only way forward, with the Holy City of Jerusalem returning to its rightful place. The Jewish people have to lead us Christians back to the path of righteousness so that, for the sake of both our great religions, we can see the Messiah return to save us all.

"Rabbi Tenenbaum, Reverend Turner thinks the world of you," continued Torrens, "and wants you to be an important part of this great project, but his greatest loyalty is to the Christian Evangelical world and to the people of the United States of America. This is what we call 'realpolitik.' When he becomes their next president, he wants to be the one who restores the word of Jesus Christ to his followers in our country, and he has had to take one of the toughest decisions he will ever have to make.

"We will be supporting the new State of Judea - and when I say 'we,' I mean the United States after Reverend Turner's election. As it's been made clear to us that supporting both sides is not an option as far as the Haredim are concerned, we will gradually phase out our support for the secular State of Israel, in all its forms; political, military, business, and more. Reverend Turner will make a statement to this effect in due course."

"Do you realize what you're doing?" Tenenbaum pleaded with Torrens. "You're jumping on board with Iran! You're getting into bed with the ayatollahs! Rabbi Bloch here is Iran's man, and his moronic cult has already tried to sell us out to the Iranians. Chief Rabbi Bermann has bought into this lunacy. This is unprecedented and ridiculous. I don't believe what I'm hearing."

"We're well aware of the Neturei Karta's negotiations with the Iranians, but we don't see it as any real stumbling block to our unilateral support of Judea," responded Torrens. "Who knows? It might be the catalyst that brings us closer to a proper understanding. After all, we're all men of religion, be that Jewish, Christian or Muslim."

"I've heard enough!" shouted Tenenbaum, picking up his black hat and heading for the door. "This is sheer lunacy. You are making a terrible mistake."

Nusbaum hurriedly gathered his coat and hat and followed his protégé out of the meeting without uttering a word.

"Tenenbaum!" bellowed Chief Rabbi Bermann, struggling to repress the smirk that danced about his lips, "Don't go firing your mouth off about this. You'll do yourself no end of harm if you do! Take time to think it over and cool off. My door is always open to you."

CHAPTER 9

May 5, 2048 (nine days to the referendum)

At 21:30 on November 4, 1995, at Kings of Israel Square in Tel Aviv, Israeli Prime Minister Yitzhak Rabin was gunned down by an apparently lone gunman, Yigal Amir. Rabin died a short time later in hospital.

Rabin had been one of Israel's iconic military leaders and played a key role in helping establish the fledgling nation as a regional military superpower. But like so many before him who witnessed firsthand the pain of war and conflict, Rabin came around to believing that the problems of Israel and the Palestinians could not be solved by military means alone. He judged that a political settlement had to be found.

Despite his mistrust of the PLO leader Yasser Arafat - a lifelong terrorist and enabler of other terrorists - and encouraged by then-US president Bill Clinton, he went ahead and signed the Oslo Accords. Agreement was reached after painstaking negotiations, cheered on by some in Israel and bitterly opposed by others, and pen was famously put to paper amid great ceremony on the lawn of the White House in Washington.

Soon after, Rabin was dead. He died at the hands of an Israeli Jewish assassin, inspired by far-right ideology, a hatred of Arabs, and steadfast in the belief that Rabin, for all his great military achievements and commitment to his people, was actually a traitor and had to die.

Among many moderates on the right-wing of Israeli politics, to those through the center and across to the far-left, they would come to view the murder of Rabin as the moment any real prospect for peace in their lifetime died too.

But almost forty years later, after much suffering on both the Israeli and Palestinian sides, a deal was done. It was the violent 2034 coup in Gaza that saw the overthrow of the terrorist, Qatari-backed Hamas regime that paved the way for a hard-fought deal to eventually be done. The seemingly never-ending negotiations bore fruit, and within a decade the Palestinian economies in Gaza and in their part of the West Bank were flourishing after receiving significant financial investment from the international community.

How ironic then that with the seemingly intractable Israeli-Palestinian conflict ended, it was internal Israeli politics that had now brought the country to the brink of disaster.

After his assassination, the square at which the ill-fated Israeli prime minister addressed the masses on that fateful 1995 evening was renamed Rabin Square. For more than half a century since then major political rallies were held at this pivotal place in modern Israeli history that could easily accommodate up to 100,000 people.

On the Tuesday evening following the televised debate a rally was held by secular and less religious Israelis who wanted out of the increasingly bitter partnership with their ultra-religious, mainly Haredi fellow Jews.

Not for the first time, Arab Israelis, many of whom were on the

left-wing of the Israeli political spectrum, were not present at this
or any other demonstrations relating to the impending referendum.
The Arab Israeli leadership asked their people to keep a low profile.
They felt it would do them no good to be seen on one side of the
argument or the other. Latest polling suggested the Arab community was more evenly split on the issue than the Jews; the last data
indicating 53% in favor of separation, 47% against.

Arab votes could be absolutely crucial in determining the outcome. They would need to evaluate whether they would be better
off staying in the State of Israel in its current form or be part of a
slimmed down country that excluded the Haredim and the national religious West Bank settlers. The Jewish nation had plenty of
flaws, but its large Arab community had been protected against the
turmoil of the surrounding Arab world by the Israeli military and
security services.

The word on the Arab street was that the Haredim had some
years earlier sought to encourage the Israeli Arab leaders to persuade their people to go back to the old tradition of having large
families. The Haredim argued that it was demographics that had
taken them to the brink of establishing a new state of their own,
and that if the Arabs hadn't stopped having large families from the
2000s onwards, they too would have been a numerical majority
when compared to secular Jewish Israelis.

The figures backed up the Haredi argument. Arab families had
once produced an average of more than seven children, but by the
2040s were having just two point three children per couple. The
reason: the younger Arabs over the last two generations had come
to the conclusion that having so many children was an unnecessary
financial burden and that they would have a better chance of an
improved quality of life if they had smaller families. That decision

had borne fruit in much better living standards for young Israeli Arabs over the last 30 years and more.

In contrast, the Haredim continued to follow their rabbis' urgings to do as God instructed and "go forth and multiply." It was His wish that they have large families, they were told, even if this meant so many of them living in extreme poverty. This was simply God's will, and the wisdom behind that will had now taken them to the brink of a Jewish land of their own. In January 2048, figures were published showing that during the previous year almost 60% of newborn Jewish babies in the State of Israel were Haredi.

But conservative, religious elements of Israeli Arab society were more pragmatic than the Haredim. Having seen the progress made in the health and education of their children and their much improved living standards, it was hard to imagine the Arab community heeding Haredi urgings to go back to their old ways in the faint hope they would eventually outbreed the secular Jews in the revised State of Israel and become an Arab majority in that country within the next 50 years.

Ten years earlier the voting age had controversially been lowered to just 16 in a bill sponsored by the Haredi parties that caused uproar across mainstream Israeli politics. But the bill had passed, because not to pass it would have prompted the collapse of that particular Likud-led coalition government.

The demographic figures for Israel at this time demonstrated how changed a society it had become over the last three decades. Of the 11 million or so citizens of voting age (out of a total of 15.6 million residents), just over 80% or 8.9 million were Jewish. Of these, around 4.7 million identified as either Haredi or other ultra-religious groups. Some 850,000 identified as national religious, while the remaining four million identified as moderately observant or secular, non-religious Jews.

It was the latter two groups, making up less than half of the eligible voters, who made up the vast majority of those required to serve in the army; they also accounted for more than 90% of the taxes paid in Israel.

***

Spurred on by the televised debate of a few days earlier, the crowds surged through the side streets before emerging onto Rabin Square in central Tel Aviv. The Haredi population had a knack of demonstrating solidarity in massive numbers, always acting dutifully on the instructions of their rabbinical leaders. Secular Israelis on the other hand took orders from no one, and no one could tell them what to do, who to vote for, or where to go demonstrate.

The democratic instinct to think for yourself then make your own judgment was one that had served the western world well, to a great extent, but in Israel, where everyone has strong opinions about everything it resulted in a myriad of political parties. Many represented very similar ideologies, but their respective leaders refused to set aside their egos and work together as a block vote for the common good.

Unsurprisingly, this resulted in many wasted middle-of-the-road votes as small, niche parties so often failed to reach the threshold for the Knesset. Their votes were worthless and ultimately only strengthened the larger parties. Getting these people to come together to demonstrate on any issue was always a challenge, and on the Tuesday night following the televised debate, just nine days ahead of the referendum itself, no one was certain how many would actually come out to support the calls led by the Hofshi Party for a vote in favor of separation.

It soon became clear that this was to be one of the biggest political demonstrations for many years. They swarmed into Rabin Square - and the masses just kept coming. Initial hopes of around 100,000 were a long way short of the mark as the square was filled to overflowing more than an hour before the event was due to begin. Soon the surrounding streets were completely blocked as well as the crowd kept on building.

Aerial shots from local news showed a mass of people swarming towards the square from all points of the compass estimated at more than half a million, among them many young people, as anticipated. What hadn't been anticipated was the presence of so many middle aged and older Israelis who had forsaken past indifference and been galvanized by the urgings of those parties that insisted this was the "last chance to save the Israel we love."

Also notable among the crowds were large groups of Ethiopian Israelis and other minority groups of color, those who so often felt marginalized but who this time wanted to add their voice to the calls for separation. Not that these and many others were against religious people; many wore a kippah and were devoted to their religion. They just opposed the perceived draconian nature of the black and white tide of the Haredi world which these days had such a dominant effect on their everyday lives.

When Ilana Shwartz stepped out onto the stage to address the masses following two previous speakers, she received an ovation the like of which she'd never had before. The roar that greeted the former Mossad boss was normally reserved for a rock star. It showed the passionate support she had - at least among this section of the Israeli populace.

Casually dressed in jeans and a short-sleeved shirt bearing the

Hofshi Party logo, Shwartz looked relaxed and confident. She assured the crowd that their time had come.

"For too long, hard-working, law abiding Israelis have shouldered the burden of this country," declared the Hofshi leader. "They've been crippled by sky-high taxes that have been diverted to the new majority of the population. So many of them don't work, refuse to serve in our army, and - worst of all - don't even recognize the legitimacy of the State of Israel because the Messiah hasn't come.

"This was bad enough when they were a small minority. It was troubling when they were a large minority. But now they are the majority! We are a minority within our own land; the land our fathers and grandfathers, mothers and grandmothers fought and died for; the land we love and are proud of; the land that we have turned into an economic powerhouse; the land that—had it been here between 1939-1945—would have been able to offer sanctuary to the six million Jews who died during the Shoah (Holocaust).

"I am not against religion. No one would be happier than me to see those millions of Haredim who currently hog the lion's share of our social security budget, fill our hospital beds, that have diverted education funds away from regular high schools and universities into the religious yeshivas, suddenly wake up one morning and say, "I want something different. I want to contribute to society; I only want to bring into this world as many children as I can afford; I want to serve in the army that defends my people; I want to work and pay taxes."

"But that's not going to happen, is it?"

"NO!" roared back the crowd right on cue.

"They're not going to serve alongside us in the military, are they?"

"NO!" came the cries once again from the masses.

"And, God forbid, they're not going to go out and get a proper job, are they? Why should they when fools like us have let them receive massive handouts every month? There are some families where no one has worked for four or more generations!"

"NO! NO! NO!"

A huge roar rumbled around Rabin Square echoing back and forth off the high-rise apartment buildings that framed the iconic venue. The applause for Shwartz continued for over a minute accompanied by repeated chanting of the Hebrew word for separation, "*Hafrada; Ha-fra-da! Ha-fra-da! Ha-fra-da!*"

When the noise died down enough for Shwartz to return to the microphone, she continued:

"One week on Thursday is our last chance. It is do or die for the State of Israel, as we know it. I cannot promise you that a successful vote for separation will mean that everything in the garden will be rosy the day after. It won't. Separation, like any divorce, is a painful and sometimes long drawn out business. But just like a family at war, torn apart from the inside out, the only way for both parties to survive is to separate and go your different ways. Then, after a few years, things calm down, relations become more tolerant, and a grown-up dialogue can take place.

"I truly hope that we'll never lose touch with the other side of this argument. I absolutely mean that. Like so many of you here tonight, I respect so many in the Haredi community, especially those who work, who have some tolerance for others, and who have genuinely tried to reconcile their lifestyle with ours. There are some very good people there, but not enough to make staying together a workable notion any longer. It will be hard for them, and it will be hard for us, but it is a decision that must be taken - by you, and the millions around the country - in order for us all to move forward and live our respective lives the way we want to live them.

"It's the biggest irony in all the furor surrounding this question, that the two sides who have least in common are actually both arguing for the same thing. It is those in the middle who naively cling on to the hope that ultra-religious minds can be changed, and who are too willing to just shrug their shoulders and accept the argument that 'This is just the way it is.' They stand between us and victory.

"Go home, go to the polling booths, and vote Yes to separation, to a renewed State of Israel, all of whose inhabitants contribute as equally as possible. Vote Yes to a country in which the minority no longer carry those that openly despise them on their backs. Go home, vote Yes, and let's start breathing again and live the life we all want and deserve. Thank you."

***

At the same time as the Rabin Square rally, another gathering took place less than 10 miles away. It was in Bnei Brak, the main center of Haredi life outside of Jerusalem. It might border Tel Aviv, but Bnei Brak was a world apart from the free and easy, some would say hedonistic city that dominates Israel's coastal plain.

Officially the poorest city in Israel, Bnei Brak was almost exclusively Haredi. Its local by-laws prevented men and women from walking on the same side of the street, reflecting the policy enforced by the Haredi majority these days on much of central Jerusalem. Men only dressed in black and white, or some shades of gray; women were very modestly dressed. Only children up to the age of nine were able to dress as most outsiders would expect children to be dressed.

Much of the city was slums in which overcrowding had reached frightening proportions. It was not uncommon for a family of 12 to squeeze into a two-bedroom apartment. Many such families only survived through the generosity of those providing food banks. Even though they might receive 10 child allowance payments from the state, it still wasn't enough to pay the bills when there was, in a great majority of cases, no proper income coming into the household other than part-time wages from the wife of the family. Israel remained one of the most expensive countries of the world in which to live, and the husband invariably would not work and would follow Haredi tradition and spend his days in study at the yeshiva.

That's not to say all Haredi men didn't work. Some did, and some were very successful. Those in the diamond business, one of the few areas in which there was genuine interaction with the outside world, were especially successful. There were Haredi property developers, shopkeepers, butchers, restaurateurs, and grocers. Many event hall owners were also successful with the Haredi world celebrating so many weddings, bar mitzvahs, circumcisions, and other family occasions.

And there was a small community of more modern thinking Haredim who had shown themselves to be capable hi-tech entrepreneurs and successful employers, and who even encouraged staff to go to university and get a degree. They represented a tiny fraction of the Haredi world though and were guided by a small minority of progressive Haredi rabbis who believed in the equal value of work and prayer.

For the Haredim in Bnei Brak the prospect of a Yes vote was a double-edged sword. Many resented being a minority in this particular part of Israel, having to constantly fight with the authorities to adapt laws to suit their way of life. They abhorred the way the secular Israelis dressed, their lack of religious observance, and the contempt of many for the religious section of society, a contempt only equaled by the low regard in which Haredim held the secular world.

But Bnei Brak, for so many Haredim, was the only world they had known. Of course they would travel to Jerusalem to visit relatives and friends, but Bnei Brak was theirs, even if less than 5% of Haredi families in Bnei Brak actually owned their home; most rented from Haredi landlords and did so all their adult lives.

The prospect of uprooting, even the fifty miles to Jerusalem, was daunting. Many felt they had managed to get by well enough to this point so why should they vote to change anything. Others wondered who would defend a new State of Judea with the Israeli army no longer available to mind their backs. Wouldn't the Arabs try and overrun the new country that had no army of its own? Would they be lambs to the slaughter once again, just as so many of their relatives had been more than a hundred years earlier in Poland, Lithuania, Germany and other countries in eastern Europe?

The gathering in the main park of Bnei Brak was to rally residents to vote No to separation, but it also attracted many from outside Bnei Brak, including moderately religious and secular Jews who were accommodated in a separate area of the park so as not to offend Haredi sensibilities. Estimates put the crowd at between 150,000 to 200,000.

In a very rare move, Prime Minister Doron Gal was the main speaker, something virtually unheard of in a Haredi community. He was accompanied by a number of senior rabbis from the town. Also on the platform was the Commander-in-Chief of Israel's army, Roni Melchik, a very big surprise as the military wouldn't normally declare any allegiance in an election or other political campaign.

Doron Gal wasn't popular in these parts, even though he was

the glue that held the coalition together that enabled the Haredi community to enjoy massive financial support from the state. He always appeared ill-at-ease in front of an audience and had a somewhat furtive persona. His forced smile didn't help either, but this sixty-six-year-old Likud leader was a shrewd politician and knew how to play the game.

Gal had managed time and again to defy those who said his days in politics were numbered. When the voting figures were against him and his coalition government, he would invariably find a way to forge an alliance with an unexpected partner, usually as a result of agreeing to divert state funds to their particular constituency and its supporters. Gal began by thanking so many people for coming.

"You may well have seen or heard about the large rally taking place just down the road in Tel Aviv," said Gal. "Well we're here tonight to send a message that they are not the only ones who can rally support." A large cheer rose from the crowd. "The State of Israel is 100 years old and, despite all the challenges we have faced, has achieved wondrous things in its first century. It's achieved these things, thank God, because all the people of Israel have stood together, shoulder to shoulder, despite their many differences.

"I look out here tonight, across this vast sea of people, and see a snapshot of Israel before my very eyes. On one side the righteous Haredi community whose prayers have helped protect this country; good people, family people who look out for one and other. And I see the other side of our great Israeli people, secular Jewish Israelis, and those from the moderately religious communities.

"I don't need to tell you that there is much crossover between these two sides of our people. There are Haredi families who have secular relatives, and secular families who have seen individuals discover the Haredi world and choose to follow that path. But they still remain one family, regardless of how differently they might observe God's commandments. If we lose the vote in nine days' time it is no exaggeration to say that some of you will be kept apart from each other.

"If a border is established it may prove very difficult to visit your loved ones when you choose. Bnei Brak will not be the same Bnei Brak. You would have family allowance cut to just the first three children; you would have to end the separation of the sexes; there will be no unemployment benefits for those who choose to study in yeshiva; and your children would have to fight in the Israeli army. Is that what you want?"

The crowd was subdued with just a few cries of "No." Gal was forcefully spelling it out in the bluntest possible fashion. The prime minister let a low hubbub role around the park before continuing.

"If Judea is created it will struggle to survive. How will it defend itself with no Israeli army on hand to watch over it? Only God knows what fate may befall the people of a new Judea if exposed to Arab armies and terror groups doubtless licking their lips at the prospect of an undefended, or only lightly defended Jerusalem. The Jewish people could lose Jerusalem! Do you hear me? *We* will lose Jerusalem if Judea is created as a result of this referendum!

"Don't believe the assurances you hear from the other side that all will be well. It won't. You must vote No and stay with the State of Israel. We will defend you; we will respect you; we will allow you to continue your way of life unhindered; we will invest in you, giving those who might want to join the workforce every incentive to do so; we will keep religious and non-religious Israelis together as one people; we will not allow our people to tear each other apart. We stand for one Israel! Vote No!"

The polite, even reverential tone of the gathering suddenly fell apart as a roar emanated from both sides of the park. Gal had given just a short speech, but it was a speech some commentators would suggest may have been the best he had ever delivered.

General Roni Milchek spoke next and took to the stage to enthusiastic applause. He then gestured to the side of the stage where on walked Rabbi Zvi Tenenbaum to a rapturous reception. He stood alongside Milchek, waved to the crowd for a few moments, but did not speak. He'd spoken enough during the televised debate. His mere presence there was a message in itself, and it was a message enhanced by him standing alongside Israel's most senior military figure.

"Thank you for coming here this evening," began Milchek. "It's heartwarming to see so many people representing so many different sections of Israeli society.

"I am the head of Israel's armed forces; I'm very proud to be the head of the armed forces. You will no doubt have noted that I am not in uniform. This is because I come here not as a soldier but as a citizen of the State of Israel, as the father of a daughter who now leads a Haredi lifestyle, and as grandfather to two Haredi grandchildren."

Applause emerged at the first-time revelation of the Commander-in-Chief's connection to the Haredi world.

"I grew up on a secular kibbutz where there was no religious teaching, although we always looked forward to celebrating the Jewish festivals. My home is kosher, but we are not a religious family. My four children have traveled the world and chosen their respective paths. Among them, my eldest daughter felt drawn to becoming more observant, studied at a women's yeshiva, then married into the Haredi community here in Bnei Brak. She may well be here in this audience this evening.

"She has made her choice - one that differs greatly from the rest of the family - but we still love her for who she is, and her gorgeous children for who they are. Our situation is repeated many, many thousands of times across this great country. Should the vote for separation prevail, opportunities for me to see my daughter and grandchildren will become far more limited. There will be significant barriers in our path. Such a change, I believe, will do no good for so many people.

"I understand and sympathize to some extent with the arguments of the other side. There does need to be a rebalancing in the way our society treats its citizens, and all citizens do need to take some responsibility for themselves, but separating into two countries would be, I believe, a terrible, tragic mistake.

"While I am not here in a military capacity, what I can say - and it echoes the words of our prime minister a few moments ago - is that a new State of Judea would be incredibly vulnerable to attack were it not to have any significant military force to protect it. Additionally, if there is any other military in the region or beyond that might have promised its allegiance to Judea, then this would be a false promise, one that would only ensure the failure of Judea and, ultimately, present an incredibly serious security threat to the State of Israel itself.

"Finally, my friends, let me remind you that Israel has survived in this very challenging neighborhood for 100 years as a country whose majority is Jewish, Jews of all colors and shades of belief. I promise you it would not have come this far if we had not stood together as one. Please, I urge you, vote No on referendum day."

***

The following day, after a massive public outcry led by the mainstream media echoing the thoughts of the vast majority of Israelis, Roni Milchek, Commander-in-Chief of the Israeli armed forces, a career soldier who placed his life on the line many times in his earlier service and who had been instrumental in successfully defending Israel against a variety of enemies, both on the field of battle and in cyberspace, resigned as the nation's top soldier.

"When it comes to a choice between kin or country," he stated in his farewell address, "every citizen has to look into their heart and decide for themselves. I truly believe I have let neither of those sides down with the choice I have made in publicly supporting the campaign to maintain the status quo."

CHAPTER 10

Jerusalem, Wednesday May 6, 2048 (three days after the TV debate; eight days to the referendum)

The Merkaz HaChaim yeshiva in Mea Shearim was situated in a dilapidated 19th century building that appeared to have undergone few if any renovations or maintenance since it was first constructed.

Its name, literally translated, means "Center of Life," and on this bright, sunny Sunday morning the yeshiva was a hive of activity. Room after room was filled to bursting with eager students of all ages attending lectures, reading the holy scriptures, and debating the nuance of individual words that might better explain the ancient texts that have guided the Jewish nation for thousands of years.

Ambling along the corridors, peering in through the reinforced glass pane of each door in turn, was a smartly dressed, middle-aged Haredi man not seen in this building before. Almost without exception those hurrying by him on their way to lessons cast a glance in his direction; there was always great suspicion of strangers, even Haredi strangers.

Arriving at the door that led to the lecture hall, he glanced through and eventually recognized the man he had been sent to contact. He produced an envelope from his right inside jacket pocket, and right on cue a teenage yeshiva boy in a wide brimmed black hat arrived at the door and asked if the man would mind moving aside so he could enter.

"Of course, but can I ask a favor of you?"

"Maybe. What is it?" the boy asked with more than a hint of suspicion.

The man pressed the envelope into the teenager's hand.

"You know Baruch Tenenbaum, don't you?"

"Of course."

"Well, please hand him this envelope right away, would you? It's quite important."

"No problem," smiled the boy and hurried inside.

The man watched as the boy did exactly as instructed and headed straight to Baruch Tenenbaum who was seated near the front of the lecture hall. He gave him the envelope. The man saw Tenenbaum look around and behind him to see who had sent this missive, then he left the building at a brisk walk and disappeared into the side streets of Mea Shearim.

Baruch Tenenbaum had lived his whole life in Mea Shearim. He was not a popular figure though and had only achieved some degree of respectability through the exploits of his youngest son, Zvi. Rumors had long circulated about him being an abusive father and husband, his gruff demeanor and famously short temper not helping dissuade people from this suspicion - one never acted upon or proven.

When he received the letter from the Office of the Chief Rabbi summoning him to a private meeting later that day Tenenbaum greeted it with mixed emotions. Never before had he been invited to meet the chief rabbi, although he had been at events (along with thousands of others) where the chief rabbi had been in attendance. His excitement at receiving the invitation was tempered though with a sense of foreboding.

He had seen the vicious exchanges between Chief Rabbi Bermann and Zvi in the televised debate a few days earlier, something that had taken the breath away from those viewing alongside him. They were stunned that Zvi could so publicly challenge the legitimacy and honesty of their leader in front of an audience that included secular Israeli society. It was unprecedented.

Baruch left the yeshiva and hurried home to change into his best suit. Yoheved wasn't home so he would have to wait until the evening to tell her the big news, whatever that might be.

Arriving at the Office of the Chief Rabbi he was taken aback by the smart interior and fine furnishings so far removed from the very modest standards of most Haredim, but he supposed they had to be that way when so many foreign officials and dignitaries visited.

There was no hanging around. Tenenbaum Snr. was waived directly through to the chief rabbi's private study where he was warmly greeted. He felt like a fish out of water but was surprised at the warmth of Bermann's welcome. He couldn't quite believe he was actually having a private audience with the great man. His eyes were everywhere, taking in the photographs, books and the general ambience of the place.

"May I call you Baruch?" asked Bermann, seeking to place his visitor at ease.

"Why, of course," stammered Tenenbaum.

"I know you must be puzzled at my invitation, and I apologize that we have never had the chance to meet before. You understand I have many people to meet during the course of my day and there is so little time, especially now. But with God's help, here we are, sitting together at last having this nice conversation.

"Of course, I'm forgetting my manners, Baruch. Would you like something to drink? Some mint tea maybe?"

"Well, that would be very nice," came the reply.

Bermann pressed a button on the intercom on his desk - a device that disappeared in mainstream society decades earlier - and asked for mint tea for two to be brought to them as soon as possible.

"You must be very proud of your youngest son. He and I might not see eye to eye on some things, but there can be no denying you have produced a quite brilliant young man - and that's a credit to you."

"Thank you, Chief Rabbi."

"I don't need to tell you that, thank God, we are living in quite remarkable times. I understand that your senior rabbi has instructed his followers, including those at the Merkaz HaChaim, to vote for separation next Thursday."

"Yes, that's right. He has been very clear that there's no alternative."

"And you too will vote this way?"

"Why, of course There are a few who say they haven't yet decided, but the overwhelming majority seem certain to vote for separation."

"That's pleasing to hear, although I hope the waiver issuers will come around in time to make the right decision as well."

"I hope so too," said Tenenbaum.

"Baruch, the main reason I asked you to come and see me - apart from finally getting to meet you, of course - is a poll published this very morning in Yediot Aharonot that indicates the gap between the Yes and No vote has closed dramatically following Sunday night's televised debate."

"Really!" replied Tenenbaum, genuinely surprised. The Haredi masses rarely, if ever, saw a mainstream newspaper or website.

"Yes. Prior to the debate there was plenty of clear daylight between the Yes and No campaigns, but since the debate there has been a move toward the No camp, and today" - he held up the newspaper with the figures emblazoned on the headline - "they are saying the gap has narrowed to just seven points; 46% in favor, 39% against, and, crucially 15% still undecided. That means the vote could still go either way."

"I'm amazed!" said Tenenbaum. "We've been clearly told there was a large majority, even on the secular side for separation. They've said that all we have to do is turn up and cast our ballot as instructed and we'll wake up the next morning with the new State of Judea a reality."

"Yes, well I'm very confident that will be the case but things in politics don't always go as smoothly as people might anticipate," murmured Bermann. "I'm of the view that the televised referendum debate proved damaging to our cause and I now regret having taken part, I don't mind telling you. We all make mistakes. I erred in agreeing to put the case in that forum.

"And one of the key problems in the debate wasn't the prime minister, or the leader of the opposition. It was, I'm afraid to say - your son."

Tenenbaum sighed and threw his hands upwards before allowing them to fall back heavily onto his lap.

"What can I say, Chief Rabbi? I feel terrible about this, but my son is his own man these days. I'm proud of him, of course, and he's much smarter than me, but he's an independent thinker. We have disagreed many times on his outreach to the seculars and his arguments against separation, but he doesn't take my views into account. If anything, he makes a conscious effort to argue the opposite standpoint to so many things I believe in. I doubt I could change his mind, if that's what you are asking me to do?"

"Baruch, we cannot afford to let this opportunity slip through our grasp." Suddenly, there was a distinct change in the chief rabbi's tone. "You are his father. You - are - his - father! You might not be able to change his mind, but you must insist that he not speak publicly on this subject again before the vote.

"I was horrified when I saw the pictures of him standing alongside the army Chief of Staff at that rally," continued Bermann. "He might not have spoken, but his presence there was worth a thousand words. Being there, standing alongside the country's most decorated soldier, a soldier, God help us, was an insult to the Haredi community, an insult to me, and an insult to you too sir! He's been defying you too long."

Leaning forward towards his guest with a knowing look on his face, Bermann whispered, "He's defied you since he was a very young man."

"A very young man? I'm not sure what you mean sir. He only entered the political arena in the last few years."

"Yes, but I have it on good authority that he was instrumental in arranging for your late-daughter to leave the community all those years ago. He reached out to the other side and had her spirited away. He's the one who enabled the events of her disappearance and the immense embarrassment caused to you when she abandoned the *shidduch* (arranged marriage) you personally worked so hard to make for her."

"What! No, you must be mistaken," said Tenenbaum, forgetting himself and raising his voice. "That girl took it upon herself to leave when she did - and good that she did. She was rotten! Zvi was only 15 then. He couldn't have known anyone on the outside. I can't believe what you're telling me."

"I assure you, Baruch, that my office was informed of the facts of the matter just a few days after your daughter disappeared. Do you think we allow disappearances to go without investigation? I know this must come as a shock to you, of course it must, but when you think about what he has become today, doesn't it fit neatly into the picture?"

"It fits neatly into the picture sir, but that doesn't mean it's the truth."

The chief rabbi pressed his intercom button and asked his assistant to bring him, "The Tenenbaum file." A few moments later, the man who delivered the message to the yeshiva earlier that day placed a plain brown file on his boss' desk.

Baruch Tenenbaum's eyes were glued to the tome. Bermann thumbed through a few pages then drew one page out and placed it on top of the file itself.

"Mr. Tenenbaum, this report is dated June, eleven, 2032. It states that after a number of enquiries, a witness came forward saying he had been present at the Or Ya'akov Synagogue on King George Street the previous Wednesday when a young Haredi man, matching the description of your son, entered the building and asked if he could place a call using their communication system. He entered the secretary's office and remained there alone for around five minutes before leaving as swiftly as he came.

"The following day, your daughter, Hila (may she rest in peace), disappeared and hasn't been seen again in this society. The synagogue secretary refused to grant us access to the records of the Or Ya'akov communication system, but we are all but certain that Zvi contacted the abominable Ahutza people and they swiftly put a plan together for her to be extracted from our community, from the bosom of your family, and from the impending *shidduch* that you personally had arranged."

Tenenbaum didn't know what to say. He sat, shoulders slumped, staring at his shoes. Bermann said nothing, leaving his guest time to contemplate the bombshell news he had just received.

"Baruch," said Bermann in a conciliatory tone, "this is not your fault. Zvi is a talented man who was showing great potential even as a boy, *before* his bar mitzvah. In so many ways I admire him, but of late he has become a renegade force and could seriously jeopardize the expected success of the Yes vote. He is so charismatic and articulate that many waiverers seem to see in him what they feel is an acceptable face from the Haredi world. He must not contribute any more to the debate on separation. Do you understand?"

Tenenbaum didn't respond.

"My suggestion is that you meet with him and lay down the law," continued the chief rabbi. "*You are his father*, regardless of what he has become in his own right. And if he refuses to see sense, then you must reveal that you are aware of his treachery in facilitating the loss of your daughter, and that you will be forced to present the Haredi public with this information if he does not cease from intervening in the referendum debate.

"Even Zvi knows that those Haredim who support him now, those who have a mind to side with his point of view at the ballot box, would dissolve very quickly away from him if such information entered the public domain. He would lose all credibility as a Haredi rabbi and scholar. I have no doubt he will appreciate the seriousness of the situation in which he finds himself and will agree not to speak out any more on the subject. He's already done more than enough damage anyway."

The chief rabbi rose to his feet and escorted his guest to the door.

"I know this has been a difficult experience for you Baruch, and I'm sorry that our first encounter has proven so traumatic. But can I rely on you to do the right thing and persuade your son, for once, to listen, *b'ezrat hashem* (with God's help), to the advice of his father? It would be a huge favor from you to the Haredi people. One that I personally would never forget."

"You can, sir. You can."

CHAPTER 11

Washington, May 6, 2048 (eight days to the referendum)

Drew Harper, running mate of Republican presidential candidate Rev. Larry Turner, rushed to contact the senior half of the dream ticket.

"Larry, you're not gonna believe what's just come through. We need to meet immediately."

"Drew, I'm in the middle of an important video meeting."

"I know, but this is very, very urgent. We gotta meet now."

"This better be something good. I'm in conversation with a very important and much appreciated party donor," replied Turner with a forced smile, pointing to the big screen in his home office where the chairman of a well-known pharmaceutical company was visible in life-size Technicolor.

"Mr. Jensen, I do beg your pardon, but something very urgent has just come up. Can I come back to you later today to continue this valued conversation?"

"Of course, Reverend Turner. No problem. I look forward to continuing our discussion whenever convenient. No problem."

Mr. Jensen's image disappeared from the screen.

"I'll be with you in twenty minutes," said Harper. "We can't discuss this on here. It has to be face to face. Just get yourself ready to go to a meeting."

***

"What the hell do you think he wants?" asked Harper, wafting his mobile phone under Turner's nose.

"I'm not sure, but you're right. It's gotta be something big," agreed Turner. "He wouldn't ask us over at short notice for anything other than a very serious matter. Let's get our things together and head over there right away."

"Sure thing."

"Oh, and please leave hell out of the equation Drew, would you?"

***

Thirty minutes later, arriving as instructed in an unmarked car via the rear entrance to avoid press scrutiny, Turner and Harper were ushered into the Oval Office where the president rose from his seat to shake hands with his two guests. Standing to his right was Lorne Simmons, Director of the CIA, who also shook hands with Turner and Harper.

"Mr. President, thank you for your unexpected invitation; Lorne, how are you?" asked the Republican nominee.

"Reverend Turner, Mr. Harper, I appreciate you both coming over here at such short notice. I'm sure you're very busy," said President Luis Dominguez. "You understand I wouldn't have brought you here if it wasn't something of the utmost importance?"

"Quite so," said Harper, receiving a steely glance from Turner, having spoken out of turn.

"Well, the presidential election is only three months away and we both aspire to occupy this office soon after that, don't we? It is due to a highly sensitive matter relating to national security that I have called you both here for this briefing. That is why Lorne has joined this meeting."

"Thank you, Mr. President," replied Turner in his unfailingly charming manner.

Harper shuffled uncomfortably in his seat and looked a shade bemused, betraying a sense of unease. Turner maintained steady, unblinking eye contact with the president.

"Few, if any people in the United States are better connected than you with the key figures in Israeli politics, Reverend Turner."

"As you know, Mr. President, the State of Israel and the success of the Jewish people is a cause very close to my heart."

"Yes, of course it is - maybe a little too close," sighed President Dominguez. "There's just a week to the separation referendum in Israel. While we don't support the country financially to the extent we did twenty or thirty years ago, Israel remains a close US ally. In particular, and as you well know having sat on the relevant committee in the past, we share much intelligence with the Israelis and they have proven - not forsaking a few bumps in the road here and there - reliable partners who have helped us protect US interests and US citizens, not only in the Middle East but across the globe."

"Mr. President, I'm fully aware of that."

"Yes, I'm sure you are, Reverend Turner. Which is why alarm bells have been ringing louder over here than Quasimodo on a drug-induced session!"

Harper sat wide-eyed and bolt upright at the president's change of tone.

"Reports have reached us that your representative, Mr. Torrens, very recently met with senior figures in the Haredi separatist camp." Turner did not react. "Not only that, we understand that he pledged your support to their cause, both as a private individual and through your foundation, and stated that if you become the next president the USA will side with the new State of Judea against the State of Israel, assuming the vote for separation is successful. What do you have to say to that, Reverend Turner?"

"Well, Mr. President, with the greatest of respect, both myself and my representatives are free, are they not, to meet with key figures on either side of the separation debate. I have also met with Prime Minister Gal, Hofshi leader Ilana Shwartz, and others. Our discussions are a private matter, and any pledges I may or may not make are a matter between me and them."

Turner spoke deliberately but with confidence, not betraying any sign of pressure.

"I don't agree with many of the foreign policy decisions you have made on behalf of this nation over the past three-and-a-half years or so, or indeed with many of the people and causes you have chosen to support. That doesn't mean you are not entitled to make those choices. I respectfully suggest that you should grant me the same deference sir."

"Reverend Turner, let me spell this out to you plain and simple. Your quest to lead the Christian community back to Zion is no secret, and your belief that such a path will clear the way for the Messiah to come and save the world is a matter for you and your followers. I have no qualms with that, although as an atheist I don't share your views. But what I, and the American security services

106

(he gestured in the direction of Lorne Simmons) do object to - and this is serious - is to you pledging that the United States will get into bed with the Iranians in backing Rabbi Bermann and co. and his side of the argument."

"Now just a minute, Mr. President, what on earth are you talking about? I've had no dealings with the Iranians. They repulse me even more than they repulse you! Are you accusing me of treason?"

Turner's face flushed red; his Evangelist ministerial stare unswervingly fixed on his Democratic counterpart. Harper appeared dumbfounded by the allegations.

"Reverend Turner, Bermann and that nutcase Bloch, of that loony Haredi sect I can't pronounce, are in the pay of the Iranians and have agreed to accept Iranian military support for their new state. They wanted to be certain they wouldn't be left exposed to attack from neighboring Arab nations once the Israeli military pull out and leave them high and dry. The Haredim have cut a deal with our arch enemies, the one state that has explicitly and repeatedly called for the destruction of the State of Israel for more than sixty years, *and* the United States of America. In effect, this moronic alliance would bring the Iranian Republican Guard to within 20 miles of Tel Aviv! And you have pledged to be part of that alliance!"

The president paused to assess the body language of his two political opponents. Neither cast even the slightest glance at the other.

"We could have leaked this to the media and blown you and your campaign out of the water right now, Reverend Turner, but, rightly or wrongly, that's not my way. Not only is this alliance you have suggested incredibly ill-judged, but it would seriously jeopardize the security of this country and our allies. That's why I'm telling you now - not asking you, I'm *telling* you - you must immediately withdraw your pledge to these people. You got it?"

Turner's mind was whirling. He knew this was a potentially career-threatening situation, and he had a feeling he knew what was coming next. Dominguez hadn't got to the top of the tree without pulling a few stunts along the way. He understood the subliminal message behind the president's play to keep this meeting quiet.

"Reverend Turner, your actions have caused utter chaos at the CIA and in the intelligence community. Now, my PR people and policy advisors, if they were here, would certainly be telling me I should expose what you've done to the media and let them rip you apart. Your political career could end in disgrace before nightfall. However, regardless of my personal views on your ministry and your somewhat extreme Christian beliefs, I do understand the place you hold in the hearts and minds of many millions of Bible-loving, decent American folk. I am not in the business of tearing into any holy man - unless he happens to be an Islamic fanatic, like the Iranian leader."

Turner could see the writing on the wall.

"Reverend Turner, it has been agreed between my office and the CIA," continued the president, "that if you step aside from the presidential race neither they nor I will leak details of your arguably treasonous tryst with the Iranians. You have my word. You can spin this however you wish, of course, but if you continue with this presidential bid, I assure you, you will be ripped apart. Not only will your political career be ended, but your ministry and your whole Evangelical organization will also be ruined too. I'm giving you the opportunity to save your ministry."

This was bare-knuckle politics at its rawest. Turner had to turn this around. He had to find a way out of this bind without failing to maintain his commitment to Bermann's side of the argument. He couldn't afford to lose his influence over the Haredim and unfettered access to Jerusalem for his fellow believers, but he had no intention of giving up on his dream of being US president either.

"Mr. President," Turner responded after a few seconds, "I appreciate what you're saying and what you're doing. Firstly, I assure you I had no knowledge that Bermann and his people were in cahoots with Iran. Truly, I didn't know. If that is indeed the case, then it does complicate matters somewhat."

"Mr. President, may I make a comment?" asked Director Simmons.

"Go ahead," said Dominguez.

"We know that your representative at this rabbinical meeting in Jerusalem was made perfectly well aware that Rabbi Bloch of the Neturei Karta, and one of Israel's two chief rabbis, are both directly and indirectly in the pay and accepting millions of dollars from the Iranians," insisted Simmons. "Your representative stated that this was not an issue that would be problematic, and that it may, in fact, lead to better relations between the USA and Iran."

"And you say this only complicates matters!" bellowed Dominguez, losing his cool.

"Yes, sir," Turner cut back in. "Just hear me out. As you acknowledged a few moments ago, I have considerable personal influence with both sides of the argument in Israel. Surely it is better to keep our lines of communication open in both camps as long as we can. Mr. Torrens, my representative at that meeting, appears to have, shall we say, been somewhat clumsy in his language. I'll deal with him for that."

"Reverend Turner, are you blind? We, the United States, already have plentiful lines of official communication in both camps. Don't delude yourself that your connections are more powerful than those of our embassy and consular officials."

"That's as maybe sir, but if what you're saying is true and Bermann's people have indeed cut a deal with the Iranians - something that horrifies both myself and Mr. Harper here with me - we should hang on in there and play dumb, as if we don't know about the Iranians. Then, when the Yes vote has come through, you tell them the United States will offer *all* necessary means of support to assure the safety of the new State of Judea. You push the Iranians out of the picture, and we're onto a winner."

The president looked aghast.

"Mr. President," continued Turner, "I have no ego with regard to this matter. Really I don't, and I understand that the deal the Haredim have allegedly cut with Iran - a deal I tell you I was not aware of until you brought me here - has serious security implications for our side." Turner was doing his best to sound contrite without completely losing face. "The security and safety of the American people is, and always will be my first priority. With regard to the situation in the Holy Land, as long as the great city of Jerusalem is safe and kept out of Muslim hands, then I will be happy, however that is achieved."

"Reverend Turner, there are two obvious flaws to your wacky hypothesis," responded the exasperated president. "The first is that the Israelis would baulk at us entering into a military relationship with the religious State of Judea so soon after separation, and it would unnecessarily complicate our bilateral agreements on defense and intelligence.

"The second flaw, sir, is that neither you, nor I, can be sure the chief rabbi and his advisors would choose our support ahead of that of the Islamic Republic of Iran. Has that even crossed your mind?"

"But—" began Turner trying to interject.

"No buts, sir. They might be Jews and Muslims, but they are

both - pardon me for putting it this way given your background - religious fanatics. They actually have more in common than divides them. I don't suppose the latter point had crossed your mind, had it?"

***

It was not by chance that President Dominguez invited the famously anodyne Drew Harper along to the meeting. He knew that Harper, for all his bland, gray personality, had the political instinct to smell blood too. Dominguez also knew that polls suggested he had a 10-point better chance of being re-elected if he faced Harper rather than Turner.

And sure enough, Harper informed Turner that if the reverend didn't step down right away, he would have no choice but to withdraw from the Republican ticket and explain to the masses what had prompted his decision.

Harper, who played no part in Turner's proposed alliance with the rabbis and the Iranians, had been gifted his chance to run for president.

The following day, to the shock of the Republican Party faithful, his millions of Christian Evangelical followers, and the international community, Rev. Larry Turner announced his decision not to run for president. He cited the strain of trying to simultaneously juggle the demands of his political career and potentially the world's top job, with his commitment to his ministry and, of course, his family.

"It is with a very heavy heart, on the one hand, but with the certainty that God is guiding me and my followers in the right direction, on the other, that I have taken this very difficult decision at this time," Turner earnestly told his supporters.

"Stepping aside now gives my great friend, Drew Harper, the opportunity to put together his own campaign team and choose the right running mate to deliver victory for the Republican Party, a victory this country so desperately needs.

"God bless Drew, and God bless the United States of America."

CHAPTER 12

11:00 A.M. Jerusalem, Thursday May 7, 2048 (seven days to the referendum)

Yoheved Tenenbaum was a sixty-something, shapeless Haredi woman characterized by an ever-present, world-weary aura. She walked with her feet at ten-to-two; actually, it wasn't so much a walk as an extended shuffle. She was wracked with arthritis and seemed to be in permanent discomfort. On this warm spring day beads of sweat soon emerged on her brow as her *sheitel* (religious wig) warmed her to a point beyond comfort.

Wife of more than fifty years to the domineering Baruch, Yoheved was mother to 14 children produced in a period of little over 19 years. Zvi, the youngest, arrived two years after the next-to-youngest, Hila. She already counted more than ninety grandchildren, and eleven great-grandchildren among her rapidly growing flock. Another two were due in the next few weeks. Her dynasty was not unlike many Haredi families, although Yoheved and Baruch had proved even more fruitful than the norm.

Her offspring had left home years earlier but the family apartment remained a hive of activity as some of her children would leave grandchildren with "grandma"; hers was an unpaid crèche which she fitted in around attending to her husband's needs and volunteering twice a week at a food bank that distributed supplies to those Haredi Jews living around Jerusalem, outside of her Mea Shearim enclave, who were struggling to make ends meet.

She would board the "women only" bus at the main junction in Mea Shearim and travel the extended mile to the distribution center in another religious area where she would often catch a glimpse of the few remaining secular Jews in the city. Every time she saw a secular woman, she would think of her youngest daughter who years earlier had fled and joined the secular world.

It wasn't easy hiding this longing for her youngest daughter from her husband. He would fly off the handle if anyone ever dared mention Hila's name in his presence, but Yoheved had for years yearned to see her daughter again. Baruch, on the other hand, hated his "dead daughter," as he referred to her. Yoheved suspected, indeed she was almost certain that his hatred was as much based on the fear of his daughter speaking openly to others about her childhood, as it was her choice to abandon both her family and her community.

She knew though that Hila would never inform the authorities of her father's inappropriate behavior to his children. She knew Hila still loved her and loved her brothers and sisters and would never subject them to the trauma of public scrutiny of their father's actions. Such a move would result in the whole family being cast out of the community - not because of the shame and the sins of the father, but for speaking outside the community of affairs that happened within - and that would be the end of Yoheved, for whom her friends and the respect in which she was held by her peers was everything.

She knew this for a fact, because for the last four years on the first Thursday of every second month, Yoheved would meet Hila in a discreet place in a small park within walking distance of the distribution center and close to the edge of Mea Shearim. She told no one of these meetings, not even Zvi. Given his outspoken views on not abandoning Israel's secular Jews that had sent shockwaves through the wider Haredi community, it was unthinkable he would oppose her clandestine meetings. But she felt it best not to risk mentioning it in case, somehow, word got back to Baruch.

Hila hadn't felt comfortable telling Ed she had reconnected with her mother after a decade incommunicado. She was fairly certain he would understand her need to reconnect, but he was well aware of the various reasons that persuaded her to flee and, on the few occasions they discussed the issue, had expressed the view that Yoheved was only marginally less guilty than Hila's father. She had remained silent when she knew or strongly suspected her husband was abusing their children.

"She's frightened," Hila once told Ed. "My father has a vicious temper. It was different for me. I was still a kid and young enough to start a completely new life. She had fourteen children to take care of, a circle of friends that respected her, and she's only ever known life within the confines of Mea Shearim."

"She looked away when he abused you and your siblings!" Ed shouted at his wife. "How could she? What sort of a mother is she?"

It was one of the rare times they raised voices against one another. She ended the discussion at that point by storming out into the garden. When she returned, Ed had gone to a late meeting at Hofshi headquarters. And that's how the impasse ended.

Central to policy decisions for the liberal, democratic party on the cusp of winning the separation referendum, Ed had little time for Hila's view of her mother's plight and the bind in which she found herself in the Haredi world. It was without a moment's thought that she decided the meetings with her mother should be kept a secret from her husband. There was nothing to be gained by bringing the subject out into the open again. It would only aggravate an old wound.

On the first Thursday of alternate months she slotted into a tried and tested routine. After dropping the kids off at school and kindergarten respectively, she then set off to Jerusalem, but not before disabling the GPS system of her driverless car so her whereabouts could not be determined. The last thing she wanted was Ed downloading the car's movements, only to see visits to Jerusalem appearing on the docket. As it happened, Ed never printed out the GPS movements; he had far more important things to do with his time. But you never know.

It was seven days before the referendum. As she drove into Jerusalem it seemed that every inch of wall space was covered in a campaign poster, the overwhelming majority urging Haredim to vote for a separate state and take control of their own destiny. Only occasionally did she see a poster calling to vote No, and many of those had been defaced with vulgar slogans equating secular Judaism with Sodom and Gomorrah.

She couldn't walk through that part of the city in her usual clothes. In fact, there was nowhere nowadays in Jerusalem where anyone could dress the way she did in Tel Aviv without attracting unwanted attention, some of it threatening. It just wasn't done. She always changed in a service station halfway along the Tel Aviv-Jerusalem highway, emerging in modest clothing typical of a married Haredi woman. She would wear a turban-like hat and dark sunglasses, her concern at being recognized by someone from her past being paramount. If she was seen there, things could turn nasty. It could make life very, very difficult for her mother.

They met, as usual, at 1100, in a corner of the park almost always devoid of visitors, apart from the hour or two before dark when local kids would come to play on the slides, swings and roundabouts; their playthings were those that occupied children the world over for generations prior to the arrival of the mobile phone more than 60 years earlier. Haredi children nowadays had no modern electronic devices following a judgment by one of the legendary rabbis in 2028 who determined they were "tools of the devil" and should never be used by Haredi children.

When they met, Yoheved would always cry.

"You're so beautiful - and so slim!" she would say. "Show me the latest pictures of your children. Oh, I'd love to hold them and kiss them. They're adorable, thanks to God."

She always brought a small picnic filled with food that reminded Hila of her childhood; homemade pickled cucumbers, chopped and fried fish with freshly made *chrain* (horseradish sauce), and fresh pita bread from the superb Gellman's bakery at the heart of Mea Shearim, to which Hila would often run in her youth to buy rugelach pastries, onion bread rolls, and best of all, delicious jam-filled donuts at Chanukah, the Festival of Lights.

It was at the major Jewish festivals that Hila felt the strongest pangs of longing for her Haredi childhood. It hadn't all been bad by any means, and despite the traumas she and her brothers and sisters experienced these festivals were joyous occasions at home and in the wider community. Their love for God, their gratitude for Him providing them with a full table, their comic drunkenness at Purim, modest but much appreciated gifts for each and every one of them at Pesach (Passover), even their communal fasting on Yom Kippur (the Day of Atonement) and other Fast days, were, in their way, an experience that bound the family and the Haredi populace together.

And somehow, despite their poverty, the most important celebration of all, the arrival of Shabbat (the Sabbath) at sunset every Friday evening, was the abiding memory of her childhood. That special moment when the neighborhood began to fall silent as the men went off to pray in the synagogue. The anticipation as the women awaited their return, the blessing of the Shabbat candles, the wine, and the bread, then dinner, with a horde of siblings. Very soon their respective husbands, wives and children all found a place at the table where somehow everyone always managed to squeeze in.

Hila would reminisce with her mother about those days. She would hear how her brothers and sisters, and her scores of nephews and nieces were doing; a couple of Yoheved's older grandchildren were soon to be married by *shidduch* (arranged marriage). Although she no longer believed in God, she offered a silent prayer to whoever or whatever is out there, that those marriages would be happy, loving ones.

They never discussed the troubles of the past, but when they embraced and looked into each other's eyes there was an unspoken message, a signal from mother to daughter that all still was not well. Hila never felt the moment was right to verbalize her innermost thoughts.

They would meet for around an hour and a half, sometimes as long as two hours, but no more. Yoheved had to put in an appearance at the distribution center before she was missed and questions were asked, and Hila had to head back to Tel Aviv in good time to prepare a late lunch for her boys who had to be collected on a Thursday at three thirty in the afternoon, having started before eight in the morning. They always returned absolutely ravenous.

Hila strode off in one direction, and Yoheved shuffled off in the other, feet always at ten to two. They would meet again, God willing, in two months' time - same time, same place.

CHAPTER 13

Noon, Jerusalem, Thursday, May 7, 2048 (seven days to the referendum)

"He'll be here soon, Shmulik," Baruch Tenenbaum told his brother-in-law. "This isn't going to be easy. You know what he's like, but we must make him see reason. In the long run it will be for his own good. He has to step out of this debate."

"I can't stay long. Anyway, this has nothing to do with me. It's between father and son. I've left one of the assistants in charge of the shop and it's already getting busy ahead of the Shabbat (Sabbath) rush. There's a big delivery of chicken coming in soon too and they can't sign. Only I sign for the stock," said Shmulik, well known in the community as the proprietor of a thriving butcher's business that also incorporated a traditional delicatessen.

He was a benevolent soul, grossly overweight and often a touch breathless, his lumbering exterior belying a gentle nature. Unlike his sister, Yoheved, his feet didn't point at ten to two; his indicated nearer five to one. Big Shmulik wasn't the kind who could look away when those without means found themselves unable to put food on their table. He would discreetly hand them a plainly wrapped parcel, ensuring their family didn't go without something modest but tasty for their Sabbath meal. He was blessed by many, including his sister, whose large family had been sustained for decades by Uncle Shmulik's sausages, wurst, brisket and chicken.

"Yes, yes. Hopefully, it won't take too long," said Baruch. "He won't like it, but he'll have to accept it."

Baruch had invited his son to meet him at 12 noon when Yoheved was out doing her rounds and wouldn't be back until mid-afternoon. This wasn't a matter for a woman - not even Zvi's mother.

Zvi had no mobile communication device. Like most Haredim he adhered to the edict laid down decades earlier by the council of rabbis that forbade the use of such devices. Some took a chance and ignored that ruling and got away with it; others didn't.

There were those in the higher echelons of Haredi society who managed to successfully argue that being without such a device might compromise their effectiveness when it came to political or financial matters and were granted an exemption from their senior rabbi. Zvi Tenenbaum could have easily received such an exemption, but he liked the independence not having one gave him. If a message was missed; so be it. It would be God's will whether or not such a communication was really necessary in the grand scheme of things.

Baruch had gone to his son's apartment the previous day on the way home from his thought-provoking meeting with the chief rabbi. As usual, only Zvi's wife, Nava, was home with the children. She didn't like her father-in-law. Any conversation they had in her husband's absence was usually restricted to a few pleasantries. Baruch had a good idea where Nava's antipathy came from. She would never leave him alone with the children.

He told her that regardless of any other business Zvi might have planned the next lunchtime, he must come to his parents' home as Baruch had a very pressing matter of the utmost importance to discuss with him. For as long as they had been married Nava had never known Baruch to demand a meeting with her husband. She understood this must be a serious issue and told her father-in-law that, to the best of her knowledge, her husband would be available as he had planned a quieter day that Thursday. He was exhausted from all the running around connected to the referendum campaign.

"I'm sure he is," observed Baruch dryly.

Twelve noon came and went. So too did 12:15. Shmulik was getting restless; he had no wish to be there. Zvi was known for his punctuality so the chances were that he wasn't going to show this far past the scheduled time.

"If they come with the chicken and there's no one to sign they won't leave it there or come back later," he moaned. "They'll just go. Then there'll be trouble tomorrow when all my regulars turn up to find we're chickenless!"

"Calm down," said Baruch, getting to his feet. They were seated at the kitchen table. He'd decided it was worthwhile having the not inconsiderable bulk that was Shmulik there, just in case his son felt the urge to run away and refuse to listen to his father's arguments.

He reached into the oak display cabinet in which the Shabbat candlesticks were kept, along with the *havdalah* (prayer) wine cup, and the eight-stemmed chanukiah used once a year during Chanukah. The shelf above contained a whisky decanter. He placed two glasses on the kitchen table and poured them a drink.

"Well, this must be a special occasion if you're offering whiskey so early in the day," laughed Shmulik. He knocked it back in one and gestured to his brother-in-law that a refill would be most welcome.

"One more then, but don't get used to it," grunted Baruch.

There was a garish crystal and mock-silver clock on the wall opposite the display cabinet that featured a prayer for the home printed alongside the face of one of the now departed chief rabbis. It chimed every half an hour and didn't let the side down when ticking around to 12:30.

"I'm sorry, Baruch. Thanks for the whiskey and all that, but I've got to go. He's not coming."

Shmulik picked up his oversized black coat and took his black hat from the stand. The front door was also the kitchen door. It burst open at that very moment as Zvi rushed in.

"Sorry I'm late, Abba (dad). Things have been crazy today. Uncle Shmulik! Lovely to see you. Have you just arrived too?" he asked, warmly hugging his portly uncle. Shmulik placed his hat back on the stand, sighed, then took his coat off and sat down. Zvi didn't embrace his father.

"Well this is all very nice. It's been ages since the three of us sat together. What's the occasion? Can I have a drink too?"

The young rabbi sat down at the head of the table with his father on one side and his uncle on the other.

"Sure. Shmulik, pass me a glass from the cabinet behind you." He dutifully obliged and Baruch poured his son a drink. Zvi said a prayer, then took a sip.

"How's Nava and the three lovely kids of yours?" asked Shmulik.

"Doing great, thank God," said Zvi glancing in his father's direction. "Thanks for asking."

"Zvi," said Baruch, seemingly oblivious to his son's previous remark, "we need to talk about something serious. You know—"

"Abba, I know what you're going to say. I've been thinking about this on the way over and it's OK. I understand. I never really expected you to vote No and support my side of the argument. Uncle

Shmulik, I suppose you too are going with the flow?"

"Well, despite what the rabbinical council says, my vote is a matter between me and the ballot box," said Shmulik in a hesitant manner. "I'll say no more on the subject. Anyway, this isn't about my vote."

"Oh, Abba, what's the problem?"

"Look, I know we don't seem to agree on very much and that you have become an important man - far more important than me," began Baruch, "but I am your father and I am deserving of respect."

"Respect," repeated Zvi quietly. "That's an interesting word. I don't have a dictionary with me, but I imagine that word would likely be defined as something you earn, not something you deserve."

Shmulik was taken aback by Zvi's pointed comment. An uncomfortable atmosphere very quickly descended on the modest kitchen.

"I'm unhappy at your high profile in the referendum campaign," said Baruch, "especially as you are a figurehead for the *hilonim* (secular Jews). They're using you; can't you see? Look, you spoke very well on that television debate prior to the insults you hurled at the chief rabbi, which were not called for. Are you going to tell me you don't respect him either?"

"That's exactly what I was going to say. He's a crooked thief who places self-interest well ahead of the real wellbeing of the community. Why should I respect him, especially after he attacked me first in the debate?"

"Look Zvi," said Baruch, his voice rising a notch or two, "you're becoming a troublemaker. People are talking. You have to stop speaking out against separation. It's causing concern in the community that your arguments might undermine the separation campaign."

"Good! I'm glad they're worried. The fact they've obviously got to you and persuaded you to try and convince me to back off gives me great encouragement," grinned Zvi.

"You fool," lamented his father. "With all your brains and charm you still don't have the sense to see that you're a tool of the leftists, the *hilonim*, the army - all the elements that have made life so difficult for us and who mock and demean us at every opportunity. You're dancing to their tune. You've got to quit the campaign right now! If the vote goes against separation, they're going to come for you, and God knows what will happen."

"Abba, you purport to be a man of God, don't you? So, if God knows best, let him be the judge as to whether I'm right or not."

"You've become a complete embarrassment to me and to the family. I'm not asking you; I'm *telling* you, this *balagan* (mess) has to end. I'm your father, and this time you must obey me and respect what I say!"

"What have they promised you?" asked Zvi, his voice lowered to almost a whisper as he leaned forward across the table and looked his father right in the eyes. "Nobody in the political word has ever looked twice at you. Who's been playing with your mind? What have they promised you that you would undermine your own son? But more than that, I doubt you have given a proper thought to the argument to separate. Have you thought about who will defend Judea once the Israeli army has gone? We're in a 'tough neighborhood,' as they say. We could easily be invaded by the Arabs or overrun by Islamic terrorists. You've not thought much about that, have you? And who's going to pay for the children, and for you and so many others to study in yeshiva each day when there is no social security dropping into your lap?"

Zvi was angry. He gritted his teeth, placed his empty glass back on the kitchen table around which he had spent so much of his time during his formative years.

"If it wasn't for Uncle Shmulik we'd hardly have had a proper meal at this table throughout my childhood," he continued. "Left to you we might have starved. Some father you are ... and you expect *me* to respect *you* for trying to undermine my career! Under this roof you've done enough damage to me and my brothers and sisters—"

"Now shut your mouth Zvi," intervened Baruch sharply, getting to his feet. Shmulik also rose from the table then hesitantly moved toward the door. Zvi also stood. The atmosphere had turned toxic.

"Who got to you, Abba? Was it Grinwald? Marks? Levinstein? Who was it?"

"It was Bermann," admitted Baruch, in a proud tone. "Yes, Bermann. The chief rabbi invited *me* to his private office. *Me*! Not you! This time it was *me*, not you, who for once was paid some respect. I sat with him and he explained the damage you're doing. He showed me evidence linking you to Hila's disappearance. He'll make it public if you don't back off from opposing separation. You, and all our family will be finished here. He is our leader, our connection to God. He insisted you must stop - and I agree with him. You're making fools of all of us. *This-must-stop!*"

"You vile man. You pathetic imbecile. You'd take the side of that conman against your own son, a son who has stood by you despite everything. Have you no shame? You disgust me. You ..."

He didn't even complete the sentence. The red mist descended on the usually calm and reasoned Zvi Tenenbaum. He rushed at his father, grabbing him by the throat as decades of pent up hatred and frustration poured out of him. Baruch, bigger and stronger, wasn't quick enough to respond, but Shmulik moved swiftly from the doorway to try to break it up, attempting to force his way between them and loosen Zvi's grip.

"Enough Zvi! Enough!" shouted Shmulik, prizing his nephew's hands from his brother-in law's throat. Baruch gasped for air and slumped against the oven.

"I don't ever want to see you again," a breathless Zvi told his father. "You'll never come to my house. You will never see my children again, and I'll do all I can to make sure that my brothers and sisters also turn you away. You fucking pervert!"

Shmulik looked on in astonishment at what he had just heard. There was silence in the kitchen. Zvi picked his black hat up and headed for the door, but before he could leave Baruch, having caught his breath again, lunged at his son. Grabbing him from behind by the shoulders, he hurled his youngest son onto the kitchen table. He landed heavily, but almost immediately gathered himself up to respond.

Before he could even raise a fist, his raging father hurled Zvi backwards a second time. This time his head smashed into the glass panel of the display cabinet behind the kitchen table. He didn't respond. Splayed across the table with the back of his head in the cabinet door, Zvi made a low, gurgling noise. His legs twitched for a few moments and his eyes stared in horror in the direction of his father and uncle. Then the twitching and the gurgling stopped simultaneously, his lower jaw dropped, and his gaze was fixed.

"God help us, Baruch. What have you done?" cried Shmulik, rushing to his nephew's side. Baruch stood motionless, dazed and confused. "Elohim *ishmor*, there's no pulse. I think he's dead. Oh my God, what have you done?"

Shmulik began to sob. Baruch, devoid of paternal instinct, remained unmoved.

"We've got to get help," said Shmulik trying to gather his wits. "Maybe it's not too late! Let me call an ambulance."

"He's gone, Shmulik. There's nothing we can do. He's gone."

The clock with the old rabbi's wizened features smiled down through the silence. The ticking filled the room, each man wrapped in their own thoughts; Shmulik distraught but making no sound.

"We have to get him out of here," said Baruch, breaking the silence.

"Get him out of here?! We have to call an ambulance!"

"You know we can't bring them in from the outside and let them have a field day with this. We'll both be hauled in for murder. We have to get him out of here and away from Mea Shearim."

"What do you mean, 'We'll both be hauled in for murder'? You killed your son, Baruch. I didn't lay a finger on him. I only tried to keep you two apart."

"That's what you say, Shmulik. Can you prove it? I'm sorry, but we'll both be finished if this gets out."

"You rat! You cold-hearted, soulless rat. I never liked you much. I heard the rumors but told people it was all drivel. But now I know it's true. You wouldn't have flown into such a rage if it hadn't been true."

"Shut it!" said Baruch with real menace. "We're in this together, and as long as you do what I say we'll get out of this together. Zvi had plenty of political enemies both here and outside. Anyone could have killed him to try and stop him speaking out. Do you understand? We can deal with this."

"Baruch, I don't believe what I'm hearing. You've just lost your son. You've just *killed* your son! You're a fucking monster."

"Shut your mouth Shmulik, grab your coat and hat, go to your butcher's shop and bring some tools. He must not be recognizable."

"What!"

"You heard me. And you've got a van, so you're going to bring it to the rear of the building and pull in right outside the back entrance, as if you're making a delivery."

"I never deliver round here. I only use the van for collecting meat from suppliers. It would look suspicious."

"Just do as I say. I'll wrap him up. Go now. Get out," Baruch shouted, "and go now. Hurry!"

Shmulik was dazed, horrified both at the callousness with which Baruch was so readily planning the disappearance of his own son's body, and at the realization that he was trapped in a situation that was none of his doing. He grabbed his things, looked back at the lifeless body of the nephew of whom he had been so proud, and rushed out. Baruch hurriedly locked the door behind him.

CHAPTER 14

12.45 P.M., Thursday, May 7, 2048 (seven days to the referendum)

Baruch knew Yoheved would probably be back around two-thirty. He had to remove Zvi's body then tidy the kitchen and come up with a story to account for the broken glass panel in the display cabinet.

Under the sink there were rubber gloves for washing up. He took them and placed them on the kitchen table alongside the body of his son, then frantically looked for black dustbin liners. Where did she keep them? He couldn't find them, so rushed into the bedroom to take some sheets, or a quilt, or something that would be enough to wrap the body in.

He scanned up and down, surveying the contents of his wardrobe: clothes, towels, winter quilts. Then he opened his wife's wardrobe, the one where she hung her dresses. He hadn't opened that door for many years, but remembered that she had told him, angrily, that said she would never get rid of it.

The large green lady's coat was the only piece of clothing Yoheved had kept after Hila disappeared. The teenager had bought it at a second-hand store on the edge of the neighborhood and loved it, even though it was far too big for her. How he hated that girl. He paused and wondered if it was the right thing to do. He was cool and calculating. An air of calmness descended over the man who had just committed the unimaginable crime of filicide. It was as if nothing had happened.

He removed the coat from its hanger and adjusted the remaining dresses so there was no obvious gap. His traitor of a son would leave this house wrapped in the only remaining item that belonged to the daughter who had brought such shame on his family. The daughter who his traitor of a son helped to leave the Haredi world. It felt like the ideal scenario; poetic justice, he thought to himself.

Re-entering the kitchen, he checked again that the front door was locked. The apartment was quiet, in fact the whole building was quiet. He moved across to his son's body and felt a brief pang of regret, one quickly dispatched from his mind. He had to think carefully. There was very little blood. Zvi's body was sprawled across the kitchen table almost defying gravity, the base of his head having been pierced by the glass of the cabinet door. It had anchored him in this macabre position.

Putting the rubber gloves on, he glanced behind his youngest son's skull, placed one hand on either side of Zvi's head, then without any hesitation, as if he was picking up a melon at a fruit stall, lifted the head up and away from the shard of glass that had so brutally and improbably impaled the young rabbi, ending his life ambitions in the space of a few seconds. It must have been a million to one chance that the glass shattered, and a shard pierced him in such a place, causing death almost instantaneously. There were just a few more drops of blood as the head came away from the glass.

Before wrapping the upper half of the body in the green coat,

Baruch had the presence of mind to go through Zvi's pockets. He left most things where they were, but removed a hand-written note that said, "*Meet Abba, 12 noon, tomorrow.*"

The engine of Shmulik's van could be heard pulling in at the rear of the building, then moments later there was a knock at the back door. Baruch rushed through and opened up, beckoning his brother-in-law inside.

"Listen Baruch, this isn't going to work," Shmulik whispered, clearly stressed. "We can't do this. We'd be better off explaining exactly what happened, how it was an accident, telling someone we trust from the community."

"No one will believe it," said Baruch in a matter-of-fact way.

"OK, I thought you might say that. Well, you know Yankele from the *hevra kaddisha* (burial society)? He's one of my best pals and I can trust him with my life, I promise you. If we make it worth his while he could help us get rid of the body and he wouldn't speak a word of it to anyone."

"We can't risk anyone else knowing. It has to be this way. Come help me lift him out to the van."

The two went through to the kitchen. Shmulik baulked at the sight of his dead nephew splayed across the kitchen table. Baruch gestured to him to lift the body and proceeded to wrap Zvi inside Hila's coat.

"Why wrap him in a coat? Couldn't you use a sheet, a blanket, a bin liner even?"

"I couldn't find the garbage bags, and she'd quickly notice if anything else is missing. Now listen, you're going to have to do exactly as I tell you. You understand?"

The fat butcher looked vacant. Shell-shocked.

"I'll stay here and clean up before Yoheved gets in. If ever she or

Nava ask about the meeting here, I'll say he didn't show up, so I just gave up on him and assumed he didn't want to come."

"Maybe someone saw him come into the building?" mumbled Shmulik.

"Yes, maybe they did. But then again, maybe they didn't. All the men are at yeshiva, the kids are at school or kindergarten, and most of the women are out working or shopping, or whatever. Those that are home don't spend their day looking in the direction of my front door to see if there's any action. We have to take a chance. Drive him far away, somewhere remote. And you're going to have to bury him. But first you're going to have to make it very hard for anyone to identify him: teeth, hands, and so on. It has to look like a brutal killing."

"Oh no! No, no, no!" sighed the big man. "I can't. He's my nephew. He's your son!"

"Strip him off, mess him up as much as you can, then bury him, but be sure he can't be identified. You can say kaddish (the prayer for the dead), if you wish."

"You bastard! You cold-hearted bastard. Those rumors about you *are* true, aren't they? I never believed them, but I understand it all now. You are a monster. You'll go to hell."

"And if you don't shut up and do as I just told you and get him out of here, you'll be going there with me."

Baruch moved to lift his dead son by his arms while Shmulik took his feet. Reaching the back door of the apartment he glanced around. There was no one in sight. He signaled to Shmulik to open the back door of his refrigerated van, then together they lifted the body inside and placed it on the floor of the vehicle. Two beef carcasses swung gently above the body as his weight caused the van to move slightly.

"Get it right, Shmulik," said Baruch with little feeling and no sign of gratitude. "I'm going in to tidy the place up. Remember exactly what I told you. Now go. Go!"

Shaking his head, big Shmulik clambered into the passenger seat of the van, placed his thumb on the dashboard panel, entered the code, and instructed it to head out of the city into the Jerusalem hills. Baruch watched the van rattle away down the cobbled backstreet, looked around again to check no one was looking, then hurried inside to get on with the cleanup.

***

1:30 P.M., Thursday, May 7, 2048

Early afternoon on a hot day such as this meant there were few people around the walking trails in the hills surrounding the holy city of Jerusalem.

Shmulik wasn't sure where he was going, but after not seeing another vehicle for at least five minutes he understood he had found his way to a particularly secluded area. Up ahead and to the right he saw a break in the trees and a dirt trail heading across at 90 degrees into the forest itself.

"Take next right," he instructed the van, and within moments felt the gears changing down as the automatic voice recognition system correctly identified the turn up ahead. Onto the dirt track and trundling along at a snail's pace, the van awaited further instructions, but none were given. The trail came to an end and the vehicle automatically pulled up.

Shmulik hauled himself out and dropped heavily onto the forest floor. He was in torment. For five minutes he circled the vehicle, dabbing his glistening brow and his eyes with a white handkerchief while muttering to himself. He knew he shouldn't go on with Baruch's plan, but the truth was that nothing would bring Zvi back.

He'd tolerated his sister's husband for so many years but never particularly liked him. Now he understood how she must have suffered being married to that man for more than half a century. No wonder she always seemed so desolate.

Shmulik was genuinely frightened of Baruch now, after the killing. He saw the emptiness in the man's soul, the callous, calculating mode into which he slipped with uncanny ease within moments of depriving his own son of a life that was on the verge of delivering so much. He felt certain that Baruch would turn on him, maybe even frame him if he didn't do as instructed.

He stood quietly, pawing the dirt beneath his feet, hands in pockets as he tried to compose himself for the awful task ahead. There was a picnic bench about thirty yards away that looked out over the wooded valley below. He wandered over and noted that the garbage can was empty, and it appeared no one had been to this spot for some time. There were no footprints in the dusty ground. On the other side of the van, away from the bench and its majestic panorama, were some bushes. He scuttled over.

"Well," he thought to himself, "this place is probably as good as any."

He went to the back of the van and began to undress. He removed his jacket, then his *tsitsit* (the tasseled prayer vest he wore over his shirt), then the shirt itself, below which he wore a singlet vest. After kicking his shoes off he slipped out of his 52-inch waisted trousers. This was going to be hot, messy and macabre. Awful, just awful. He went around and placed his clothes on the back seat of the van, moved away, then remembered he was still wearing his kippah.

"As God is my judge, I'm not going to insult Him by wearing a kippah," he whispered to himself, adding it to the pile of clothes.

Into the back of the van where Zvi's lifeless body lay. He closed the door and began to strip the clothes away from his nephew's corpse. As he took off the last garment he started to cry again.

"Poor Zvi. That lovely boy. How could God allow such a thing to happen?"

"The teeth and the hands," he chuntered to himself. "Oh my God! God help me."

Inside the butcher's van were a variety of tools. He selected a cleaver, its blade razor sharp.

"The hands, oi, the hands."

His chest was heaving. He removed Zvi's wedding ring - he'd get it back to Nava somehow when the time was right - and Zvi's watch, then laid the left hand of the corpse flat on the floor of the van, placing the blade on the dead rabbi's wrist. He breathed in, raising the cleaver to above shoulder height - then halted and lowered it again. Could he do it? He wasn't sure he could.

He needed some air and stepped out of the back of the van in his underwear and circled around three, four, five times. Still the wooded hillside was silent. He took another deep breath then half-trotted back, opened the door, grabbed the cleaver before he could think again and Wham! Then turning to the other side of the body while his own adrenalin was still pumping, Wham! but no clean-cut, so Wham! for a third time.

There was blood, but not a great deal. Shmulik began to shake ever so slightly, then more and more noticeably. Within moments he was trembling with shock at what he had just done. He realized he had to finish the job as quickly as possible so took a mallet used for flattening steaks and schnitzels and began tapping at Zvi's teeth, to little effect.

Shaking his head, he said a prayer to himself then raised the mallet high and began repeatedly smashing it into Zvi's face. He drove that mallet at least 20 times into the face of the nephew he loved. Most of the teeth were smashed out, the nose splattered and collapsed, and his mouth was torn to pieces. He was unrecognizable. A few of the blows missed the target and hit the corpse in the eyes during the frenzy.

Shmulik rubbed blood away from his own face then turned his back on his nephew's body. He sat facing the doors of the van and wept again. He wept for a couple of minutes, all the time remembering Baruch's sinister threat that Zvi must not be recognized.

He glanced behind and saw what was left of the body. It was a dreadful sight. He felt physically sick. But Zvi still had his *payot* (sidelocks). He must remove the curls and leave no trace of him having been Haredi. He reached over to a pair of scissors used for cutting fat from meat and began to cut at the curl on the left side of Zvi's face. It didn't cut cleanly but eventually came away. It was the same story on the right.

Pushing the back door of the van open Shmulik gulped at the hot, dusty air as if it was Alpine fresh. He looked around again. Still and silent. Back into the van, he dragged the body to the doorway, looked around again, then bent a good way at the knees and hauled the corpse onto his back and began trotting, with difficulty, to the bushes. He was desperately unfit, and deeply traumatized. Just as he reached the edge of the dense greenery his legs gave way under the burden and he fell heavily to the ground, the corpse slipping off his right shoulder and into the thick foliage.

Shmulik was hurt. He was no youngster and was grossly overweight. Panting heavily, writhing in pain, more mental than physical, it took him at least a minute before he managed to haul himself to his feet. His knees were bleeding. So was his right elbow. He'd gone with a hell of a bang, his own 280-pound bulk compounded by the 160-pound dead weight of Zvi's body.

The job had to be finished though. Hobbling back to the van he looked like an old man. Clambering inside to retrieve a spade he placed there prior to arriving at Baruch's house, he reckoned he could dig the grave in sixty minutes or so, even though he was already exhausted.

Back out of the van and five paces in the direction of the bushes, he stopped bolt upright. Distant voices, probably walkers. Panic, utter panic!

He couldn't risk being seen. There was no time to dig. He ran to the van, grabbed the green coat and rushed back to the bushes, wrapping his nephew up as best he could, then rolling him a couple of yards deeper into the undergrowth where the coat provided good camouflage.

That would have to do. He hobbled back to the van as fast as he could, hurriedly locked the rear doors, and still clothed only in a vest and boxer shorts jumped in and ordered the car to head straight back to Jerusalem.

A mile back onto the main forest road he saw a small parking area with no vehicles in sight. He told the van to stop, stepped out, then using the rear door to shield himself from view, took a bottle of drinking water and soaked his handkerchief, rubbing as much blood off his skin as he could before replacing his clothes as fast as possible. A few specks of blood on a butcher's face wouldn't prompt even a passing glance.

Back into the van, an instruction to go "Home", and innocent Shmulik the butcher was now a prime accessory to a dreadful crime. He began to cry again and cried sporadically throughout the half-hour journey back to Mea Shearim.

CHAPTER 15

15:00, Thursday May 7, 2048 (seven days to the referendum)

Baruch Tenenbaum felt he'd done a good job cleaning the house after the horrific events of an hour or so earlier. He walked through his forthcoming conversation with his wife and planned for every question she might ask when she saw the damage to the display cabinet in the kitchen.

Yoheved, of course, had secrets of her own and had been running through answers to any questions *he* might ask *her* that evening about her activities and whereabouts that day. He had a naturally suspicious nature. She prepared herself every time she returned from the clandestine meetings with her estranged daughter.

Yoheved arrived to find her husband sitting in the lounge reading a page of the Talmud. He was usually at the yeshiva until early evening, so she was taken aback to find him at home.

"What are you doing here?"

"Have you had a good day?" he enquired.

"Yes, fine. Nothing out of the ordinary, but why are you home? Is everything alright?"

"Actually," said Baruch, "I came home before noon to meet Zvi, but he didn't turn up. I wasn't feeling so good anyway. I felt a little light-headed and decided to stay home."

"You arranged to meet Zvi here?"

"Yes, I wanted to talk to him about something important to do with the yeshiva, but he must have had some bigger fish to fry."

"Listen Baruch, he's a public figure now. Everyone wants a piece of the boy. I'm sure he meant no offense to you. Anyway, how are you now?"

"I'm alright, but I had a fall when I was in the kitchen. My head started spinning and I lost my balance, stumbled and fell into the cabinet. I'm afraid I smashed one of the panes of glass. Sorry, I know it was your mother's, but I'll get it fixed soon enough."

"It's only a piece of furniture," said a concerned Yoheved, taking a seat on the sofa next to her husband. "Has the dizziness passed? Maybe you forgot to take your blood pressure pill?"

"No, I took the pill, but, well … neither of us are getting any younger, are we. Maybe I've been overdoing it lately. I swept the glass up and checked for any fragments. I wouldn't want any of the grandchildren to step on a piece."

"Oh, well done. You managed to find the sweeping brush then?" she said sarcastically. "Wonders will never cease. Anyway, I'll have a look in a minute as well, just to be certain. Do you want a cup of mint tea?"

"Ah, that's a good idea. Thank you."

Yoheved shuffled into the kitchen and switched the kettle on, then surveyed the damage to the cabinet, shook her head, and went into the utility room, bringing out the sweeping brush. She searched for any stray pieces of glass that might have traveled across the floor but found none. Baruch had done a very good job of cleaning up considering he'd never cleaned before or helped in any way with the kitchen or the housework. It made sense though that this time he had the wherewithal to sweep the glass up. It could have been dangerous, as he said, if she or the grandchildren had walked around there unawares.

She opened the glassless cabinet door expecting her husband to have missed a few pieces that would have fallen inside, but despite moving all the items on the shelves there wasn't even the tiniest shard to be found. Then, like a police dog trained to latch onto the scent of illegal drugs, she began sniffing the air. There was a faint smell of disinfectant.

"That's strange," she thought. "Why would he use disinfectant if there had been no liquid on the floor? You don't put disinfectant down on broken glass. He must have cut himself."

"Baruch," she called through to the lounge, "did you cut yourself?"

Within moments he filled the doorway between the lounge and kitchen.

"It's a funny thing," he said. "I went with such a bang, but I don't have a scratch on me."

She approached him and ran her finger around the inside of his shirt collar, peering in. "You're right, you haven't cut yourself."

"Well I told you, didn't I. I think I'd know if I had cut myself."

"So why did you use disinfectant on the floor?"

"The disinfectant? Oh, I don't know," he responded quick as a flash. "I think I must still have been dazed when I started cleaning up and I put disinfectant down before realizing there was no need for it. It made cleaning up much tougher! All of a sudden I'm seeing your complaints about how hard the housework is in a much more sympathetic light," he chuckled.

"Well go sit down now before you fall over again. I'll bring the tea."

She returned the sweeping brush to its place just as the kettle boiled, then soaked a teabag in a clear glass mug and added fresh mint from the fridge, along with two teaspoons of sugar. After squeezing the teabag, she opened the cupboard door under the sink, fully expecting the shattered glass to be in there, but the can was empty. In fact, there had been a few pieces of trash in there that morning when she left home. Baruch *never* emptied the garbage.

She took him his tea then returned to the kitchen before sneaking out the backdoor to check the outside garbage bin. There was no bag of trash there either. There should have been, because the bin was emptied the day before and wouldn't be emptied again until Sunday.

"Where's he put the broken glass?" she asked herself. "He's up to something. Home at such a time; he doesn't look sick; he's being uncharacteristically pleasant too, but I'm not going to say a word."

***

8:00 P.M., Thursday May 7, 2048

When Zvi Tenenbaum failed to come home that Thursday evening, Nava, his wife of 11 years instinctively knew something was wrong.

The fact he wasn't home was nothing unusual, but he'd promised to be home for dinner that evening and, had his plans changed he would have let her know. He always found a way to let her know when his schedule changed, or he was running late.

Shuli Ross, her neighbor and best friend, popped in at around eight that evening as she'd run out of plain flour for a cake she was baking. She found Nava in a concerned state. The three Tenenbaum kids, two boys aged 10 and 8, and a daughter aged 7, were oblivious to their mother's anxiety. It was normal for their high-profile father to be out until late at night on political business.

Shuli insisted it was too early to jump to any conclusions, pointing out the likelihood that he had so many demands on his time since the TV debate that he just hadn't been able to get a message to her. Maybe he hadn't been able to find an old-fashioned landline from which to call.

"He'll be in later, you'll see," said Shuli with a degree of certainty. There was a knock on the door. Nava strode over and opened it to find Baruch. She didn't invite him in.

"Shalom Baruch," she said. "What brings you here?"

"Shalom Nava. I was wondering if I could have a word with Zvi. It's about this lunchtime. I was very disappointed that he didn't come to our meeting and didn't even let me know."

"He didn't meet you? But only this morning he said he was going to meet you at noon. He was quite certain of that. And he was due in for dinner some time ago but hasn't come home yet."

"Well. He didn't show. Something must have come up. I'm quite aware that I'm not high on his order of priorities, but I thought he would at least have had the decency to send a note or telephone me at home to save me wasting my time."

"Look Baruch, I'm sorry, but it must have been something fairly serious that caused him not to keep his meeting with you, and not to arrive home yet. I'll make sure he gets in touch as soon as I see him. Send regards to Yoheved. *Lila tov* (Goodnight)."

She closed the door on her father-in-law and looked directly at Shuli.

"Something's wrong, I know it. I've just got this bad feeling."

"It's probably indigestion," laughed Shuli, never one to make a drama out of a crisis. "So he stood his father up. So what! He doesn't even like the man. No one likes that man," she giggled. "I'll drop by later and check that he's back home and all's well. Call me if you need anything."

"Thanks," Nava replied hesitantly as Shuli disappeared out through the front door.

By 11:30 p.m., with the children long since asleep and still no contact from her husband, Nava was starting to panic. It was late, but Zvi and his long-time assistant Yossi Hartov often spoke by telephone into the early hours, even though they regularly spent much of the day together at his office. She decided to call Yossi to see if he knew where Zvi was. The phone rang out a dozen times before a bleary voice answered.

"Zvi, it has to be you," mumbled Yossi, clearly dragged from his bed to answer the phone in his kitchen.

"Actually Yossi, it's Nava. I'm really sorry to call at this hour."

"No, Nava, it's OK. Is everything alright?"

"That's the thing," she said. "I don't know. Did Zvi have anything planned for this afternoon and evening? He hasn't come home yet, and I know he missed a meeting with his father this lunchtime, and he didn't come home for dinner, as we'd arranged."

Yossi suddenly sounded clear as a bell. "He was at the office this morning. We had a meeting at around ten-thirty. He left in a hurry at about twelve fifteen, and said he was late for a meeting with his father. You know he hates being late for anything. He hadn't made many other plans for the day, apart from scheduling a few calls to the States from the office, but I wasn't there this afternoon so can't tell you if he was there later on."

"I'm worried, Yossi. It's so out of character."

"Yes, I understand. It does seem strange. I'll contact Judith from the office and find out if he was there this afternoon. If he was, then she probably knows where he's got to. Maybe there's been a big development on the referendum? I'll call you back in five minutes. Hold tight, and don't worry."

True to his word, he called back within five minutes.

"I just spoke to Judith and she said he didn't come back to the office this afternoon. She expected him to make those calls to the US I mentioned before. He didn't contact her to tell her to cancel the calls. I think one was to Reverend Turner, and that would have been important."

"Yossi, I know something's wrong," said Nava in a deliberate fashion.

"Look, don't get yourself upset. I'm sure there's a reasonable explanation. I'll call my friend at the *mishteret kehilla* (Haredi community police) and ask him to find out if anyone has seen him today. I'll come over to you soon. You should ask a female friend to be there when I arrive."

"Yes, of course. Thank you, Yossi."

She placed the ancient phone back on the receiver. It was the only kind of telephone permitted by the rabbinical council, then put her coat on over her nightdress and hurried across the hall to Shuli's. Shuli was always up until around midnight cooking for the next day.

Yossi arrived within half an hour to find Nava, Shuli, and Shuli's husband, Dov, all wearing anxious expressions.

"Any news?" said Shuli, before he'd even had time to say hello.

"Nothing yet," replied Yossi with a forced smile. "The *mishteret kehila* are checking into things. They normally have their fingers on the pulse of the neighborhood, as you well know. I told them I'd be here, I gave them your phone number, and they said they'd be in touch by one, if not before."

For over an hour the four sat in the lounge making polite

conversation and trying to talk about anything but Zvi not coming home. Every 10 minutes either Shuli or Dov would nip back across the hallway and check on their six children. On one occasion Dov returned with their youngest child, an eighteen-month-old daughter who had woken when he peered around her door, but she fell asleep again almost instantly once snuggled into her mother's arms.

The toddler continued to sleep soundly but the four adults jumped when the phone rang at 1:15. Nava answered. The others watched on closely. She said little, nodded her head a few times, then placed her right hand on her forehead before running her fingers down to her chin. She was upset.

"Thank you, thank you," she said. "*B'ezrat hashem* (with God's help)," then dropped the phone back down.

"Nothing," she reported. "They said to call them first thing in the morning if he still hasn't come home. They tried to reassure me everything's alright and told me not to worry too much. I don't think they like Zvi so much though. They're probably angry at him - so many people are angry at him and, well you know Yossi, he gets so many nasty messages. They were no more than polite."

The other three rose from the sofa simultaneously.

"It'll be fine, Nava. You'll see," said Dov. "He's probably going to surprise us with some great announcement to do with the campaign that he's been working on all night."

"I'll sleep here on the sofa tonight or at least until he comes home," declared Shuli. "I'm not going to leave you alone. No arguments." Nava smiled a grateful smile.

"Look Nava, I'm going to head home," said Yossi, "but call me any time of the night when he shows up, will you, to put my mind at rest."

"Thanks for coming over so fast. He knows you're a good friend."

Dov went back across the hallway with the baby, and Yossi headed home.

"Try get some sleep, Nava. I'll be here if you need me," Shuli said, pointing to the sofa. "I don't need a blanket; this housecoat is like a furnace on its own!"

"Thanks Shuli. There's a phone extension in our bedroom, so if it rings, I'll answer. Lila Tov."

***

9:30 A.M., Friday, May 8, 2048

By morning, with no word from Zvi, there was serious concern about his welfare. Nava and Shuli both struggled to sleep and spent much of the night chatting and wondering what might have happened.

By eight thirty in the morning, Yossi returned with Judith and three others connected to Zvi's referendum campaign. Yoheved dropped by to see Nava and the kids and received the news of Zvi's absence with dismay. An hour later the Haredi community police called in to say they had still come up with nothing.

"It's like he's disappeared into thin air," one blurted out.

Once the "kosher cops" had left, as they were known colloquially, Nava asked everyone to gather in the lounge. She had something to say.

"I'm grateful to you all for being here and I know how much you all care about Zvi. There's no hiding the fact that something is wrong. He wouldn't go without contacting me for this long, especially as we had plans to eat here yesterday evening. He didn't make the meeting with his father yesterday lunchtime and, as far as we can make out, no one has seen him since he left his campaign office yesterday lunchtime.

"The *mishteret kehilla* have come up with nothing and I'm very, very concerned about his safety. He's a high-profile figure these days and he's made a lot of enemies, many of them living close by. I know it's not the done thing, but I think we have to report his absence to the Jerusalem police."

There were glances cast back and forth across the room.

"Before anyone says it, I know this is frowned upon, I know it could cause trouble for me and the children, but my husband's welfare comes before the need to keep matters private and within the confines of this community. Zvi mixed with a lot of people from outside. He's been traveling the length and breadth of the country meeting all sorts of people. He's been threatened many times. He could be somewhere, desperate for help, somewhere outside the community."

"Nava," said Yoheved, "I'm his mother and I'm as concerned as you are about this, but maybe we should give the *mishteret kehilla* a little more time before making such a controversial decision?"

"Controversial decision," echoed Nava raising her voice in frustration. "What on earth is controversial about reaching out to people who might be able to save your son's life? *Pikuach nefesh* (saving of life), the Torah tells us, is paramount, above and beyond all other Jewish laws. I know Zvi is in danger. I just know it. We have to do everything we can. I'm not being paranoid. A wife just knows when something is wrong."

"Nava, let's give it just a little more time and wait till lunchtime," suggested Yossi trying to defuse the tension between daughter-in-law and mother-in-law. "I agree that it's very worrying, but maybe he's had to lock himself away in some kind of secret negotiations.

He has, on occasions, produced big surprises, hasn't he Judith?"

"Well, he does keep quite a lot of his discussions and meetings private and plays things close to his chest, I suppose," said Judith, doing her best to back up her immediate boss.

Nava let out a massive sigh of frustration.

"We'll wait until one o'clock," stated Yossi. "Agreed."

Everyone nodded in agreement.

"If there's still nothing by then we'll have to call the police and to hell with what people say or do."

CHAPTER 16

11:00 A.M., Jerusalem, May 8, 2048 (six days to the referendum)

"So how do you want it?" asked the young, female assistant in the shawarma take-away on Jerusalem's Jaffa Street.

"Are you always so direct!" came the response.

She feigned half a laugh, but no more.

"OK, lafa bread; with humus, red cabbage, chopped salad, tehina - plenty of tehina - pickled cucumber, and lots of *harif* (spicy sauce). And when I say 'a lot,' I mean a lot. Don't hold back."

"You got it man. I'm bathing this baby in *harif*," laughed the server. "And when you're done - just so you know - there's a public toilet just fifty meters across the street!"

"You think you're funny, eh? Well put another spoonful on, you tight fisted …"

The phone rang.

"Sure. I'll be there in around twenty minutes. Just having my lunch, man. Don't start your moaning. I gotta eat. You can eat too when we're done. He's not going anywhere, and you won't starve."

Solomon Rada. Detective Inspector Solomon Rada, Israel's most senior officer of Ethiopian descent.

Many Ethiopians were tall, elegant and slim, but Rada was short and stout, his penchant for Israeli fast food doubtless a factor in his rotund physique. 44-years-old, married with two children, he'd shattered the glass ceiling that kept other policemen and women of Ethiopian origin in the lower ranks of the force for a long time.

More than 60 years had passed since "Operation Moses," the 1985 airlift of Ethiopian Jews to Israel that saved the lives of thousands suffering from the terrible drought in Africa that eventually killed millions. The Jewish state received much international praise for its intervention to save the people many referred to as "The Lost Tribe."

But while most citizens celebrated the saving of Jews from near-certain death, there were those in Israeli society, just like every other country in the world, who were less than delighted at an influx of black people - Jewish or not - into their fold.

Not for these dark-skinned newcomers the opportunity to integrate immediately and taste the best Israel had to offer. Most were shuttled off to dusty development towns in the Negev desert, or found their way to the poorer neighborhoods in central Israel where jobs were scarce, crime was high, and life opportunities were at a minimum. With limited Hebrew-language skills the older generation found life particularly tough. Many worked in menial, low-paid jobs.

Like the Russian immigrants to Israel immediately before and after them, many Ethiopians found it incredibly hard to adapt to their new life. They were poor where once they had a decent standard of living; they didn't speak the language where once they had been articulate and capable; and they found it too hot where once they had lived in temperate surroundings. Most had lived in mountainous areas with a relatively cool climate, and now they found themselves in the dusty, humid, no holds barred Middle East.

But like it or not, there was one great equalizer. The Israeli army.

For young Ethiopians raised in their new country the army offered a chance to serve and be treated as an equal to the white Ashkenazi youngsters of Tel Aviv and the center of the country, to a great extent the educational and business elite. And to the Sephardic youngsters, those hailing from families who arrived in Israel in the 1950s after the expulsion of whole Jewish communities from the Arab world.

That mass ethnic cleansing by the Arab nations of their Jews had only recently started to be recognized by the international community and the worldwide media, for so long obsessed with the complex Palestinian issue. What happened more than nine decades earlier had devastated huge communities of Jewish people around the Middle East and North Africa, for whom the Arab world was their world. They were as much immersed in Arab culture as European or American Jews were in their adopted cultures.

But black, white, blue or pink, it made no difference when you got your call-up papers at the age of 17 before being drafted after high school at 18. That was, of course, unless you were one of the million and more Haredim exempt from military service - the prime condition their political leaders had demanded of each and every Israeli coalition government in which they had sat since the 1990s.

It was in the army that Solomon Rada excelled. Short in stature, but smart, sociable, and with a burning desire to succeed, he rose quickly through the ranks after signing up beyond the initial three years and left at the age of 27 having risen to the rank of major in the parachute regiment. Married soon after to his long-time girlfriend

Oksana - whose family had arrived in Israel two generations earlier from the Ukraine - after leaving the army he joined the police and shot up the ladder there too, repeating his rise through the military echelons just a few years earlier.

His was a career to inspire Ethiopian Israeli youth, but still, sadly, somewhat of an exception that proved the rule.

***

The unmistakable whiff of cleaning fluid was always the first sensory experience prompted by entry into Jerusalem's forensic and pathology laboratory.

Through security with a cursory display of his police credentials - his face was its own pass; he was an unmistakable figure - Rada headed down to floor -3 where he found the fifty-something, balding and bespectacled Nahum Greenberg, furiously munching on a rather unappetizing homemade sandwich.

"Playing hooky again?" smiled Rada.

With his mouth full, Greenberg shrugged his shoulders and offered a half-smile, taking his time to fully digest his food.

"Solomon. Nice to see you. Go fuck yourself!"

"Oooohh!" laughed the detective inspector. "Someone's a bit cranky today. Has the lovely Mrs. Greenberg been making life hard for hubby, I wonder?"

"I hardly think I'm going to share my innermost thoughts about my dear wife with you, old pal. Let's go see the man, and then I can go upstairs for a fruit juice. I want to leave fairly soon as I promised to help prepare Friday night dinner."

"What a thrilling life you lead," mocked Rada. "No, actually, that's nice."

Out of cold storage and placed on a dissection table was the corpse found in the Jerusalem hills a few hours earlier. Greenberg had already performed the autopsy on the gory remains that had put such a damper on Roi and Adva Bruner's Friday morning picnic.

"Here's what I know. Some of it is quite obvious, but no doubt you're recording me, so I want it all there for the record," stated Greenberg in his usual, thoroughly professional manner.

"We're talking about a white, Caucasian male, mid-twenties to early-thirties, around 160 lbs., five foot ten inches tall. He's circumcised so is almost certainly Jewish; he's almost certainly too fair to be Arab. He could, of course, be a European visitor, and some non-Jews still circumcise their boys, as you may know."

Rada nodded confirming he was aware of the aforementioned details.

"He's obviously too old to have been microchipped at birth; that came in just 18 years ago. He has average muscle tone and is unlikely to have been a sporty type. He has an appendix scar. Hands have been hacked off; most teeth have been smashed out. There are no signs of trauma on his torso or arms, suggesting he didn't put up a fight before he was killed. He may well have been surprised. He has a low level of alcohol in his blood."

"No DNA?" asked Rada.

"We've run it and he's not on the system, so he probably has no criminal record. Obviously, due to his facial injuries it would be impossible to match up any dental records," continued Greenberg. "You'll be aware there have been no reports of a missing person to match his description, so he could have been a loner; the foreign tourist theory applies as you wouldn't necessarily be concerned about not hearing from someone for a few days while they're away enjoying themselves; but I think he's a 'frummer' [slang; religious person], probably Haredi."

"How do you come up with the '*frummer*' theory? Man, that's not easy to say after wolfing down a spicy shawarma! My lips are still tingling!"

Greenberg rolled his eyes and continues regardless.

"Well, he's pale all over, including his face, so he wouldn't have been one to sit out in the sun or be outdoors for any great period of time. That tallies with the complexion of most Talmudic Ashkenazi students. But, more significantly, take a look at his hair."

"I'm looking, but I'm not seeing," whispered Rada in a quizzical tone.

"His sideburns are all over the place, aren't they?" questioned Greenberg, inviting a response, but getting none. "I think he had *payot* (sidelocks) and they've been hacked off with a knife. You see how the cut of the hair is uneven while the rest of his hair is - given the trauma his head has been through - relatively well groomed. No barber worth his salt would make such a bad job, don't you think?"

"I do think. I think you are better at your job than you look - although you've not met my barber!"

"Cut the wisecracks, for God's sake. You're such a pain in the ass."

"Consider me chastised."

"One final thing leads me to believe he may have been a 'frummer'. There are no inoculation scars anywhere on his arms and, as you know, plenty in the Haredi world still didn't agree to their kids being inoculated when this guy was a boy."

"OK," said Rada. "So we're looking at a young male; probably married - 'cos if he's a 'frummer' he could have already been married ten or more years and probably has a houseful of kids; he's had his appendix out; he's not on any database; he didn't put up a fight, so he was either surprised or he may have known his killer; and no one's reported him missing."

"Yup," nodded Greenberg, "but you haven't asked me about the cause of death?"

"Well I haven't asked you because I thought the fact that someone smashed his face to pieces might well have been the main contributing factor. Am I wrong?"

"Yes, you're wrong. His face was almost certainly smashed in and his hands removed after death in order, no doubt, to make identification more difficult for your good self and your esteemed colleagues. He hasn't been dead for much more than 24 hours, by the way. He died as a result of a severe trauma to the upper spine area just below the skull itself, close to the brainstem, which appears to have been inflicted by, most likely, a piece of glass forced into him at an upward angle. There were very small glass fragments around the entry wound. He would have died almost instantly."

"So I can probably rule out the possibility of him having been targeted in a hit, which was where I might have been going first with this. When was the last time a hitman killed someone with a piece of glass?"

"Yes, I concur with that view. This probably wasn't a professional job."

"The only thing that doesn't quite fit is the fact that if he was the family man you suggest," mused Rada, "no one has reported his disappearance to the authorities. We're going to have to check the database of recent missing persons again. Surely such a family man would check in at least every couple of days to see how the wife and kids are doing.

"If though, as you suggest, he is Haredi, well they don't come running straight away to the likes of the police, do they. That might explain why we haven't heard anything yet. This is a strange one."

"Fair point, but remember he's probably not been dead much

more than a day," acknowledged Greenberg, covering up the body and sliding him up and back into his refrigerated resting place. "I agree. It's a bit of a puzzle."

"Just one minute." shouted Rada. "What about the green coat the report mentioned he was wrapped in. It was read to me in the car on the way in. Did you do the tests on that?"

"I was wondering when you would latch onto that. We won't get the DNA within the next couple of hours so it will have to wait until Sunday morning, or after Shabbat. But close to the cuff of the left sleeve of the coat, very faded, I found the name, Tova Smotkin. I ran a check and, believe it or not, only one Tova Smotkin came up and she had plenty of data on the system having been hospitalized for a long period."

"Bingo! I'll run a check and get an address or a number for her. We need to talk to her."

"You'll have a job as she's been dead for sixteen years! I immediately ran her details through the system myself and called her daughter who lives in Tel Aviv. She said her mom was ninety-three when she died of cancer at Shaareh Zedek hospital. I have her family contact details for you and will zap them over to you in a few moments. She said they gave all her mother's things to a charity store within a couple of weeks of her death. The coat was almost certainly among the things they gave away."

Greenberg took out his communication pad and said "Tova Smotkin." The details appeared on his screen and he forwarded them to the detective.

"You've earned your fruit juice," said Rada, disappearing through the swing door. "Hell, treat yourself to a chocolate bar as well! Shabbat shalom!"

***

2:30 P.M., Friday, May 8, 2048

Rada arrived home and had just kicked his shoes off when the call came through from head office.

"Solomon, we just had an interesting missing person call that might tie in with the body found in the hills earlier today," said Rita, Rada's assistant on the homicide desk. "A Haredi woman reported her husband didn't come home last night, and before you make any wisecracks, you're not going to believe who her husband is!"

CHAPTER 17

7:00 P.M., Friday, May 8, 2048 (six days to the referendum)

The last weekend before the referendum. Dusk fell across the Holy Land, the State of Israel. From the apple and pear orchards of Metula in the north on the Israel-Lebanon border, to the searing heat of the Red Sea resort of Eilat at the southernmost tip of the country's Negev desert, from the great nonstop metropolis of Tel Aviv on the Mediterranean, and to the fabled city of Jerusalem just forty miles to the east; Shabbat, the Jewish Sabbath, had arrived.

Until 2036, the Israeli public had been free to mark Shabbat as they wished. Secular Jews and Arabs used the period to go on day trips, enjoy family picnics or barbecues, dine at a restaurant, hang out with friends. It was the one time of the week when they could take a much-needed break from the heavy work schedule most endured. For the religious communities Shabbat was a time when no work of any kind, and no travel were permitted. It was a time for reflection, prayers in the synagogue, and the togetherness of the extended family unit.

In religious areas of the country such as Jerusalem, Bnei Brak, the Israeli West Bank, and others, no businesses of any kind were open and there was no public transport. A hush would fall on these areas as prayer, family, and each individual's connection to God were central to the Shabbat tradition.

As the growth of the Haredi vote gathered pace, so too did their political power. In 2035, a bill was proposed that sought to force the whole country - with the exception of Arab towns and villages - to observe the Jewish Sabbath in the traditional way.

There was massive opposition from secular Jewish society, from a large proportion of the moderately religious Jewish sector, and from Arab society too, but under the threat of them pulling out of the ruling coalition that would force a political crisis and a general election, the Haredim succeeded in getting their way and the bill became law, the Knesset voting 62-58 in favor.

From January 1, 2036, it was illegal (with the exception of the police, the military, and the emergency services), to drive any vehicle in Israel from one hour before sunset on Friday, until one hour after sunset on Saturday. Anyone breaking this law immediately had their license revoked. The whole nation - as had previously been the case solely on Yom Kippur (the Day of Atonement) - now ground to a halt. It was a massive victory for the religious block but caused enhanced resentment among the rest of the population.

Many businesses that relied primarily on weekend trade to help them make ends meet, went to the wall in that first year. There was a $10,000 fine per offense for any shop, store, or food outlet that broke the new, draconian Shabbat Law. Unemployment rose sharply for the first time in a generation. The freedom of choice of which the democratic Israel had so long been proud, was seriously eroded and devalued.

The Haredi world was convinced that the law had been approved by parliament because it was God's will that Shabbat be observed in the proper manner. God had enabled them to bring about this landmark change to the Israeli way of life. It would enhance the value of togetherness and strengthen the family unit. At last, people would have time to step back from the usual frantic routine and enjoy each other's company without distraction. Hopefully, they would start attending synagogue, or at least say a family prayer together. Maybe they would eventually discover the joy and consolation some religious observance would bring to their lives.

Undoubtedly, the new Shabbat restrictions brought some people closer to their religion. Attendance at mainstream synagogues increased, and there was much to be said for the stillness and quiet that roads without traffic provided. People who normally sat at the office or behind a driving wheel found the only option was to walk if they wanted to meet friends; many admitted they had increased their exercise as a result of a Friday evening or Saturday walk and their health had improved. And air pollution, a huge problem these days, especially in the big cities, had already dipped noticeably as a result of the roads and highways lying deserted for at least 26 hours a week.

But like Christmas or Thanksgiving in so many other parts of the world, having extended family under one roof for any period of time often caused tensions. Incidents of domestic violence and family disputes rose markedly, but at least to this point people could lock themselves away and interact with friends on social media. Now, twelve years on from the introduction of the Shabbat Law, even that pastime was in serious jeopardy.

A new bill had been put to the Knesset in early-2048 prior to being frozen once the referendum issue overwhelmed the political dialogue. It proposed legislation that would make it illegal for

Internet and telephone companies, and any other company that facilitated mobile communications in the State of Israel, to provide a service to customers during Shabbat. To do so would have resulted in the cancellation of the trading license of such a company in the Jewish State.

This was yet another pertinent issue filtering into the decision-making process of the electorate when it came to voting Yes or No to the question of separation.

**

Hila Sonfeld was stressed. She bathed her boys earlier than usual. Ed read them their bedtime stories and had them in their pajamas by six-thirty. Their dinner guests would arrive in an hour.

At first she had been exasperated when Ed told her that his boss, Hofshi Party leader Ilana Shwartz, the woman who could become the first prime minister of the new-look State of Israel, had agreed to come for Friday dinner - the very last Friday before the referendum. She had panicked. She'd only met Shwartz and her husband, Avi, a couple of times before, and that had been in the company of many others at party events.

For ages Ed had been trying to get Shwartz to come for dinner. For her to accept would be a sign that he was in favor and might be set to rise further up the party ladder. Shwartz's willing acceptance of the invitation on this significant weekend was much more than a nod and a wink in the right direction for the young party fixer; Ed hoped an offer of a more prominent role in the party might be forthcoming.

They arrived on the dot at 7:30 in the evening, having enjoyed a half-hour stroll through the streets of central Tel Aviv that had fallen relatively silent a couple of hours earlier. Shwartz vehemently opposed the Shabbat travel ban arguing it was an infringement of civil liberties, even human rights, but there could be no denying the tranquility was a welcome change from the usual bumper-to-bumper daily grind.

Along the way she'd been recognized by many people, some shaking her hand and assuring her they were voting Yes on Thursday. Others spontaneously broke into applause. Only once was she heckled, an elderly man shouting, "Ilana, where did all the money go?" a reference to a financial scandal that engulfed a military software company some years earlier of which she had been chairwoman.

She and Avi reached the Sonfeld household in relaxed mode, looking forward to a great dinner.

Once upon a time Israel had been the land of home cooking. Everybody cooked and there was great debate and competition as to which national cuisine offered the best food. These days, despite all the labor-saving devices, few young people outside of the religious communities regularly went to the trouble of cooking a meal from scratch. Nearly everyone worked full-time (a minimum nine-hour day), debilitating long hours for modest pay. Time pressures meant ready meals and takeaways were more often than not the easiest, if not the healthiest option.

Hila, however, was noted as a fine cook. She grew up in a household where her mother would cook every day. Yoheved taught her eight daughters the skills of the Eastern European "*haimishe*" kitchen, based on the Polish and Russian Jewish cuisines that reflected the family roots. For ages, Ilana Shwartz hinted she would have to come over to taste for herself this food she'd heard so much about.

Ed poured wine and the four raised a toast to "the right result on Thursday," then Hila invited Avi to join her in the kitchen as she served the first course, chopped liver pate with cranberry sauce and a side salad. The stove was active with a large soup pan on the boil and the oven emitted the unmistakable aroma of roast chicken.

Hila and Avi hit it off immediately, both bemoaning the long hours their spouses had been putting in over the last year and the pressure it had placed on the family. Avi worked full-time too, as a university lecturer. The Shwartz's three children had already completed army service; one was traveling abroad, the other two were studying at university, one in Tel Aviv, the other in the United States.

They brought the first course to the elegant dinner table and tucked in. The conversation flowed, there were plenty of laughs, and a second glass of wine was poured before the starter was completed.

Hila returned to the kitchen to serve borscht. This beet soup containing small meatballs was for generations one of the staples of Russian cuisine. It's a signature dish of the traditional Ashkenazi kitchen.

"Oh my God," sighed Avi after taking a first spoonful, "this is fantastic! Where did you learn to cook like this? It's just delicious."

"It really is delicious," added Shwartz. "You're more than living up to the reputation you've earned at Hofshi HQ. Avi's right, how did you learn to cook like this? It's so rare these days to find a working mum that has the skills to make such a superb, traditional meal?"

"Tell her, Hil," said Ed. "You won't believe it."

"No, it's no big deal. I just used to watch my mother cooking and helped out from as far back as I can remember. That's all. I enjoy it too. I find it therapeutic."

"Oh, Hila, therapeutic! I still get stressed out trying to make pasta for the family," laughed Ilana.

Shwartz, the former Mossad boss, sensed there was more to Hila's story. Turning on her famous charm she tried to delve a little deeper.

"Yours is obviously a traditional Ashkenazi family, Hila. Mine too, but my grandparents were the last to cook in this way. I still remember some of the great food Safta (grandma) made when I was a child; *tsimes*, potato kugel, that kind of thing. The skills died with her though. Where did you grow up?"

Hila shot a glance across to Ed. Before she had a chance to speak for herself, he revealed that she was from Jerusalem.

"Really," said Shwartz. "That must have been hard growing up there given the restrictions on secular life?"

"I'm from a Haredi family, Ilana," said Hila, "if that's what you wanted to know. I grew up in Mea Shearim, in a big family. I left when I was seventeen and started a completely new life. I met Ed when I was in the army, and this is where I am today," she declared, raising her hands and pointing to the home around her.

"Wow, that must have been such a hard thing to do," said Avi. "I can't imagine what you must have gone through in order to reach a decision to leave that world, then trying to adjust to this way of life. I think it's amazing."

"Not amazing," replied Hila. "I'm not the only one, as you know. It was hard, but it's no different to what Jews have had to do throughout their existence. We're like chameleons, changing into something new in order to adapt to whichever society and environment they move to. In my case, the move took place within the borders of a Jewish nation. That's the only difference."

"And that's how you came to be such a great cook," nodded Shwartz. "It's a bit ironic, isn't it, that on the last Friday before we vote to separate ourselves from the Haredi communities, we're here, in your lovely home in Tel Aviv, center of democratic Israel and the secular society, enjoying the most wonderful traditional Jewish dinner. I'm sure many Haredi families who will vote the other way are having a similar meal. Do you stay in touch with your family?"

"No. I haven't seen any of them since the day I left. They said kaddish for me."

"Oh, how awful," railed Ilana. "How can any family treat their child as deceased just because they want to live a different life? That, I just don't understand. Especially the mothers. How can any mother who has weaned and loved her child suddenly close the door and treat them as dead? I just think it's barbaric."

"Well, unfortunately, that's the way it is," said Hila, in a matter-of-fact way. "Can I take your plates?"

The stuffed roast chicken, served with roast potatoes, broccoli and green beans, and rich chicken gravy was even better than the previous two courses. They opened another bottle of wine. There was plenty more laughter. Hila and Avi cleared the table - Ed insisted he'd straighten up the kitchen later.

"Well you kept that quiet," whispered Shwartz, leaning across to her host. "I mean about Hila's background. *Kol hakavod la* (good for her). On a different subject Ed, after we win on Thursday, I'll speak to you about taking on a little more responsibility within the party. What do you say?"

"I'd be honored. Can't wait for the vote to be behind us then we can start getting on with returning this country to its former glories."

"Yup, it's going to be a unique ride - but it won't be easy, you know that."

"Of course. Did you have time to look through the ideas for the ten-year-plan I sent you a few weeks ago?"

"To be honest, I've not had time to even scan through it, but I will. Let's get Thursday out of the way then we can look ahead to the new dawn."

An hour later they'd done justice to a fresh fruit salad with Cointreau liqueur, accompanied by dessert wine, then arrived at the espresso coffee.

"Hila, what can I say," grinned Shwartz. "This has been terrific. What a great meal, and what a great evening. You two are really special. I'm really proud to have Ed as an important part of my team."

"Ilana, it was our pleasure," responded Hila. "It was so kind of you to come over tonight given all the pressure you've been under over the last few weeks."

"You know, Ed," said Shwartz, "it's a shame you never told me about Hila's Haredi upbringing. It could have been useful in the campaign."

"Ilana, with the greatest respect," responded Hila, "my husband may have chosen to work in the political field, but I haven't, and I'll always keep my private life just that. Private. I'd really appreciate it if it remains that way," she added before Ed had a chance to say anything.

"I'm with you, Hila. It's no fun being in the public eye, believe me. I just don't know how I'm gonna cope if she becomes prime minister," said Avi. "I hate even having my photo taken, never mind standing in front of lots of people."

"Ilana, you wouldn't believe it if I told you who Hila's brother is," blurted out Ed, clearly the worse for wear.

"It's a private matter Ed, so let's leave it that way," snapped Hila.

The Shwartz's stared momentarily at each other, he sent her a look that suggested it would be unwise to pursue the matter. She didn't pay any attention.

"Well, you can't just throw it out there Ed and leave it hanging in mid-air. Who is he?"

"Ed! It's not up for discussion," Hila insisted.

"Oh, Hil, it's not a big issue. We're here with close friends who can keep a confidence. She's Zvi Tenenbaum's sister. Can you believe it? Zvi Tenenbaum!"

Hila got up from the table, furious with her husband, and stormed into the kitchen.

"I don't believe it. You're having me on?" gasped Shwartz. "Hila is Zvi Tenenbaum's sister! The same Zvi Tenenbaum I debated on TV earlier this week. Your brother-in-law!"

"Technically, but I've never met the man," Ed sheepishly muttered, quickly realizing he'd gone too far.

"One of my main opponents in this bitter battle, and we're having Friday night dinner with his sister just days before the referendum. You couldn't make this up!"

"His *estranged* sister. She hasn't had anything to do with her family since the day she left. That was in another life. It's not her fault who her brother is, is it? Ah, I shouldn't have mentioned it. I've had too much to drink."

"But you did, Ed, didn't you?"

"Well, what does it matter," said Avi. "I think it just makes her an even more admirable person. Look what she's gone through to be the impressive woman she is today. I think she's great, and we've had a wonderful evening, haven't we Ilana?"

"Oh yes, absolutely. Great."

Hila emerged back into the lounge, her eyes betraying that she'd shed tears. Avi put his arm around her and gave her a kiss. Shwartz also kissed her and thanked her again for a great meal and a wonderful evening. She said she hadn't meant in any way to make her feel uncomfortable.

"You and Ed are something else," she shouted as they made their way down the garden path to the street. "Thanks again."

"That was unforgivable," Hila told her husband once the front door had closed. "We agreed it would never be brought up. Why on earth did you do that, especially in front of her?"

"Oh, Hil, I'm sorry," said Ed, trying to hug his wife but being firmly pushed away. "I've had too much to drink. I meant no harm. I'm just so proud of you. It's no big deal anyway. She won't say anything. By the way, she's offered me a promotion."

"You know where you can stick your promotion …"

The bedroom door slammed shut before she completed the sentence. Ed, in a stupor, was left to tidy the kitchen on his own.

CHAPTER 18

4:00 P.M., Tel Aviv, Saturday, May 9, 2048 (five days to the referendum)

It was too good not to use. Ilana Shwartz had turned it over in her mind from the moment she and Avi left the Sonfeld's late the previous evening.

She told her husband that a gem like this rarely came your way at such a late stage of a crucial political campaign. Not to use it to drive home her message, she said, would be a dereliction of her duty as leader of both Hofshi and the Yes movement. Avi had flown into a rage, forcefully pointing out to his wife that details of Hila's past and the fact she was Zvi Tenenbaum's sister were told to them in the strictest confidence.

"She's not a political figure," Avi insisted. "She's entitled to her privacy, and she is in no way connected to the campaign. It's her private life and it should remain private, as she said. You must not, I repeat *not* mention what was discussed over dinner last night to anyone. Do you hear me, Ilana? I'm warning you. *You must not betray their trust.*"

All the way through lunch Shwartz continued to mull over the pros and cons of using the information gained the night before. Ed Sonfeld would be furious - and with good reason - but she could take care of Ed. He was an ambitious young man who had always been loyal and hard-working. Confirmation of a step up the ladder, as she'd mentioned after dinner, would probably be enough to take the heat out of the situation.

Facing Hila would be quite another matter. She could see she was no pushover, but she'd faced much worse during her time at the Mossad and could handle her. One thing her intelligence training had impressed upon her was that when you're in a dogfight, or at war, it can be the smallest detail and the tiniest fractions that might sway the balance in your favor. You've got to know not only precisely what to do with an intelligence gem, but when to use it.

Any nagging doubts or pangs of conscience lingering in her mind were quashed by a mid-afternoon phone call from her main campaign pollster. The first news broadcast after Shabbat would show the gap between the Yes and No campaigns narrowing to 50% in favor, 43% against, and now only 7% still undecided. That meant that with 52.5% representing the winning post, victory was no longer assured. It was becoming a little too close for comfort.

Of the once legendary social media sites plenty had come and gone over the previous twenty years, but good old Twitter still remained one of the most powerful tools for reaching the masses. Ilana Shwartz had well over 2 million followers. At 4:26 p.m. she Tweeted:

You heard Rabbi Zvi Tenenbaum on the televised debate stating: *"I am not willing to give up on so many millions of Jewish people in Israel and around the world who choose not to be as observant as us."* I said at the time,

"He's a fraud. Nothing more, nothing less." Information
has subsequently reached me that Tenenbaum has a close
family member who left the Haredi world some years ago
to join secular society and he has not had any contact
with that person since! Sounds to me like a classic case of
"Do as I say, not as I do." He and his vote No campaign
cannot be trusted. HE'S A DANGEROUS PHONY!"

Within half an hour Shwartz's tweet had received more than 24,000
likes, more than 6,500 retweets, and more than a thousand comments, almost all slamming Rabbi Tenenbaum for his "two-faced",
"hypocritical" behavior.

It still being Shabbat, there were few comments defending the
rabbi or his side of the campaign.

CHAPTER 19

10:00 P.M., Jerusalem, May 9, 2048 (five days to the referendum)

Around an hour after Shabbat ended members of the Israeli and international press received a message that an extraordinary press conference would be held at ten thirty at night at the central police headquarters in Jerusalem.

No details of the subject of the press conference had been included, other than the somewhat cryptic message that it was connected to the referendum campaign.

The press corps piled into a room where 100 seats had been arranged facing a table where just two seats had been prepared, set against a backdrop that included the Israeli flag and the emblem of the Israeli police. There was sufficient space at the perimeter of the room to allow television crews to set up and broadcast live.

By the appointed hour the room was packed, and a wide variety of rumors were circulating. Some had it "on good authority" that the announcement was going to be confirmation of criminal charges being brought against Prime Minister Gal on one or more of the three investigations into his affairs that had dogged him for more than two years. If so, pressing charges so close to the referendum, they said, would be seen in many quarters as an act of political sabotage by the prosecutor's office against the No campaign.

Others had heard that the gathering was related to historic Israeli intelligence activities that might have crossed the gray line between acceptable investigative processes and criminality and had taken place under the watch of Ilana Shwartz during her time at the Mossad. The Mossad's activities were primarily conducted overseas, but there were occasions when their path crossed with the Israeli internal security agency, Shabak. It wasn't uncommon for such cases to cause massive tension in the Israeli intelligence community, and speculation was rife that those who tangled with Shwartz and came off second best during her time at the top were now looking for the perfect moment to exact their revenge.

Plenty of other suggestions were spouted involving a host of characters connected to the referendum campaign, the only issue in town. All attention understandably focused on what was certain to be a momentous decision for the country, whichever way Thursday's vote went.

Nearly ten minutes later than scheduled, two men walked out to a barrage of flashes and occupied the seats facing the media. Ofir Carmel was Israel's most senior police officer and head of the Israeli constabulary. To his left sat Solomon Rada.

"Ladies and gentlemen," began Carmel. "Thank you all very much for coming here at such short notice. This press conference was called to present details of a very serious crime that has been committed and to answer, as best we can, any questions you may have on the subject. Seated alongside me is a figure many of you may recognize. Detective Inspector Solomon Rada is the senior investigating officer on this case. He will make a statement in a few moments' time.

"Before we get to the statement, I want to make it very clear that the press has a duty to accurately report the facts. Speculation, supposition, unnamed sources, and unattributed quotes are often harmful to an investigation and give little credit to the journalistic profession. In the current political climate, I urge all reporting this case to tread very carefully. We will not hesitate to look very closely at prosecution of any reporting that is judged to be inflammatory or prejudicial to the public good."

Looks of surprise and raised eyebrows filled the room. The sense that this was going to be something really juicy had the normally blasé members of the press sitting up and taking notice.

"And now, I'll hand over to Detective Inspector Rada."

"Er, thank you Chief Inspector Carmel," Rada began. "I shall present a timeline of the events, as best we know them, and with those details we're able to disclose at this time that have led to you being invited to join us here this evening.

"At ten o'clock yesterday morning, Friday, May eighth, a call was received by the police here in Jerusalem from two hikers in the Jerusalem hills, reporting the discovery of a mutilated adult male body, about 3 kilometers from the village of Kisalon. Emergency services attended the scene and removed the body to the city forensic laboratory for postmortem investigation. The police service is performing a detailed forensic search of the site where the body was discovered."

A buzz surged across the gathering. Flashlights blazed again and TV cameras zoomed in closer on the face of Solomon Rada as he continued.

At approximately 13:30 yesterday afternoon, a missing person report was filed with the Jerusalem police by an immediate relative, along with friends of a man whose failure to return home on Thursday evening had been a cause of great concern and was completely out of character. A plain clothes police unit attended the missing man's home to obtain DNA samples. They also interviewed the man's wife and work colleagues who happened to be present and were able to help establish a good timeline of his movements up until the point that he was last seen."

"Because of the weekend break, analysis of these DNA samples could not be completed until immediately after the end of the Shabbat period, but that process was concluded at approximately nine-thirty this evening, after which an invitation was sent to you all to attend this press conference."

The room was completely silent. You could hear a pin drop.

"The DNA samples obtained from the home of the missing man, and the DNA from the dead body are, without a shadow of a doubt, one and the same. It is therefore with great regret that I have to inform you that the deceased male found yesterday morning in the Jerusalem hills is thirty-one-year-old Rabbi Zvi Nahum Tenenbaum, of Mea Shearim, Jerusalem."

The room erupted into unbridled pandemonium. There were shouts of horror, bemused looks on the face of many, a few tears, and a cacophony of questions fired in Rada's direction. He appeared dazed by the lights and the shocked reaction that surged through the room with electrifying force.

The press conference hadn't been carried live to that point, but news of the stunning subject matter was immediately transmitted to the respective headquarters of the competing Israeli news organizations, all of whom cut into their programming to switch to a live broadcast of the remainder of the statement. Even US networks Fox News and CNN cut into their programming to carry coverage of the event on what was an otherwise quiet weekend news day.

"Ladies and gentlemen, can we please have some order," bellowed Chief Inspector Carmel. He repeated his request five times before the room settled down sufficiently for Rada to continue.

"I'm not taking any questions just yet," he said, in response to a barrage of enquiries fired at him. "I'd thank you all to just calm down while I finish my statement, then I'll move on to answering a few of your questions."

"The deceased obviously had a high public profile, but this is a terrible tragedy for all those connected to Rabbi Tenenbaum, in particular his wife and three children, his family, friends and colleagues, and his community. The Israeli police offer our sincere condolences to all affected by this tragedy. Following on from the comments of the chief inspector, I urge all the media to respect the privacy of Rabbi Tenenbaum's family at this very difficult time, and not to engage in any wild speculation. We have already drafted in extra manpower and other resources to do all we can to try and catch whoever is responsible for this truly despicable act as swiftly as is practicable.

"Now, I am happy to try to answer a few of your questions."

Chief Inspector Carmel took charge of selecting the questions as a forest of hands were raised. It went without saying that this shocking news could have a truly profound effect on the outcome of the referendum itself.

"Yes, Channel One news," said Carmel, pointing at their main crime reporter, Moshe Brodi.

"Detective Inspector Rada, can you give us details of how Rabbi Tenenbaum died?"

"Our postmortem examination established that the rabbi died from a single wound located at the top of the neck, just under the base of his skull. We believe death would have been almost instantaneous."

Another buzz surged through the gathering but shouting over the hubbub Brodi followed up his initial question. Glancing down as he spoke and referring to his notes, he asked, "Detective Inspector Rada, in your statement you said that the body was mutilated, but just now you indicated that the late rabbi died from a single wound beneath the base of his skull. Can you clarify this as the one fact doesn't obviously tally with the other?"

"I can, sir. It is our belief that the deceased died, as I mentioned a moment ago, as the result of a single entry wound below the skull, at the top of the spine. We have not ruled out the possibility that the murder and the subsequent mutilation of the body took place in different locations; the latter appears to have been a crude attempt to make identification as difficult as possible."

"Dorit Lillenblum, Channel Two news," bellowed Carmel, pointing to that channel's sometime newsreader and regular crime reporter.

"Detective Inspector Rada, can you specify when and where Rabbi Tenenbaum was last seen alive, and by whom?"

"At this point in time we believe the deceased left his campaign office, which is situated just outside of Mea Shearim in central Jerusalem, at about twelve-fifteen yesterday lunchtime. We understand he was on his way to see his father, who lives inside Mea Shearim, but he never arrived."

More murmurs flew around the packed press conference.

"As you will no doubt appreciate, we will be looking at as much CCTV recording as we can, but most of you will know that close to the perimeter of Mea Shearim the CCTV coverage ceases out of deference to the religious sensibilities of the Haredi residents of that quarter. If Rabbi Tenenbaum set out to meet with his father at his father's home - which is no more than one kilometer away - it should have taken him no more than ten minutes or so to arrive."

"Joe Henderson, CNN!" roared Chief Inspector Carmel.

"Thank you, sir, for the opportunity to put a question," nodded CNN's Jerusalem correspondent. "The televised referendum debate last week was shown with simultaneous translation in the United States, and Rabbi Tenenbaum was, according to the post-broadcast reaction, viewed favorably by the majority of our viewers, regardless of which side of the referendum argument they support. I'm sure I speak for all our viewers and others across the US and beyond in expressing our heartfelt sympathies to his family at their tragic loss.

"Detective Inspector Rada, given the geography of the last sighting, and picking up on what you just said about the deceased's intended destination after leaving his campaign office, are you able to indicate whether your lines of inquiry center on members of the late rabbi's own Haredi community?"

"Well, we are pursuing a number of lines of inquiry. It's too early at this stage to narrow down the field, sir. You will be aware that as a high-profile public figure at the center of what is a very heated, hard-fought referendum debate, Rabbi Tenenbaum received plenty of support but also plenty of criticism from different quarters, some of it somewhat vitriolic, shall we say. It would be wrong to rule out any line of inquiry."

"But you believe that his death is connected to the campaign?" Henderson fired back.

"I didn't say that."

"Three more questions and then we'll have to let the detective inspector get on with leading this investigation," said Carmel. "Rafi Raphaeli, Israel radio."

"I just want to follow-up on the point raised by the previous questioner." Rada nodded. "We all saw the fiery exchanges between

Rabbi Tenenbaum and Chief Rabbi Bermann, as well as Rabbi Tenenbaum and Hofshi Party leader Ilana Shwartz in the debate earlier this week. Have you ruled out the possibility that either of these figures might have had any sort of role, however peripheral, in inciting someone to commit the terrible crime that you revealed a few moments ago?"

"As I said, Rafi, we haven't ruled out any particular lines of inquiry at this point."

The room erupted again almost to the level following the identification of the victim just moments earlier. Raising his voice to be heard above the din, Rada continued.

"Let me just make one important point, and that is that all involved in the political campaign, as well as the general religious-secular debate that has been raging in this country for years, must understand that words can have consequences. There have been some very inflammatory statements made on both sides of the referendum issue of late, and I would urge all those who have a major voice in this issue to choose their words very carefully. As the chief inspector pointed out earlier when referring to press coverage of this investigation, there are laws in place that facilitate the prosecution of anyone found to have been inciting racial hatred or violent actions. I'll take two more questions."

"Shmuel Brandt, representing the Haredi media." bellowed Carmel.

"Thank you. This news is a huge shock to all in our community and I want to express our sincerest condolences to the family of the late Rabbi Zvi Nahum Tenenbaum, *zichrono l'bracha* (of blessed memory). I am sure I speak for everyone in the Haredi world, those both for and against the idea of separation, when I send our thoughts and prayers to his dear wife, Nava, his three young children, the rabbi's parents and siblings, and all those who have known this brilliant scholar. My question relates to the funeral arrangements. Will he be buried this evening, or tomorrow?"

"Shmuel, there will certainly be no funeral tonight, and we can't say with any certainty at this point when exactly the body will be released for burial. It very much depends on any developments in the investigation in the coming hours - or days."

"But detective inspector," insisted Brandt, "his community will demand that the body of this holy man be handed over for burial, certainly by no later than lunchtime tomorrow. There will be outrage if he is not buried according to the timeframe proscribed in Jewish law. There will be thousands, if not tens of thousands attending his funeral. You cannot keep the body much longer, out of respect for the family!"

Rada refused to respond. "Just one final question," he said, gathering his things up from the table.

"Shirley Levi, Galei Tzahal (army radio)!" shrieked Carmel, reiterating, "Last question!"

"Detective inspector, both you and the chief inspector have gone to some lengths at this press conference to point out the potential dangers of inflammatory statements and rhetoric posted on social media, and elsewhere. At sixteen-twenty-six today, during Shabbat, Ilana Shwartz, leader of the Hofshi Party and the Yes campaign released the following Tweet. I quote: 'You heard Rabbi Zvi Tenenbaum on the televised debate stating: "I am not willing to give up on so many millions of Jewish people in Israel and around the world who choose not to be as observant as us." I said at the time, "He's a fraud. Nothing more, nothing less." Information has subsequently reached me that Tenenbaum has a close family member who left the Haredi world some years ago to join secular society and he has not had any contact with that person since! Sounds to me like a classic case of "Do as I say, not as I do." He and his vote No campaign cannot be trusted. HE'S A DANGEROUS PHONY!'"

Another buzz whipped round the press corps like wildfire, but Levi continued, "Given your comments of just a few seconds ago, can you tell me if that statement falls into the category of inflammatory public comment, and if it does, whether you will be questioning Ilana Shwartz during the course of your investigations?"

"Well Shirley, there are a few points there. First of all, any decision on whether a public statement can be classed as inflammatory and deemed worthy of prosecution is not a matter for me; it's a matter for the public prosecutor's office. And on the second point, I am not prepared to begin a dialogue here and now on who we are and are not questioning as part of this investigation. OK."

"I have a final statement, if I may," said Rada. "I urge anyone who thinks they might have any piece of information relating to the death of Rabbi Tenenbaum, no matter how small it might seem, to come forward and contact us as a matter of urgency on ten-ten-ten. I appreciate that in some religious quarters there is often a degree of, shall we say, reticence, about working with the police, but in this particular case I hope people will set aside any misgivings they might have. I can assure you that all those coming forward will be dealt with in the strictest confidence and with the utmost discretion. Thank you all for your time."

With that, Rada and Chief Inspector Carmel strode out of the press conference to a final barrage of flashes and the accompaniment of countless questions shouted across the room in their direction. They sought refuge in an ante-room where they simultaneously heaved a sigh of relief.

"Solomon, this is arguably the biggest case since the Rabin

assassination. You know what I'm saying," said Carmel, eyebrows raised.

"I know, sir. I'll give it all I've got."

"I'm sure you will. I'm not going to tell you how to do your job, but one thing I ask is that you somehow find a way to return the body to the family as soon as possible. This could be toxic if they're not able to bury him very soon. You understand?"

"Understood."

CHAPTER 20

11:30 P.M., Saturday May 9, 2048 (five days to the referendum)

Even as the press conference was still in progress lurid headlines began appearing across the world. This was a huge story. As if the battle for the hearts and minds of the Israeli public wasn't enough, now there was the horrific murder of one of the main protagonists leading the fight for Israel to remain as one.

Both senior officers who spoke at the press conference appealed to the media to act with restraint and report responsibly, but those appeals fell on deaf ears. Before Saturday had turned into Sunday there were a host of scurrilous rumors doing the rounds. One major media outlet very heavy-handedly hinted that Ilana Shwartz might have used her Mossad contacts to eliminate the "poster boy" of the opposing campaign; another intimated that Tenenbaum's death may have been the result of a long-standing feud between the deceased rabbi and Chief Rabbi Bermann, who exchanged barbed insults on the televised debate a few days earlier, exposing a fracture in Haredi opinion so rarely witnessed outside of that world.

A local Israeli news channel interviewed an individual

- purportedly once connected to the Prime Minister's Office - whose identity was blurred from view and whose voice was distorted to avoid easy identification. He said he had it on good authority that the PM had privately been furious that Tenenbaum was grabbing all the headlines and stolen his thunder, and that Doron Gal had made comments hinting he would be better off if Tenenbaum "disappeared from the scene."

And in the US, a major Democratic-leaning news outlet published an editorial suggesting that a long-standing friendship between the late Rabbi Tenenbaum and the now former Republican presidential candidate Reverend Larry Turner, had turned sour immediately prior to the reverend announcing he would no longer run for presidential office. Without making any specific allegations, it left questions hanging in mid-air about an alleged sudden end to their friendship, and the shocking subsequent murder of the young Israeli rabbi might in some way be connected.

***

Just a few minutes before midnight on this last Saturday before the referendum breaking news reports came in of a pitched battle taking place between crowds of Haredi and secular youths in the area traversing Bnei Brak and Ramat Gan, close to Tel Aviv.

Large numbers of police had been drafted in, but by the time they managed to take control of the situation three people were confirmed dead - two Haredim and one secular - and more than 20 seriously injured and requiring hospital treatment. The dead were all males under 20 years old; the two Haredim died from stab wounds, while the secular fatality had been beaten to death.

The violence appeared to have flared when the two groups,

representing opposing sides of the referendum question, had faced off. At its height, witnesses suggested that as many as 500 people may have been involved in what turned into a vicious melee in which knives, bricks, baseball bats, glass bottles and at least one firearm had been used.

No sooner had that incident been quietened, leaving behind a scene of devastation not seen on the streets of the greater Tel Aviv area in living memory, than at around 0100 another, smaller confrontation flared up in the normally sleepy southern town of Kiryat Gat, not far from the Gaza Strip. Again, secular and Haredi sides were involved in fighting in which around 100 people were reported to have been involved, but in this case most of the combatants were much older than those in the earlier incident near Tel Aviv.

One 59-year-old secular man was reported in critical condition after being stabbed, and two Haredim were hospitalized with broken bones.

The simmering mistrust - some openly characterized it as hatred - between large sections of both the religious and secular Israeli Jewish communities, had erupted in serious violence and fatalities triggered by the news of the death of Zvi Tenenbaum.

Messages from leaders on both sides of the debate were immediately issued calling for restraint and urging their respective supporters to calm down. In the early hours of the morning Prime Minister Doron Gal warned that if there were any more battles or riots on the streets of Israel, he would be forced to mobilize the army to restore order. He urged everyone to calm down and take a step back.

Then, without even consulting the senior investigating officer in Jerusalem, Gal went on to announce that Rabbi Tenenbaum's funeral would definitely take place later that day, with a precise time to be announced by nine in the morning. This came as an unpleasant surprise to Solomon Rada and the police team in the capital.

"What the fuck!" exclaimed Rada, woken by an 0230 call from the few hours' sleep he had desperately anticipated. "What did he say?"

The caller repeated the news of Gal's surprise announcement of a short time before.

"OK. Get Nahum Greenberg out of bed right now and tell him he has to get down there immediately to take as many samples from the body as he thinks he might need. My guess is they'll come to take Tenenbaum away sooner than later, like the PM said. What an asshole that man is! How could he do this, removing the main piece of evidence without even speaking to us first? It's obvious why he's done this, but Jesus Christ, he's forced us into a very difficult position now. We'll be lynched by the Haredim if they don't get that body this morning like he said!"

Greenberg worked through the night with two assistants. In a break from the usual protocol Rada insisted the second postmortem be filmed in order to satisfy any questions that might arise later on. It didn't reveal anything additional to the findings of the original examination.

Around 0930, a plain black transit van followed by two black cars arrived at the gates of Jerusalem's main forensic and pathology center. The whole scene was broadcast live, as would now be the case with almost every development, large or small, connected to a crime that had caused such a sensation. The remains of Rabbi Tenenbaum were duly handed over with solemnity to the delegation from the *hevra kaddisha* (religious Jewish burial authorities) who transferred them to the black van. It rolled very slowly away in the direction of Mea Shearim. The funeral was already set for 1700 later that day on the Mount of Olives.

Solomon Rada had been in some tough situations during his time in both the military and the police, but the pressure he was under with every move followed by masses of cameras and reporters wherever he went, was something he'd never experienced before. Nahum Greenberg had also dealt with plenty of pressure during his time working on high-profile cases, but this was a completely different league. Both men were already tired having been up most of the night. Rada, for sure, still had a long day ahead. They adjourned for coffee at the laboratory canteen.

"I can't quite believe this is happening," said Greenberg with a half-smile.

"Well, I can. My eyes are already telling me they want to close the shutters for a while," shrugged Rada.

"You know we should get the DNA report back on the coat any time soon. It might well offer up some kind of a clue."

"Maybe it will, maybe it won't," sighed the detective. "Wow Nahum I've got so much to do. We're heading to Tenenbaum's office to speak with his staff and have a root around, then we have to speak with his wife and parents. That's going to be hard when they're getting ready for the funeral. I can already see the 'insensitive cops' headlines, and all that. You know how it is though with the first seventy-two hours always being critical."

"I don't envy you," said Greenberg, stretching and stifling a yawn at the same time. "I'll be in touch if there's anything to report."

***

10:30 a.m., Mea Shearim, Sunday May 10, 2048 (four days to the referendum)

By the time Rada and two police colleagues arrived at the late Rabbi Tenenbaum's campaign office, a short distance from one of the entrances to the Mea Shearim neighborhood, a large crowd had gathered in a silent vigil. The sight of Haredim and a number of the few remaining secular Jerusalemites standing together in contemplation was something rarely seen.

Inside the office, Judith, Tenenbaum's secretary, was still distressed as Rada sat down to talk to her. Yossi Hartov, the rabbi's close friend and colleague, was also on hand to answer questions.

The police team were shown Tenenbaum's modest work desk on which an old-fashioned landline telephone sat alongside a large blotting pad. The rabbi, in a nod to tradition, wrote with fountain pen and ink. Various prayer books, a set of tefillin, the black prayer boxes attached to leather straps that are ritually bound and placed at the upper arm and forehead respectively, sat to the left of the blotting pad along with a photograph of the rabbi's wife and children. It was a poignant scene.

"Wouldn't he have taken the tefillin with him when leaving the office?" Rada asked Yossi Hartov.

"No, he has other sets at home and at the synagogue. Anyway, as far as we know he planned to go visit his father then return to take a few calls later on. He would often come back to the office to work late and make calls to people in the US. Obviously, he had no communication device at home."

"So you think he planned to come back in the evening?"

"I know he planned to come back later on, probably after he and Nava had put the children to bed," suggested Judith. "I'm certain he

arranged to speak with Reverend Larry Turner because Turner tried
to call him a number of times from ten pm Israel time."

"How do you know that if you've only got these old fashioned,
antique telephones?" asked Rada with a hint of a cheeky smile.

"How do I know?" responded Judith in a sarcastic tone. "Well,
connected to Zvi's 'antique telephone' is an antique answering machine! It shows the phone rang four times between ten and eleven,
but no message was left. Then, on the fifth call, Reverend Turner
left a … well, it wasn't the most pleasant message I've ever heard. He
obviously assumed Zvi would be the only one to hear it as everyone
else would be at home at that time. And Zvi made a point of always
deleting messages once he'd heard them, the reverend knew that."

"Can I take a listen?" asked Rada.

"Of course."

Judith opened the top left drawer of the rabbi's desk and placed
the answering machine on the desktop. She pushed a button.

"Hello, this is Rabbi Zvi Tenenbaum. I'm away from my desk at
the moment but please leave me a message and, with God's help, I'll
get back to you as soon as possible."

Hearing Zvi's voice Judith broke down. Yossi also looked
glassy-eyed.

"I can't believe he's gone," cried Judith. "I just can't believe it."

"Beep … click … beep … click … beep … click … beep … click."

"Wait," said Judith, "here it comes."

"Zvi, this is Larry. Where the hell are you?" Turner sounded extremely agitated. "I've been trying for the last hour to get a hold of
you, although I'm not surprised you haven't got the guts to answer.
After all I've done for you, well I … I just can't believe you'd betray
me. I can't believe you'd do such a dirty rotten thing after the millions of dollars my followers have plowed into your organization.

You probably haven't got the guts to face me 'cos you know that I know it's because of you I lost my chance to bid for the big one. Zvi, I know you're listening to this right now. I wasn't born yesterday. I made the right choice for my people, and if you but knew it, for yours too!"

There was a short pause.

"I'm telling you Zvi, you'll pay very dearly for what you've done, you son of a bitch! You'll burn in hellfire!" Click. The call was finished.

"Well, that's quite a message!" observed Rada.

"I can't believe how he spoke," said Hartov. "As far as I was aware, Zvi and Reverend Turner had a great relationship. I'd even say they were close friends. I just can't understand why he would leave such a vile message. Maybe he's cracking up after deciding to drop out of politics? Maybe he's been drinking? It doesn't make any sense."

"I'll have to take the answering machine with me as evidence," said Rada. "Do you mind if I take a look through the rest of the drawers? I haven't brought a warrant."

Both nodded their approval. Judith asked the officers if they'd like some lemon or mint tea. They were all happy to accept whatever she prepared.

"Check everything," Rada told his colleagues as Yossi watched on. "Go through all the books and see if anything falls out. Look under and behind everything - and don't forget to put your gloves on."

There was nothing of any obvious consequence in four of the five unopened drawers, but the final drawer, the lowest of the three on the right side of the desk, wouldn't open. It was locked.

"Any reason why this drawer should be locked?" Rada asked Yossi.

"I've never looked in his desk," he shrugged. "I wasn't even aware that any of the drawers locked."

"Well, we're going to have to open this one up. Where would you guess the key might be?"

"I'll ask Judith. If anyone knows, she'll know."

Judith arrived right on cue, placing the tea in the main area outside of the rabbi's private office. She told Yossi she knew the bottom drawer locked but had no idea where the rabbi kept the key, or what was in there.

"Sorry folks, but we're going to have to pick the lock. Tzahi!"

Rada called across to one of the two officers searching through the shelves.

"This is your specialty."

"I'll give it a whirl," Tzahi said eagerly.

It took less than a minute for the lock to release. The small drawer was duly lifted out and placed on the desk. It contained just one item. Rada picked up the photo and examined it closely. Tzahi, his colleague Yoni, Judith, and Yossi watched on as Rada considered the picture. For the time being they could only see the matt white back of the image.

"Do either of you know who the woman is?" he asked, turning the picture around.

They looked bemused. Tenenbaum was pictured standing alongside an attractive young blonde woman. She wore sports shorts and a tennis shirt, the top two buttons of which were open. He was without his black hat, wearing just a black kippah. He had removed his jacket, his sleeves were rolled up, and he looked as informal as anyone had ever seen him.

"Who is she?" Yossi wondered out loud. Judith was speechless.

"Well, hopefully we'll find out sooner rather than later," said

Rada, looking in the direction of Tenenbaum's two bemused colleagues. "If only they hadn't banned facial recognition a few years ago, we'd find out sooner!"

He placed the photo in a plastic evidence bag.

"Please, do not mention this image or the contents of the telephone message to anyone. Do you understand? They are now pieces of evidence in this investigation."

Rada left his two assistants to continue the search of Tenenbaum's office, asking them to check if there was a safe and to interview both Yossi and Judith. He headed back to his car, steeling himself for what was sure to be a very delicate meeting with Tenenbaum's bereaved family.

CHAPTER 21

Sunday, 12:00 P.M., May 10, 2048 (four days to the referendum)

Hofshi Party headquarters in Tel Aviv was in meltdown. A campaign that seemed on its way to almost certain victory had gone completely off the rails in the aftermath of the news of Rabbi Tenenbaum's murder.

The death of the young rabbi would have been expected to garner a sympathy vote, but the angry, threatening tweet published by Ilana Shwartz less than five hours before Tenenbaum's death was announced had sparked a severe backlash against the Yes campaign.

Social media was awash with accusations focusing on Shwartz; on her ill-tempered exchange with Tenenbaum on the televised debate a week earlier; on her speech at the Rabin Square rally; and on "that tweet."

Panic was setting in among campaign workers anxious for reassurance from their leader that the ship was not going down. No one here believed Shwartz had played any part in what happened to Tenenbaum, but they needed her to be there to raise their spirits and offer reassurance and guidance on how they should respond to the media allegations. A few Hofshi activists on the street had already had insults hurled in their direction as they arrived at the office wearing Yes campaign T-shirts.

Shwartz was nowhere to be seen though. She was holed up at home where dozens of reporters and cameras were camped outside her front door, waiting for her to emerge and answer questions. Inside, the former Mossad chief was in a video conference meeting with her senior campaign team. Only Ed Sonfeld was absent from the group discussion. Ed's absence had been noted by a couple of those on the call, but Shwartz had quickly moved on to discuss other issues.

"You've got to carry on as though nothing has happened," one said, before being shouted down by the others. How can she do that, they snapped back, after the tweet she'd put out? The consensus of opinion was that Shwartz would have to make a statement to the media expressing her deep sadness at what had happened, insisting she supports all measures taken by the police to apprehend the perpetrators. She should apologize for the tweet, which she would say was ill-judged but was never intended to cause any personal harm to Rabbi Tenenbaum.

Jules Denton, formerly a campaign advisor in Britain for the successful Labor Party at the most recent British elections, had been brought in some weeks earlier to offer advice to the Hofshi campaign.

"You have to be quite clinical about the timeline," he told Shwartz, "even though at first it might seem a bit cold. The police announced the murder last night, six hours or so after you posted the tweet, didn't they? But they made it clear Tenenbaum's body was found on Friday morning. Your tweet was posted on Saturday afternoon, at which point you were completely unaware that the rabbi had died the previous day. It stands to reason you wouldn't have published that post and landed yourself in this mess if you had any prior knowledge of Friday's terrible event."

There was a pause, then an instant change in the atmosphere of the meeting. In all the panic, no one else had bothered to spot the glaring timeline issue that could save Shwartz's metaphorical bacon.

"Cynics might say it's a double bluff," Shwartz eventually responded. "And the media will want to know who the relative is that I mentioned, otherwise they'll say I was making it up."

"Well, who is the relative?" asked Denton, before anyone else managed to ask.

"I can't say."

"What do you mean, 'I can't say.' You've got to say. If you don't say who the relative is - and let's be straight about this, does it really matter now the rabbi is dead? - then you may be able to persuade much of the public you weren't involved in the killing, but you'll be roundly condemned instead as a brazen liar! That won't be much less damaging to a campaign that is starting to stall, unless you come clean."

"I just can't say," repeated the usually calculating Shwartz, for once betraying an element of torment. "I just can't."

"Look Ilana, I wasn't going to bring this up just yet," fired back Denton, "but a new poll came out about fifteen minutes ago and you're not going to like what it says."

Two of the others in the meeting simultaneously asked for the numbers.

"It's the poll of polls, averaging the five main polling companies as of 1000 this morning. They give us 47.5%, No 48%, and the 'don't knows' 4.5%. We're being crucified!"

"It's a knee-jerk reaction," Shwartz answered, showing little emotion. "People are certain to be distressed at what's happened, but when they go to the polling booth and think again about the country and where it's going, they'll come back to us."

"I agree that's likely, to some extent," said Denton, "but we're still more than three days away and a lot can, and in my experience will happen between now and then - and it might not all be to our benefit. You have to prove you weren't making up what you tweeted about the rabbi's 'close relative.'"

Shwartz knew Denton was right. She had to nip this mess in the bud as fast as possible. Not for the first time she wished she'd listened to her husband when he told her not to reveal anything that had been discussed at dinner on Friday evening. She would have to bend over backwards to make things right with Ed.

"I'm sure it hasn't gone unnoticed that Ed Sonfeld isn't with us for this call on what is a very difficult day for us. Under normal circumstances he would be an integral part of this discussion," began Shwartz. "Well, he couldn't make it into the office today because it's an even more difficult day for him than it is for me. I can see the puzzled looks on your faces, so I'll come straight to the point. Ed's wife, Hila, is the late Rabbi Tenenbaum's sister."

"What!" exclaimed Denton, along with the others. "You're telling us that one of our key campaign strategists is married to the sister of our main political rival!"

"That is correct."

"So, for all we know, she could have been passing on our campaign plans to the other side, for God knows how long!?"

Denton and the others looked and sounded incredulous at the news.

"No, absolutely not," said Shwartz, getting to her feet. "I only found out about them being siblings on Friday night, after dinner at their home. She fled the Haredi world 16 years ago and hasn't seen anyone from the family since. That's how I knew Tenenbaum was being a hypocrite when he spoke so sincerely in the debate about welcoming others who are less religious into the fold. That's why I felt obliged to expose him, because I found out he'd been stringing everyone along."

"I know Hila pretty well," chipped in Maya Taylor, Hofshi Head of PR. "She's a lovely person. I'm stunned she used to be Haredi and never mentioned it; nor did Ed. Then again, it's her private life, I suppose. She might not have been in touch with the family for ages, but she must still be devastated at what's happened to her brother."

"You're going to have to reveal the truth about Ed's wife then. I can't see a way around it," shrugged Denton. "Let's just hope for all our sakes she hasn't been working secretly for the other side all along. Maybe we can even spin it by hinting what a great person she is, and show her as an example of what can be achieved by people leaving the Haredi fold and having the guts to follow a different path ..."

Half an hour later, Ilana Shwartz appeared on the steps of her family home, flanked by her husband. He eventually agreed, after a tense stand-off, to stand alongside her for her statement to the press.

She presented the timeline as discussed in the meeting after first offering sincere condolences to Rabbi Tenenbaum's family. She pointed out that political rough 'n tumble was one thing, but such a senseless tragedy was beyond the imagination of anyone involved on either side of the referendum divide. She went on to explain that she had not lied in her tweet, revealing she had only recently learned that Hila Sonfeld, wife of Ed Sonfeld, one of her own campaign team, was the estranged sister of the late rabbi - and that Hila and Zvi Tenenbaum had been incommunicado from the day she left the Haredi community. This was why she called out the rabbi on his claim of tolerance and understanding of those less religious than himself.

Shwartz fielded a number of awkward questions following her statement, but there appeared little doubt that, for the most part, her words had taken much of the heat out of the situation. At Hofshi HQ there was a massive sigh of relief.

***

A couple of streets from the home of the late rabbi's parents, Solomon Rada found his way blocked by a black and white mass. He ditched the car and set off on foot in the same direction as the hundreds of Haredim.

After showing his police badge he managed to force his way through a ten-deep crowd gathered at the entrance of the modest four-story apartment building. The traditional black framed notice was displayed at the entrance, and again on the wide-open front door of the raised ground-floor apartment, inviting those mourning the late Rabbi Zvi Tenenbaum to make their way inside.

Even before he scaled the few steps up to the family home Rada heard angry male voices emanating from the apartment. He waited in the stairwell, out of sight of the mourners. They were in the middle of a heated argument. The majority of those speaking stressed that Rabbi Nusbaum, Zvi Tenenbaum's long-time mentor, should officiate at the funeral, while a lesser group seemingly headed by Tenenbaum's father, was insisting that the family would absolutely accept the "honor" of having Chief Rabbi Bermann preside over the ceremony.

There was uproar when Baruch Tenenbaum insulted Rabbi Nusbaum, saying he blamed Nusbaum for planting the seeds in his son's mind that set him on a path that ultimately contributed to his death. The argument teetered on the brink of turning violent as the larger group screamed that Zvi would never have wanted Bermann to speak at his funeral. He disliked the chief rabbi and had made it his life's work to oppose his plans for separation.

When Rada entered the house of mourning the screaming and shouting abruptly stopped. It was a rarity to see a black face in Mea Shearim, and few of those present had seen the detective inspector speaking at the press conference the night before. They didn't have access to TV broadcasts.

Rada introduced himself and offered the traditional message of joining in their sorrow. He said he hoped he wouldn't disturb the family for too long at this very difficult time, but he needed to ask a few questions of the late rabbi's wife and parents. Might it be possible for him to speak to them alone?

Baruch Tenenbaum asked the mourners to grant the detective's request and they dutifully filed out into the hallway and kitchen from which both Yoheved and Nava Tenenbaum emerged.

"Baruch, we could have spoken with the detective in the kitchen," said a red-eyed Yoheved, seeing so many people leaving the apartment.

"It's more comfortable here," came the response.

Rada again offered his condolences to the wife and parents of the deceased and assured them he would take up as little of their time as possible. He said he understood how shocked they must be and how hard the rest of the day and the subsequent seven-day shiva (traditional prayers) would be. He first asked Nava to explain when it was that she became concerned about her husband not coming home. She ran through the timeline, including calling her next-door neighbors, then Yossi Hartov, later in the evening.

Nava explained how difficult a decision it had been to eventually report their concerns to the police and expressed fears she and her family may be punished by the community for stepping out of line. She appeared completely numb at her loss. Beyond tears.

"I'm sure that won't be the case," Rada told her, then moved on to her father-in-law.

"Mr. Tenenbaum, I understand you were scheduled to meet with your son on Thursday lunchtime. Is that correct?"

"It is, but he didn't show up. I waited for a while, but it became clear he wasn't coming. As I wasn't feeling too well anyway, I decided to stay home and didn't return to the yeshiva for the rest of the day. If he had turned up at any point on Thursday afternoon, I would have been here to see him."

"So this was a meeting between the two of you, and no one else."

"Just the two of us."

"Can you say what you planned to discuss?"

"Nothing special. He knew I was going to vote Yes in the refer endum, but I wanted to let him know how proud, as his father, I had been when I saw him arguing his corner so impressively in the televised debate. But I never got the chance ..."

Tenenbaum appeared visibly upset at recalling that last, missed opportunity.

"And Mrs. Tenenbaum, you weren't home on Thursday lunch-time when your husband and son were planning to meet?"

"No. I didn't even know they planned to meet. Anyway, Thursday is one of the days when I volunteer at the shelter and help with food parcels. I didn't get home until around three o'clock."

"So Nava, you last spoke to your husband when he left for his campaign office on Thursday morning, and Mr. and Mrs. Tenenbaum, you last spoke to your son when?"

"It would have been at Shabbat dinner, the previous Friday," said Baruch. "I saw him again on Saturday in the synagogue, although I wasn't able to grab a word with him. He was inundated with worshippers both supporting and having a go at him about his stance on the referendum issue."

"Nava, had Rabbi Tenenbaum mentioned any threats against him of late?"

"He said the office often received unpleasant messages calling him a traitor and saying he would pay for defying the guidance of the rabbinical council. But he also got plenty of messages of support; more than most people would imagine. He didn't take the threats seriously."

Rada wished the family members "long life" then excused himself. The black and white mass assembled outside the apartment and on the pathway to the street parted like the Red Sea as the detective left the house of mourning.

***

12:30 P.M., Sunday May 10, 2048 (four days to the referendum)

"Solomon, it's Nahum."

Rada was driving back from Mea Shearim to police headquarters just a couple of miles away when the phone rang.

"Are you sitting down?"

"I'm in the backseat of my car doing my best to grab a few minutes sleep."

"Well this'll wake you up, I promise. There are three sets of DNA from the green coat. One is the old lady that died years ago, we haven't been able to identify the second yet, but we got a positive ID on the third. You're not going to believe this?"

"Try me," said Rada, deadpan.

"The DNA belongs to a 33-year-old Tel Aviv woman called Hila Sonfeld.

"OK, do we have a name and address for this lady?" asked Rada. He'd not seen Ilana Shwartz's press conference half an hour earlier at which Hila's name had been mentioned.

"Of course, we do, but her maiden name was Hila Tenenbaum. She's the rabbi's estranged sister!"

"Fuck me!" exclaimed Rada.

"Wait a minute, that's not all. Solomon, you're not going to believe this," said Greenberg, his voice becoming higher pitched by the second. "She's *hiloni* (secular) these days. Her husband is one of Ilana Shwartz's closest advisors!"

"Meet me in ten minutes at my office, would you? And Nahum, don't mention this to anyone else. Do you understand? Not a word."

CHAPTER 22

5:00 P.M., May 10, 2048 (four days to the referendum)

Jerusalem hadn't seen a funeral like it for over a decade. Chaim Levi, the President of Israel, Prime Minister Doron Gal, and a host of other prominent politicians were there. Ilana Shwartz, in view of the controversy surrounding her social media post, felt it best not to attend but sent her deputy.

But even allowing for the attention the presence of ambassadors from many nations created, including from the United States, Russia, the UK, France, China and Germany, this was about a human tragedy. It was about the loss of a young life that promised so much, of a man who had the potential to bridge an ever-widening divide between Jews in Israel and around the globe, be they religious or secular.

Screened live on Israeli television and in countless other countries, the spectacle of more than 100,000 black and white clad Haredim swarming through the streets on the way up to the fabled Mount of Olives where Rabbi Zvi Tenenbaum was about to be laid to rest was awe inspiring. His body, wrapped in a simple prayer shawl, no coffin, was wheeled out and set down on a plinth in full view of the sea of mourners.

Before kaddish, the traditional prayer for the dead, and other elements of the burial ceremony, one by one dignitaries stepped up to the microphone to say a few words about Zvi Tenenbaum. First to speak was Prime Minister Gal, who in a speech for which he gained much credit spoke of his admiration for the young rabbi whose charisma and belief in the value of all Jews had resonated so strongly with so many people at such a critical time.

"The shock of his loss and the void left by his passing can hardly be imagined. Our thoughts and prayers are for his dear wife Nava, his three young children, parents, relatives and friends," Gal concluded, "but his passing must not be in vain. The greatest tribute we can pay to this remarkable young rabbi who had the world at his feet, is to help fulfill his vision of how our society should be, for each and every one of us."

After the dignitaries had each said their piece it fell to Baruch Tenenbaum, father of the murdered rabbi, to say a few, final words before the burial ceremony could begin. To those who knew him well he seemed a shadow of his usual self. Glancing across to his wife, herself supported by two of her daughters who held her under each arm for fear she might collapse, Tenenbaum lauded his youngest son, saying that even though thirteen children had come before him, the family knew from very early on that Zvi had something special about him.

"God moves in mysterious ways," said Tenenbaum with tears in his eyes. "My son moved among the highest echelons of our Haredi world, and at a similar level outside of our community. If people didn't always agree with his ideas, they undoubtedly still respected him greatly for the way he spoke and the wisdom beyond his years he imparted to all who knew him.

"I loved my son," Tenenbaum concluded in an insistent manner.

"We all loved Zvi and would have done anything in our power not to be standing here today. May his dear soul rest in peace."

The father's words over the body of his son drew many a tear from the masses at the graveside and those watching on from afar. The religious ceremony then commenced at which Chief Rabbi Bermann and Zvi Tenenbaum's friend and mentor, Rabbi Nusbaum, jointly officiated.

During the hours prior to and during the burial ceremony, the bitter battle for the hearts and minds of the Israeli people that would conclude with the referendum in a few days' time was set aside. This shocking death had potential recriminations for so many people.

Although granted the usual respect from his followers, Chief Rabbi Bermann sensed an atmosphere among some of the mourners. His bitter words of criticism of Tenenbaum and the verbal battle they fought in full view of a huge audience just days earlier, gave a somewhat surreal edge to the burial ceremony. He insisted he would not abdicate his responsibility in conducting the service and, despite plenty of opposition, his presence there had been assured by Baruch Tenenbaum's steadfast refusal to allow Rabbi Nusbaum alone to conduct the ceremony.

Reverend Larry Turner watched on from Montana, conflicted by very mixed emotions. He was certain Zvi Tenenbaum had "ratted him out" and informed the CIA of his intention to side with the Chief Rabbi and draw America close to the new State of Judea once he became president. Tenenbaum, he determined, had pulled the rug from under him when he was within touching distance of the biggest prize of all. He had greatly admired the young rabbi though; they'd shared some good times, plenty of jokes, and a joint passion to see the Jewish people flourish in the Land of Israel. He couldn't help feeling a real sense of loss.

In Tehran, Ayatollah Sanvani, Chief Minister Samtalan, and the supreme religious council were also watching. There had been a near ecstatic atmosphere at the top level of Iranian politics as the Yes vote gathered momentum over the previous weeks. Even the most politically naive Iranian appreciated that dividing Israel would present a momentous opportunity for them to exploit the open sore that had enveloped the Holy Land.

The icing on the cake for Sanvani and Samtalan had been receiving word from Rabbi Bloch of the Neturei Karta that Reverend Turner, most likely the next president of the United States, had also pledged to support the pro-separation side. This meeting of minds on the question of the Holy Land could open a myriad of doors to dialogue, and a swift warming of relations between the long-standing bitter enemies. Now, following Tenenbaum's death, victory for the Yes campaign looked far less certain. The Iranians weren't happy.

Israel's Arab community sent representatives to Rabbi Tenenbaum's funeral. His appeal had not only bridged the divide between the religious and secular Jews of Israel, but he had also extended a hand of friendship to its Arab citizens, shown them great respect, and was looked on as someone who genuinely sought to fully integrate the Arab community into the Israeli mainstream.

And watching the live broadcast of the funeral from their home in Tel Aviv were Ed and Hila Sonfeld. Their two young boys, six-year-old Tomer, and three-year-old Nir, played together out on the lawn under the supervision of Ed's parents, drafted in to keep the boys occupied while their mum and dad viewed the ceremony.

Hila had taken Zvi's death very badly, but not as badly as she was able to show her family. As far as they knew she had been estranged from them all, as stated at that fateful Friday night dinner less than 48 hours before. For the first time in 16 years she saw her heartbroken brothers and sisters, her father, even her beloved Uncle Shmulik, who sobbed uncontrollably and looked inconsolable. Her greatest empathy was for her poor shell-shocked mother. All Hila wanted to do was to reach out to her mom and hug her and tell her she loved her, and everything would be all right.

She saw Nava, Zvi's widow, distraught and utterly anguished. She looked such a good person. She saw the world she left behind, a world that had never left her memory, suddenly encapsulated within the bounds of her TV screen as she sat on the sofa; a box of tissues by her side, her husband's arm around her shoulders, and her beautiful boys giving their grandfather the run around on the front lawn.

Those first seventeen years had been so utterly different to her second sixteen years. Two completely different worlds. Of all of her Haredi family she loved Zvi the most. He was the one who helped her change her life. He didn't judge her. He just wanted her to be happy and live her life as she wanted. How could anyone have killed him? It was beyond belief.

***

Tel Aviv, 6:30 P.M., Sunday May 10, 2048 (four days to the referendum)

The Sonfelds hugged each other as the broadcast of Zvi Tenenbaum's funeral drew to a close. The boys were upstairs being bathed by their grandmother. Ed's father was attempting to chop a salad in the kitchen.

Throughout the broadcast both Ed and Hila failed to notice two cars parked up opposite their house - or if they did, thought them of little consequence.

The first they knew of it was when Ed noticed a group of six people - five men and a woman - making their way toward the front door. He thought he recognized one of them. The others he'd never seen before. He wondered if they were to do with the campaign but felt uneasy the very moment the doorbell rang.

Hila was still in a world of her own and hardly noticed as Ed went to answer the door.

"Ed Sonfeld? I'm Detective Inspector Solomon Rada of the Jerusalem police. Would it be OK for myself and my colleagues to come in? We'd like to have a chat with your wife."

Ed directed Rada and the other four men and a woman into the lounge where Hila was still sitting on the sofa. She didn't look overly surprised.

"Mrs. Sonfeld, hello. I'm Detective—"

"I know who you are, detective inspector. I saw you at last night's press conference. I thought you might want to have a word after Shwartz's tweet. Please, sit down."

"Can I get you folks something to drink," Ed asked.

"No thanks," said Solomon. "Hila, I know that you've been estranged from your family since you left the Haredi community, but I hope you don't think it improper of me to offer our condolences for your loss. After all, he was your brother."

"Thank you. He was a great man."

"I need to ask you some questions and I think it would be best if your husband and the gentleman in the kitchen went to another room, if that's OK?"

"I'd prefer to stay here with my wife, actually," said Ed. His father trotted off upstairs to help with the boys.

"Fine. Hila, when was the last time you saw your brother?"

"She hasn't seen him since she left the community sixteen years ago," answered Ed.

"Mr. Sonfeld, with respect, the question was put to your wife, not you. If you jump in again, I'll have to ask you to leave the room while I'm discussing things with your wife. Let's try again. When was the last time you saw your brother?"

"The last time I saw him was the morning I left my family in Mea Shearim sixteen years ago."

"And you haven't seen him since?"

"No."

Rada rubbed his chin for a few moments. "Mrs. Sonfeld, can you tell me where you were on Thursday, three days ago, between nine and three?"

Hila stopped to think for a moment.

"I took the kids to school and kindergarten at around eight, came home, tidied up, kept myself busy and collected them a little before three o'clock in the afternoon."

"So you were in Tel Aviv all day on Thursday?"

"Yes, I was."

"Where are you going with this, Mr. Rada?" Ed butted in. "What has Hila's daily routine got to do with your inquiries?"

"Mr. Sonfeld, I'm not going to tell you again."

"Ed," said Hila, "it's OK. Calm down."

"Mrs. Sonfeld," Rada's tone became far more formal, "when was the last time you visited Jerusalem?"

She gazed at Ed. "I haven't been to Jerusalem for some years. I think the last time we went there was to a museum three or four years ago."

Rada reached into his jacket pocket and produced a black and white image.

"Take a good look at this picture, Mrs. Sonfeld. Do you recognize the car in this image and the person seated next to the driving position?"

Hila looked stunned and didn't reply. Ed grabbed the picture from the detective's hand. One of the other policemen jumped up to stop him, but Rada waved at his colleague to sit down.

"Do you recognize the car and the woman sitting in the front seat, Mr. Sonfeld? This was taken just before eleven on Thursday morning - in Jerusalem."

"Hila, don't say another word. I'm calling Izzi Linde (the family lawyer)."

"Mr. Sonfeld, sit down right now," ordered Rada. "Mrs. Sonfeld, I'm asking you to accompany myself and my officers to Jerusalem. We have further questions to put to you. You can come with us of your own free will - which would be highly preferable - or we can wait here for half an hour or so, for a warrant to be approved."

"I'll get my things," said Hila. "There's no need for a warrant."

"Very good," said Rada. "Noga (the female officer) will accompany you while you collect a few belongings. You've just a couple of minutes then we'll be on our way."

"I don't understand what's going on here," said Ed struggling to process the image of his wife in Haredi clothes taken just a few days earlier.

"I expect it will all become much clearer in the next few hours, Mr. Sonfeld. It might be a good idea for you to call that lawyer of yours now."

Hila came back down into the lounge having hurried upstairs to kiss her boys and Ed's parents. She slipped on a jacket and a pair of sports shoes.

"It'll be alright Ed," she whispered. "I promise. Look after the kids, please. Don't worry."

CHAPTER 23

11:00 P.M., Sunday May 10, 2048, Police HQ (less than four days to the referendum)

It's one of the first rules of interrogation. Rada and his colleagues delivered Hila Sonfeld into the interview room at Jerusalem police headquarters then left her there to stew for a couple of hours. Leaving a person alone with their thoughts is challenging for anyone yanked out of their home environment and dropped into an unfamiliar and frightening situation. She wasn't mistreated or put under any more pressure than simply being in that stark environment created on its own.

They brought her lemon tea and some biscuits; she was offered a meal but declined. She was fully aware they would be videoing her every move and made every effort to appear as relaxed as possible.

Hila was no fool. She understood she was in trouble but was struggling to figure out how exactly to explain herself without landing her mother in an impossible situation on top of the grief she was already suffering. At the funeral her mother stood out (along with Uncle Shmulik) as looking more shattered than anyone else at Zvi's death; no surprise there - she idolized her youngest son. He made her often miserable life bearable with his remarkable achievements - "*nachas*" was the Yiddish word she used for the way he made her glow inside.

Rada looked a decent guy when speaking at the press conference the previous day but hadn't got close to the top of the tree without being a smart cop, she told herself. Surely he'd see that any suggestion she harmed her brother was preposterous. He was just doing his best to be seen to explore all avenues.

There were other reasons for delaying the start of the interview. First, Hila's lawyer had been down in the southern holiday resort of Eilat and was flying back to be with her as she gave her statement. It was only a 40-minute flight, but he needed to get to Ilan Ramon Airport, north of the Red Sea resort city, then fly to Ben Gurion Airport near Tel Aviv, then on to Jerusalem.

Second, it was crystal clear that someone within the police had tipped off the press that a possible suspect in the Tenenbaum case had been brought in for questioning. Thankfully, Hila arrived at the Jerusalem police station before the media got wind of the development, but by eleven at night there were dozens of reporters and their TV crews erecting makeshift gazebos on the lawn outside the station. They gave every impression they would be there for the duration.

"Sir, someone has ratted us out!" Rada angrily told Chief Inspector Carmel. "We've got to find out who tipped off the press - and they need to be fired on the spot. It's a relatively small pool of people who knew I was going to Tel Aviv to interview Hila Sonfeld. We need to plug this leak now!"

"I'm aware of that," said Carmel, trying to calm his increasingly agitated senior police officer, "but you getting worked up about it isn't going to do anyone any good. You need to focus on this interview. Do you hear me?"

"Yup."

"What's your gut feeling? Did she do it?"

"Eighty percent certain. Some things don't quite add up though. She's been lying so far, but I'm still looking for a motive."

"Well as soon as her lawyer gets here you better crack on. I'm already inundated with calls from the top asking what's going on. You calm down and do what you're paid to do, and I'll look into this blasted leak."

At 23.35, with Izzi Linde, her lawyer, by her side, Solomon Rada began questioning Hila Sonfeld. She had been cautioned that all her comments could be used in evidence against her if she was charged with any offense.

"Hila, how hard a decision was it for you to flee your community sixteen years ago?"

"It was very hard - very hard indeed. My family and community in Mea Shearim were all I had ever known. They were my life."

"So, why *did* you leave?"

"My father agreed a *shidduch* (arranged marriage), which I opposed. I didn't know the man. I'd only ever met him once, but my father said he was a decent person, he was from his yeshiva, and so on. I was told the decision had been made and that was it."

"I see. So how did you manage to get away?"

"I contacted Ahutza and they arranged to meet me just outside of Mea Shearim the following day. I couldn't tell anybody. I just left home in the usual fashion but continued walking until I was out of the enclave, met a woman at the agreed place, they put me in a car, and we drove to Tel Aviv. It sounds quite easy when you say it like that, but it was the most difficult thing I've ever done in my life."

"Hila, do you recall what were you wearing the day you left Mea Shearim, back in 2032?"

"Pardon me?"

"Can you remember what clothes you wore that fateful day you upped and left?"

"My clothes? Wow! Well, it was a warm day and as far as I can recall, I wore a pale blue blouse with a gray cardigan over. I had a dark blue skirt and stockings, black shoes, and a small hand-bag. I don't think I wore anything more than that. They were the only clothes I took with me; to take any more might have raised suspicions."

"OK, thanks for that. Hila, would you describe yourself as a truthful person?"

"I don't think you should answer that," Linde intervened.

"It's a perfectly reasonable question, Mr. Linde," said Rada.

Hila remained silent.

"Let's put this another way then. Are you a person who can be trusted with a confidence?"

"I'm not sure what you mean?"

"If a friend or relative tells you something and confides only in you, are you the type of person who keeps that information secret?"

"I would say so."

"From the day you walked out of your family home in Mea Shearim back in 2032, until his death just a few short days ago, did you ever meet or have any contact with your brother, Rabbi Zvi Tenenbaum."

"No, I didn't."

"Are you quite sure?" Rada stressed.

"Quite sure."

Rada reached into a file in front of him on the interview desk and placed a photo in front of Hila.

"Then can you explain this image showing you and your brother, clearly taken some years after you left Mea Shearim. It was found in a locked drawer of his private desk during a police search of his campaign office earlier today."

She looked at the photo, felt a welling up of emotion that she effectively concealed from her questioner, but did not respond.

"For the record, can you confirm that the image is of you and your brother?"

"Yes."

"And can you tell me when and where it was taken?"

"I don't think Hila will be answering that question, detective inspector," said Linde. "She's already said enough in relation to that image."

"I'll move on then," Rada said calmly and deliberately.

"Hila, at your home in Tel Aviv a few hours ago, I showed you the CCTV image of your car taken on Thursday, May seventh at ten forty-five am. You didn't confirm that it is you in this image when asked earlier today. Will you confirm it now?"

"Don't answer that," said Linde.

"Mr. Linde, it is clearly Mrs. Sonfeld in this image," Rada insisted. "She's doing herself no favors by not answering."

She followed her lawyer's advice and remained silent. Rada was getting irritated by Hila's stonewalling.

"OK, well I have another three images for you, taken just over half an hour earlier at a gas station on the Tel Aviv-Jerusalem highway. The first is timed at just after ten am. Here you are entering the washroom area wearing jeans and a T-shirt, having parked your car a few moments before. Six minutes later in this image" - Rada pushed another photo in front of Hila Sonfeld – "you emerge from the washroom in what can only be described as clothes typically worn by a Haredi woman, including the head covering. And just for the avoidance of doubt, in this third picture you can be seen, Haredi clothes and all, stepping back into the car you parked a few minutes earlier. What do you have to say about these pictures? How do you explain this very suspicious behavior?"

"I've nothing to say," said Hila gazing into a corner of the room, refusing to make eye contact with the detective.

"Hila, let's say we give you the benefit of the doubt and suggest that - not unlike others who have been through the trauma of leaving their family then later find it hard to stay away - you engaged in this subterfuge, clothes changing and all, in order to re-enter your one-time Haredi community without arousing suspicion, because you were going to meet your brother; the same brother pictured with his arm around you in that picture I presented to you a very short time ago."

Rada produced another CCTV image showing her car parking itself in a street not far from a small park just inside the official border of Mea Shearim. He confirmed that from this point on, due to the restrictions on placing cameras in this religiously sensitive neighborhood, this was the last image of Hila. It was taken at 10.53.

"The next time we see you is when you returned to your car in a hurry - see these three CCTV images, we also have video - and that is shown as being at five after one. Your brother was last seen alive at around twelve-fifteen on Thursday when he left his campaign office to attend a meeting less than ten minutes away. He never arrived. Can you tell me where you were between twelve-fifteen and five after one on Thursday?"

For the first time Hila's demeanor betrayed signs of her feeling the stress. Her fists were clenched, and she was blinking more than usual.

"Are you able to account for your movements during the times I stated?" Rada asked again.

Still no response.

"Detective inspector," said Izzi Linde, "where are you going with this? You assert that the woman in the image is my client—"

"Of course, it's your client! It's as clear as day," snapped Rada.

"My client has neither confirmed nor denied anything other than being in an old photo with her brother. The timeline you have presented is no more than circumstantial evidence, and you know it."

Ignoring the lawyer, Rada returned to Hila Sonfeld.

"You are a serial liar, Mrs. Sonfeld. You have been lying to your husband about never having had contact with your family since you were seventeen. You lied to Ilana Shwartz on Friday night by telling her the same, and it was on that basis she published the tweet that caused such furor when she accused your late brother of not practicing what he preached in the televised debate a few days earlier. You misled Ilana Shwartz and exacerbated an already tense situation on the streets that sparked fatal violence a few hours later after your brother's death was reported.

"Your lies have caused havoc at a time when the nation is already at boiling point, and I believe, actually I know you're still lying now. All the evidence suggests that you planned to kill your brother for some unknown reason. Did he betray you? Was this a politically motivated act? Why did you do it?!"

"I didn't do it."

"Ah, she speaks," Rada responded melodramatically.

"Everything you have stated is pure supposition, Mr. Rada," Linde cut in. "You're spinning a good story, but you have no evidence. You're trying to intimidate Mrs. Sonfeld."

"Right, let's get to the crux," continued Rada, again ignoring

Linde. "There is one piece of crucial evidence relating to the killing of Rabbi Tenenbaum that wasn't made public at yesterday's press conference."

Hila was listening carefully. She was sure Rada was bluffing and was ready to try catch him out.

"The rabbi's body was found wrapped in a garment. That garment was sent away for DNA testing. Three sets of DNA were found. The first belonged to an old woman who died more than 16 years ago; none of us need to be Sherlock Holmes to rule her out of the equation. The second set has yet to be identified, but the third set of DNA belongs to someone who is still very much alive, making them the prime suspect. That DNA belongs to you, Hila Sonfeld."

"You're making this up," Hila responded in deadpan fashion.

Rada produced an image of the green coat and pushed it across the table for her to see. Her eyes grew wider as she recognized the coat she had last worn just days before fleeing her community back in 2032. She was stunned.

"Really? Making this up? Your DNA was all over this coat in which the mutilated remains of your brother were found in the hills not very far from here. Your brother, who disappeared off the face of the earth at the very time you were in fancy dress disguised as a Haredi woman in his neighborhood, a neighborhood that you have long asserted you have not revisited since your departure sixteen years ago. Your brother, who set off from his office to a meeting ten minutes away and never arrived and was found dead the next morning hidden in bushes in the Jerusalem hills. We know he died soon after he left his office. He was found draped in this coat with your DNA on it!"

Rada was waving the photograph of the green coat in Hila's face.

"It doesn't look very good now, does it, Mrs. Sonfeld?"

The detective inspector got to his feet and left the interview room, slamming the door behind him. Hila and Izzi Linde both stared at the picture of the green coat. Neither uttered a word. They knew the evidence was really stacking up now.

CHAPTER 24

12:30 A.M., Monday, May 11, 2048 (three days to the referendum)

The referendum-related violence that flared up in both Bnei Brak and Kiryat Gat the night before was repeated in three more areas across Israel as Hila Sonfeld continued to be held for questioning in Jerusalem into the early hours of Monday morning.

In the city of Tiberias on the western shore of the Sea of Galilee, where around three-quarters of the town was Haredi, a full blown riot developed after clashes flared, not between Haredim and secular Jews, but between secular groups supporting different sides of the referendum question. The trouble escalated when both sides turned on the police as they attempted to intervene to quell the fighting. One rioter died, one police officer was critically injured, and dozens more people were hospitalized. Shop fronts were smashed, looted and burned; cars were overturned. Reports indicated that as many as a thousand people may have been involved in the anarchic episode.

The beautiful, ancient port town of Jaffa, adjacent to central Tel Aviv, was also the scene of violence. The trouble started when car loads of Haredim with loudspeakers entered the majority Arab area and implored the locals to vote for separation. While the initial spark that caused bitter clashes was unknown, it appeared residents had taken exception to the arguably racist content of some of the Haredi slogans and en masse surrounded the dozen or so vehicles that entered the Arab neighborhood. The situation turned violent, a 20-year-old Haredi man died from stab wounds, and eight people required hospital treatment.

Even in the city of Be'er Sheva, down on the edge of the Negev desert there were clashes, this time between Haredim and secular Israelis. In this incident the secular side was supported by a large group of Bedouin Arabs. Violence broke out in the city center, there were no fatalities, but a city long lauded for its multicultural and tolerant atmosphere, a city that since 2025 had been the administrative center of operations for the Israeli army (following its departure from the Kirya building in central Tel Aviv), was transformed into a battleground. It took hundreds of police a number of hours to quell the violence.

Israel had seen nothing like this in its 100-year history. There were just three days to go to the referendum.

***

The investigation into the murder of Rabbi Zvi Tenenbaum was leaking like a sieve. Highly emotive media reports quoting unnamed sources were contributing to a febrile atmosphere of claim and counterclaim from both sides of the referendum debate.

These days there was no such thing as unbiased reporting. Had there ever been? Each major Israeli news outlet was privately owned, and that channel or website's reporting almost always reflected the political viewpoint of the owner. Like most people, Israelis preferred reading what they wanted to read, and hearing what they wanted to hear. Instead of offering pause for thought with a different viewpoint, the media of 2048, as had been the case for decades in so many parts of the world, only served to further harden entrenched views and political trains of thought.

This trend was epitomized by sensationalist headlines backed up by lurid claims containing few, if any hard facts. They only served to add fuel to the already heavily fanned flames:

"Rabbi's sister, wife of Hofshi Party aid, arrested" was one of the less sensationalist headlines. She hadn't been arrested; she was being questioned. "PM said he "wants rid of Tenenbaum" claimed one leading Israeli news website. A leading TV news outlet opposed to separation trumpeted in a less-than-subtle hint Shwartz may have been involved: "Ex-Mossad head Shwartz dined Friday with suspected murderer." "Did Chief Rabbi get his revenge?" asked one vehemently secular outlet. "Rabbi's ex-Haredi sister questioned for murder" reported a pro-separation website.

These headlines were of no interest to Solomon Rada; he treated them with the contempt they deserved. They were merely irritating. But the widely read Ma'ariv website, one of the few news sources that was still broadly respected, carried a story that made the investigator's blood boil: "DNA links Sonfeld to Tenenbaum murder." No matter how hard Chief Inspector Carmel had apparently been trying to get on top of the situation, the leak had most certainly not been plugged.

***

1:00 A.M., Jerusalem police HQ, Monday May 11, 2048

"Are you going to charge her?" Carmel asked Rada as they sat in his office one floor above the interrogation rooms. "You've got the DNA, you can place her close to the scene of the disappearance at exactly the right time, she's trotted out a pack of lies, and ... well, she has a number of possible motives."

"You think so? What motives?"

"What motives? Well, her husband and his party are vehemently opposed to the late rabbi's stance on the referendum question. Tenenbaum was single-handedly turning this referendum around. It doesn't take a great leap to imagine the separation side was getting jumpy and felt the greater national interest would be served if Tenenbaum was silenced."

"You really believe that?" Rada sounded incredulous. "We don't have any evidence to back up what you've just said."

"Why then did she go to such great lengths to avoid detection? There is clear premeditation in whatever she was doing. And why has she lied, each and every step of the way throughout your questioning?"

Rada remained unmoved.

"Listen Solomon, we don't have any other suspects, do we?"

"Not at this point."

"Look, off the record, I'm really getting it in the neck from the very top. They're demanding this be taken care of as fast as possible. The country's on fire! It's a huge issue. People have died in the violence."

"First of all, we can't be certain the violence is connected to this case. Second, what you're suggesting, chief inspector - off the record, of course - is that you're being pressured by people high up the governmental or political chain who, one way or the other, might have a vested *political* interest in Hila Sonfeld being charged. You know as well as I that it's illegal for politicians to interfere in a police investigation. I'll forget you ever mentioned that, and I'll thank you not to mention it again.

"I've got to tell you, sir, I don't think she did it. She's covering something up, or maybe protecting someone, but my gut instinct tells me she's not the killer. The murder scenario just doesn't stack up."

"You really surprise me," said an exasperated Carmel. "I know there are still gaps to fill, but she must have been *involved* in this killing, at the very least."

"Look, we impounded the car and checked it out. Its onboard computer shows she disabled the GPS before she left for Jerusalem then reactivated it when she returned to Tel Aviv."

"Well for God's sake, doesn't that tell you she was trying to cover her tracks?!"

"Of course it does, but the printout also showed she'd done the same thing once every two months for the two years she's had this particular vehicle - and nobody died on any of the previous trips."

"Fine. So what. Maybe she met her brother every few months and went to great lengths not to be recognized because of his high profile, at the very least," reasoned Carmel. "After all, she's an outcast from the Haredi world. They said kaddish for her! Maybe this time they had a fight over something, and it ended badly for her little brother?"

"Maybe sir. But then there's the body. If we assume he was killed in Mea Shearim - and we've had people checking the CCTV from all points bordering the enclave and there are no sightings of him after he left his campaign office on Thursday - how did she manage to kill him, then transport the body all the way up the Jerusalem hills in a vehicle other than her own - 'cos hers never moved from its parking spot - and then get back within the maximum fifty minute time frame. It's more than half an hour to the Kisalon site even on a good day! It's impossible."

"Mmmm. She could have had an accomplice," suggested Carmel.

"That is true, and I'm working on that theory. But there's one big, stinking red herring in this whole evidence trail, isn't there?"

"Solomon, I know what you're going to say. Don't think it hadn't crossed my mind as well."

"OK. First, why on earth would she wrap the brother she had just murdered in her own coat, obviously implicating herself? And second, she wasn't even wearing the green coat when she parked the car. It's been planted to try and frame her, hasn't it?"

"That seems a reasonable conclusion," conceded Carmel, "unless her accomplice decided to use that coat for some other inexplicable reason."

Solomon got up from his chair as his boss looked fixedly at him.

"I'm going to forget we had this discussion. You gave me full charge of this investigation. Do you wish to change that in any way?"

"Of course I don't, but we need results - and fast!"

"I'm going to keep her here overnight and see if anything comes out of the woodwork - either from her, or from whoever else is involved in this."

***

At one fifteen, in the early hours of Monday morning, Rada returned to talk to Hila Sonfeld. He told her she was being held for further questioning and that she would be escorted to a cell within the police headquarters where she could rest for the remainder of the night.

He asked her to think long and hard about the answers she had given him to this point. They would meet again at 1100 when the interview would continue.

Izzi Linde headed off to find a local hotel room for the night. Hila was escorted down to a cell and left alone with her thoughts.

CHAPTER 25

9:00 A.M. , Mea Shearim, Jerusalem, Monday May 11 (three days to referendum)

The mourning period (shiva) for their son gave relatives and friends seven days to visit the Tenenbaum family home and pay their respects. Tradition dictates the family itself cannot do any serving for the guests in their home; all food was brought in by other mourners who contributed toward a number of tables that sustained the hundreds of people pouring into the modest home of Baruch and Yoheved Tenenbaum.

Zvi's widow, Nava, arrived early in the morning. She slept at home with her children but they stayed the day at their grandparents' apartment where so many people were milling around. The shiva period is difficult for any family trying to come to terms with someone's passing and subsequent burial within 24 hours, as dictated by Jewish tradition. This shiva was particularly difficult, the palpable sense of shock at the loss of Zvi Tenenbaum overwhelming all present.

The Haredi press was the only media source the family and

mourners could turn to and newspapers were circulating at the shiva house, often being superseded within hours by new editions due to the mass of new developments and information. When they read that Hila Sonfeld (nee Tenenbaum) was the prime suspect in the killing, the estranged daughter of the bereaved parents, it sent shockwaves not only through the shiva prayers, but through the whole Haredi community.

Yoheved, already struggling to come to terms with Zvi's death, fell apart at the news of her daughter's reported involvement in the killing and suffered a collapse. She was escorted by female relatives to her bed and a doctor was soon on hand to prescribe something to help lower her blood pressure which was dangerously high. Never in the best of health with a raft of chronic pre-existing conditions, the doctor instructed her daughters to keep a close eye on their mother and inform him immediately if she failed to improve soon.

Outside of her bedroom raised voices could be heard. One of the daughters went out to see what was going on and found Shmulik, Yoheved's brother, insisting he see his sister. It wasn't the done thing for a male to enter even an elderly sister's bedroom unescorted, but her two daughters saw no harm in it, knowing how close their mother and Uncle Shmulik had always been.

Big Shmulik took a seat by his sister's bed and began to cry before he could say a single word. Yoheved waved at her daughters to go out and give her and her brother some privacy

"Shmulik, Shmulik, come on," said Yoheved. "You're meant to be here to make me feel better!"

The fat butcher, the rock the family so often leaned on, chuckled through his tears. His nose was running, and he frantically rifled through his pockets searching for a handkerchief.

"It's just so terrible," he said. "It's the most awful thing. That wonderful boy. Where is God in all this?"

"I don't know," answered Yoheved quietly, "but there must be a reason. Poor Nava, and the children. Those gorgeous little kids. It's going to be so hard for them without their father. Zvi was a very good father, you know. We'll all rally round and be there for them, but what will their future be?"

"Yohi," said Shmulik, calling his older sister by the pet name he'd used since they were very small, "did you see the reports in the newspapers about the investigation?"

She nodded, her lips began to tremble. "I lost her once, and now they're going to take her from me again," she moaned. "I don't believe she did it, not Hila. She was always such a good girl, regardless of all that happened."

Shmulik didn't pick up on the inadvertent slip his traumatized sister made as she fought to hold back her tears.

"I know she didn't do it," he said. "I know she didn't kill anyone."

"You didn't condemn and curse her the way the others did all those years ago when she left. I've never forgotten that, Shmulik. Don't think I didn't notice. I saw how you behaved, and I've never forgotten it."

"You shouldn't have favorites among children, even nieces and nephews, but I always had a very soft spot for Hila. She was a delightful girl. She didn't do it, Yohi. You know she didn't do it, don't you?"

"I know," Yoheved replied. "I hope God is watching over her. She needs all the help she can get at this time. They're saying terrible things about her. Awful. As if losing Zvi isn't enough to bear. Shmulik, I don't know if I can take it, I—"

"What the hell are *you* doing in here!?"

Baruch Tenenbaum burst into the room where his wife and brother-in-law had been speaking together. Alone.

"How dare you?" he raged. "Get out! Get out! Have you no shame!"

"Baruch, she's my sister. I was concerned about her."

"Well you can show your concern in the lounge, along with the others. Now get out!"

They looked daggers at each other. Shmulik truly hated Baruch now. He'd seen him for what he was at that fateful lunchtime meeting just a few days earlier. Not uttering another word, he exchanged glances with Yoheved then stormed out of the bedroom and didn't return to the shiva, hurrying out of the front door past people taking the few steps up to the apartment. Out in the street he picked his head up, put his shoulders back, and headed away.

"You're such an unpleasant man!" said a despairing Yoheved, in a tone only marginally short of hatred. "God only knows how I've managed to put up with you for so long. He's my brother! He just came to talk to me! We're both so upset. More upset than you seem to be, you cold, unfeeling man. Our-son-is-dead!"

"Don't *ever* do that again, do you hear me? You should be ashamed of yourself," Baruch shouted at his wife, loud enough for mourners in the adjacent rooms to hear. Then he realized he'd gone too far and hurried back outside.

Painting a benign expression on his face and seemingly without a trace of shame, he emerged back in the lounge, telling the mourners, "Yoheved's feeling a little better. Thank God."

***

0930, Mea Shearim, Monday, May 11, 2048 (three days to the referendum)

Half an hour later a large crowd had gathered outside the Tenenbaum home. The street was packed. Baruch looked out from the lounge window, stunned to see so many people swarming around. He hurried down to find out what was going on.

"The chief rabbi's coming to the shiva," an excited teenage yeshiva boy told him. "They say he'll arrive here in the next few minutes."

For these Haredim from the Ashkenazi side of the Jewish divide, their chief rabbi was no less important to them than the pope to Catholics, or the US president to the American people. Hundreds more, mainly young Haredim, arrived by the minute, blocking the road down which the chief rabbi's car arrived soon after.

The black luxury car moved patiently down the street as the crowds moved aside. Chief Rabbi Bermann looked out at the mass of black and white in front of him, just a tiny portion of his followers. The Tenenbaum home had been inundated with mourners as soon as the news broke of Bermann's imminent arrival, scores of family and friends wanting to take the opportunity to get as close as they could to see the great man. Maybe he would shake their hand, or bless them? Now that would be something to cherish.

Stepping out of the rear of his vehicle, Haredi security men around him, he emerged wearing the ceremonial long kaftan-like gown, ironically not unlike that worn by the ayatollahs. The chest of his black gown, embossed with both gold and silver thread, represented an awesome sight for true believers.

Baruch greeted Chief Rabbi Bermann outside the building where Haredi press photographers pictured him offering his sincere condolences to the bereaved father. The images would soon be out there on the newspaper stands; the Haredim were the only ones nowadays still publishing an old-fashioned daily print newspaper. It was their only official window on the world.

Inside the shiva house Bermann offered his condolences to Yoheved, hauled out of her bed to receive her religious leader. The chief rabbi could see the loss written all over her face, despite her best efforts to keep her emotions under control. The couple's twelve children also met the chief rabbi, each being told quietly and with sincerity that he shared their pain. For twenty minutes he also spoke with non-family mourners, repeatedly saying how shocked he was at the loss of such an outstanding young rabbi but insisting it must be God's will.

Eventually, when the time was right, he asked if he might speak privately with Baruch, and was shown through to the kitchen from where a large group of women hurried out to leave the pair alone.

They sat opposite each other at *that* table. The cabinet with the shattered glass, directly behind the chief rabbi's head, had been fixed the morning after it was broken. Baruch paid the glazier double to ensure the glass was replaced as fast as possible.

Bermann took Baruch's hand and again told him he shared his loss. God would protect his family and help them through this difficult time, he said.

"Baruch, is there anything you feel you should tell me, or anything I can do to help you?"

"I don't think so, chief rabbi," Tenenbaum responded calmly, "but I very much appreciate your offer and the honor of you being here, in my home, at this difficult time."

"How could I not come? I can't imagine how you feel. To lose any child is the worst thing any parent can experience, but one such as Zvi (may he rest in peace) … As I told you the other day, your son and I had our differences, but I respected him. What has happened is so shocking and, at such a delicate time, is of great significance.

"I've seen the news reports stating that he failed to arrive here for your meeting. Is that exactly what happened? He just didn't show up?"

"I'm afraid so, chief rabbi. He was usually so punctual and reliable. I felt a sense of unease within fifteen minutes of him missing our appointment. I planned to discuss the issues you raised during our conversation the day before but ... God works in mysterious ways, doesn't he."

"Indeed he does," said Bermann rising to his feet. "Baruch, have you heard the reports about your late daughter?" Tenenbaum nodded. "It seems extraordinary when looking from the outside in, but given what I mentioned to you the other day, in confidence, about her flight from this community, it can be viewed somewhat differently from the inside out. As some say, "When you play with fire, you usually get burned.""

"God bless you and your family, Baruch," said Bermann, clasping Tenenbaum's right hand between both his hands. "If you need anything, remember, my door is always open."

CHAPTER 26

10:00 A.M., The Prime Minister's Office, Jerusalem, Monday May 11, 2048 (three days to the referendum)

After convening an emergency meeting an hour earlier to which the heads of Israel's national police force, the military, and the intelligence services were invited, Prime Minister Doron Gal's press office informed the media there would be an important announcement made at ten o'clock.

There were just 70 hours left until the polls opened for the separation referendum. Gal had led the fight for the No campaign and over the previous days, since the death of his co-campaigner Rabbi Zvi Tenenbaum, a battle that looked almost certain to be lost was now transformed. Victory, and with it the prospect of holding Israel together as one nation, was tantalizingly in sight.

All opinion polls indicated that the No vote was now ahead. With 52.5% required by the Yes campaign to win, Gal's side of the argument had opened up clear water. The public seemed repulsed at the death of the young rabbi who had gained so many admirers. The revelation that his sister, now a secular Jew, was in custody and being questioned about the murder, had dealt those arguing for separation a severe blow once it was revealed that the suspect's husband was a prominent figure in the Yes campaign and close to its leader, Ilana Shwartz.

Tensions had been sky-high across the nation even before Tenenbaum died. That spark lit a touch paper that contributed to five major riots and other smaller disturbances in different parts of the country in the previous 36 hours, resulting in a number of fatalities. Against this background of a breakdown in law and order, Gal spoke to the media:

"You'll all be aware of the variety of violent incidents that have taken place over the last few days. Israel is a country guided by the rule of law. At this critical time in our history, with just a couple of days left to decision day, we cannot allow the upcoming referendum to be used as a pretext for mob behavior, vandalism, and even murder.

"Acting upon the advice of a committee including the most senior figures in our military, police and intelligence services, a decision has been taken and a decree already signed declaring a temporary state of emergency that will begin immediately and remain in place until Sunday, May seventeenth. At that point, dependent on the circumstances on the ground, a similar meeting will take place between the aforementioned senior figures at which we will discuss the feasibility of lifting the state of emergency.

"All public gatherings scheduled between now and May seventeenth are canceled and are deemed illegal. It has been decided that all campaigning relating to the referendum will immediately cease, and a temporary curfew will be introduced each night from this evening until Sunday the seventeenth, effective between nine pm to five am , with the exception of referendum day, May fourteenth, when the polls close at ten pm. The curfew will not come into force on that evening until eleven pm. Police and military units will patrol the streets of all towns, cities, and villages, including in both Arab and Haredi population centers. No one will be above the law.

"The safety of the Israeli public, the protection of public property, and the rule of law and order are paramount in this decision, one not taken lightly, but one that was unanimously approved and reflects the deep concern we have at the events of the last few days. Thank you."

Gal took no questions and returned immediately inside the Prime Minister's Office.

Within seconds, utter outrage was expressed on social media. TV and internet sites suggested the unprecedented action was sure to be viewed in some quarters as only marginally less than a coup. Most commentators argued this was a cynical decision taken by the PM to stifle debate and silence the voice of those who had planned rallies the length and breadth of the country supporting the vote for separation. Ilana Shwartz and the leaders of the smaller parties who formed the alliance supporting the Yes campaign, insisted they would make an immediate legal challenge.

"Israeli democracy is under attack," Shwartz told supporters outside her party office in Tel Aviv. "If you needed any clearer example of why Doron Gal and his cohorts cannot be trusted with the future of this country it has been spelled out plain and clear in the last few moments. In seeking to remedy the issues that have blighted this nation over the last couple of days, the prime minister has metaphorically thrown the baby out with the bathwater. This is the first time in the history of the State of Israel such draconian measures have been taken.

"This decision will backfire. He might want to stifle debate and try and lock in his alleged lead in the campaign until Thursday, but the Israeli public are not fools. They can see him and his gang now in all their glory; corrupt, cynical, and having no respect for the rights of the people they purport to represent. We will respect the law. There will be no civil disobedience on our side. We will win Thursday's vote and the Yes campaign will secure the freedom for the honest, hard-working, taxpaying citizens of this country they so desperately deserve."

***

11:00A.M., Jerusalem police HQ, Monday May 11, 2048 (69 hours to the referendum)

Late the previous night, Solomon Rada promised Hila Sonfeld they would reconvene at eleven in the morning, and true to his word he entered the interview room right on the dot.

She looked tired after a night in the police cells. Ed had been going out of his mind with worry and caused a scene at the main desk of the police station, insisting he had to see his wife. His pleas bore no fruit.

Izzi Linde was close at hand as the interview reconvened.

"I hope you didn't have too tough a night? Did you manage to shower and have some breakfast?" asked Rada.

"Yes, thank you."

"Hila, you've had all night and this morning to think about our conversation. Have you anything to add to what you said to me yesterday? Anything you wish to tell me?"

"Nothing. I'd just like to go home to my husband and my boys. I haven't done anything."

"Mr. Linde, is there anything you wish to say on your client's behalf?"

"Nothing," responded Sonfeld's lawyer.

"Well, although there is much in your statement yesterday that suggests you may not have been truthful, I'm going to release you for now. You're free to go, although you will be kept under surveillance and must not leave your home address. You may not leave home until we officially inform you that you may do so. Do you understand? This doesn't mean we won't be pressing any charges in due course, by the way."

Hila was shocked at this turn of events. She'd expected to be charged.

"So I'm free to go?"

"You are. I probably don't need to tell you this, but I'm placing on the record my warning to you not to speak to any media, under any circumstances. If there is anything you need to tell me, you can contact me immediately. Understood? Finally, your husband is out front. He's been going crazy. You'll both be directed to leave via a side entrance to avoid the press who are acting like baying wolves. Head straight home."

Hila was already halfway to the door with Linde only one step behind, juggling his client files.

"She's not in the clear, Mr. Linde," said Rada, one hand on the lawyer's shoulder. "You understand that, don't you? The investigation is continuing."

Hila and Linde were escorted one way out of the interview room, and Rada went the other. A minute later he emerged onto the steps of the police station where he was mobbed by scores of reporters already fired up by the prime minister's shock announcement of a short time earlier.

"Ladies and gentlemen, I have a statement to make, but I won't be making it until everyone calms down and we have a little decorum here."

It took a few seconds, but order was quickly resumed with everyone desperate to hear the detective inspector's statement.

"Despite pleas from myself and Chief Inspector Carmel on Saturday evening - asking that reporting of this case be done responsibly and without baseless speculation or sensationalism - having fallen on deaf ears, I am keeping my side of the bargain and updating you on a development in this very sensitive case.

"Yesterday evening, Hila Sonfeld of Tel Aviv, sister of the late Rabbi Zvi Tenenbaum whose body was found on Friday morning near Kisalon in the Jerusalem hills, was brought here for questioning in relation to the death of her brother. Mrs. Sonfeld remained here overnight and after helping us with our enquiries was released without charge a short time ago."

An immediate volley of questions was fired at Rada by reporters who had expected Sonfeld to be charged with her brother's murder. Rada refused to continue until calm was restored.

"Investigation of this shocking case is continuing and progressing well. I will not be taking any questions today, but despite our frustration at the damage scurrilous reporting might have caused to our endeavors, and the role such reporting may have had in further inflaming tensions running at an all-time high between people with different views on the referendum question, I want to share a new piece of evidence with you ladies and gentlemen.

"My colleagues are moving among you now with an image of a green lady's coat that we believe is of some importance in this case. It was found, along with Rabbi Tenenbaum's body, at the Kisalon site. Publication of this image is permitted. We ask that anyone with any information about this green coat contact us immediately on ten-ten-ten. Thank you."

Without further ado, Rada turned around and walked purposefully back into the police station, refusing to respond to any of the many questions fired at him by the press pack.

***

Only minutes before the news broke that Hila Sonfeld, his niece, had been released from police custody without charge, Shmulik Glass set off in his butcher's van to get away from the stifling atmosphere of Mea Shearim. He hadn't been to the north of the country for some years.

There was a time when he, his wife, and their six children would holiday at the Sea of Galilee, a favorite getaway spot for the more successful Haredim. Here they could combine the sights and sounds of the Israeli countryside with visits to any one of a host of graves of the great rabbis buried on the shores of, or within close proximity to the fabled body of water.

Nowadays, he and Feige, his wife of more than forty years, spent their time busily working in or around his thriving butcher's business. It had been her idea to expand and open up the delicatessen side of the business. When they weren't working, they were heavily occupied in helping to look after their many grandchildren. They had little spare time but had been content with their lot and thanked God for their success.

Shmulik had seen a little more of life "on the outside" than many of his contemporaries.

Back in the early 2000s he had been among the 5% or so of young Haredim who answered the call-up to serve in the Israeli military.

He spent three years in a special Haredi unit that received much praise; he became an officer and reached the rank of lieutenant. Those three years had been among the very best in his life. It wasn't such a big deal to find time for serious prayer and observance of the Torah alongside his military duties. In fact, as one who never found solace in yeshiva study, he actually became more religious during his time in the army than he had before he received his papers.

But even before his time in the military was up the backlash against conscription had really gathered pace and the small minority who wanted to serve came under severe pressure not to answer the draft. Nowadays, no Haredim served in the Israeli military.

He had no radio in his van, of course, and carried no phone or other communication device. He was away from it all, alone with his thoughts on the two-hour drive north.

***

12:00 Noon, Mea Shearim, Jerusalem, Monday May 11, 2048

Ruth, Yoheved's eldest daughter, burst into her mother's bedroom. Yoheved had fallen back into bed the moment the chief rabbi left her home.

"Hila has been released," said Ruth excitedly.

"Oh, thank God, thank God," said her mother springing back to life.

"It seems they didn't have enough evidence to charge her. They've let her go home. The detective that was here yesterday published a picture of a lady's green coat he said was an important piece of evidence. It was found with Zvi's body. Imma (mother), it looks a bit like that old second-hand coat Hila got all those years ago."

"It might be similar, but Hila's coat is hanging in the far right-hand corner of my wardrobe, so it can't be hers. Take a look for yourself. It's the only thing of hers I managed to save from your father when he burned all her belongings. He knows it's there, but he daren't touch it."

Ruth looked in the wardrobe but couldn't find the coat.

"Don't be silly, it's there on the right side."

"I can't see it."

Yoheved sighed and dragged herself out of bed to look for herself. Back and forth, flicking through the dresses, coats and shawls. Faster and faster, back and forth, then slowing down as she moved the hangers around and it dawned on her. That nagging doubt in her mind. The suspicions she'd told herself were baseless. His unusual behavior that had set her mind racing time and again over the last few days, drilling away with the persistence of an over-zealous woodpecker. She slumped back onto the bed. Things were falling into place now.

"Ruth, I know we're not meant to have anything to do with the authorities, but things are different now. You have to help me."

"Help you? Help you with what?"

"I'll explain everything later. You must go home right now and call the detective and tell him to come here immediately. Right now. Don't tell anyone what you're doing, you understand - especially your father. Act normal. Don't let him suspect a thing. Go now and call the detective. He *must* come right now. And he must speak *only* to me, not your father. Do you understand? Only to me."

"But Imma, what's going on? Are you sure you're alright? Do you want me to call the doctor?"

Ruth was confused as crazy notions raced through her head, but she always did as her mother instructed. Then, completely out of character, Yoheved pulled her eldest daughter close and kissed her on the forehead.

"Please do this for me, Ruthie. Trust me. God bless you."

Ruth was taken aback. She couldn't remember the last time her mother kissed her or addressed her by her pet name. Making her excuses, she left the shiva prayers, hurried home, and called ten-ten-ten from her landline.

Within 15 minutes Solomon Rada and Tzahi, the detective who picked the lock on Rabbi Tenenbaum's office desk a few days earlier, arrived at the Tenenbaum house where just a few mourners were present for the shiva prayers following the earlier mayhem caused by the arrival of the chief rabbi.

Baruch Tenenbaum had heard that Hila had been released from police custody a short time before. It annoyed and concerned him in equal measure. He was standing by the lounge window when he saw the two detectives pull up outside his building but wasn't unduly concerned. He greeted them at the entrance to his apartment.

"Good afternoon, detectives. Thank you for calling by again. Can I offer you something to drink?"

"No thank you, sir. We'd like to speak to your wife please."

"My wife? Well, she's in bed. The last few days have been so hard for us all. She's in fragile health and collapsed earlier on. She's resting. I wouldn't want to disturb her."

"I'm very sorry to hear that," replied Rada, "but we need to talk to her."

Yoheved emerged from her bedroom, fully dressed. She looked frail.

"Mr. Rada, would you come through to the kitchen please," she said.

The two policemen walked into the kitchen with Yoheved right behind them. Baruch joined them at the kitchen table.

"Not him," sighed Yoheved, waving a finger in her husband's direction. Baruch was horrified. There was a look on his wife's face he'd rarely, if ever seen before. She couldn't make eye contact with him.

"After all these years, there's nothing my wife can say that can't be said with me here too," he laughed nervously.

"Mr. Tenenbaum, please would you give us some privacy and wait outside in the lounge? We'll speak to you soon."

"But—"

"Mr. Tenenbaum, the detective inspector isn't asking," Tzahi cut in, "he's telling you."

Tenenbaum got angrily to his feet and fired his chair back under the table. He looked at his wife, a withering look of anger and betrayal. The door closed behind him.

"Now, Mrs. Tenenbaum," said Rada, "I know you're not feeling too well so we'll keep this as brief as possible. We received a message from your daughter, Ruth, insisting we come here to speak with you right away. What do you have to tell us?"

"This is very hard for me. You know how things work in our community, don't you, but I had to talk to you because I think ... I think Baruch was involved in what happened to Zvi."

"Really!" Rada was genuinely surprised. Might this elderly, sickly lady who had collapsed so recently be confused?

"Explain to me why you would think such a thing," he asked in his best bedside manner voice.

"Do you have a picture of the coat that was on Zvi's body?"

Rada gestured to Tzahi who produced a picture from his inside jacket pocket. He passed it to Yoheved who raised her spectacles above her forehead and held the picture close to her eyes. She looked at it very carefully, scanning it up and down, back and forth.

"Mr. Rada" she said, dropping the picture onto the kitchen table, "the day Hila disappeared all those years ago and Baruch said kaddish for her, he took everything that belonged to the girl and burned it all. The only thing I managed to hide from him was a green coat she was very fond of - even though it was far too big for her. I've kept it ever since then in my wardrobe, something *he* never opens. It was the only keepsake of my youngest daughter.

"Just a short time ago, Ruth came to see me to tell me you have released Hila. Thank God. She hasn't done anything, I promise you. Ruth told me you'd published a photo of a green coat that was found with my Zvi in the forest, and she said it looked quite like the coat Hila wore back in the day; she hadn't known I kept the coat. I told her it couldn't be Hila's because hers was hanging in my wardrobe. She went to look - I was in bed - but she couldn't find it. So I got out of bed and looked too, but it wasn't there.

"Mr. Rada, that green coat has hung in my wardrobe since the day Hila left. I am absolutely certain it's the same coat in the picture you just showed me."

"When did you last see the coat hanging in your wardrobe, Mrs. Tenenbaum? This is really important."

"I saw it a few days ago, before ... well, you know. With all that's happened since I never paid any attention. I've been in a complete daze. It was definitely there as recently as Wednesday, at the very least. I'm sure of that. *He knew* it was in my wardrobe, but he would never dare touch it even though he hated Hila so much for what she did. I made that clear to him years ago."

"OK. That certainly is very interesting."

"I feel so conflicted telling you this. He's my husband of over fifty years, but I've lost my wonderful boy, and Hila … well, Hila …" She began to cry.

Tzahi got up and tore off a piece of kitchen roll, handing it to Yoheved who took it, with thanks.

Outside the kitchen, Baruch was pacing around. He couldn't hear what was being said but the longer they stayed in there the more he suspected there would be trouble. He grabbed his hat and left the apartment without catching the attention of the few mourners there at the time.

"There's something else though," Yoheved eventually said after stemming the flow of tears.

"What else, Mrs. Tenenbaum?" Rada asked.

"Well, when you've lived with someone as long as I have with Baruch, you get to know just about everything about them. People are creatures of habit, aren't they."

"Yes, most people are."

"When I came back on Thursday afternoon, Baruch was home. That was a bit unusual because he normally spends the whole day at the yeshiva and comes home after sunset, but he explained he'd come home before noon to meet with Zvi (may his memory be blessed), but Zvi didn't arrive for the meeting, he said. They never met during the day, so having a lunchtime meeting was unusual. They didn't have the best father-son relationship, you know. Baruch said he decided not to go back to the yeshiva because he hadn't been feeling too well. In fact, he said, he'd had some sort of dizzy spell when he was here in the kitchen, and he lost his balance and fell into the cabinet behind me.

"He said he'd broken the glass as he fell and that, amazingly, he hadn't been cut at all. OK, these things happen, it's not the end of the world."

She heaved a heavy sigh. Both Solomon and Tzahi sat quietly waiting for her to continue.

"Well, he then said he'd tidied up the glass and cleaned the kitchen thoroughly because he was concerned the grandchildren might come in and step on a fragment. Sounds plausible to you, I suppose, but it seemed very strange to me. Never has *that man* tidied anything in this kitchen, even when food has fallen on the floor, or anything else. He would leave things where they landed until I was there to deal with it.

"First, he says he's unwell, he's dizzy and has fallen, but in the next breath he says he went to great care to tidy everything up. And do you know what? I couldn't find even the tiniest fragment of glass either inside or outside of the cabinet. Also, he said he'd taken the remaining glass out from the panel so that no one could get injured from it."

"Well, that's interesting," acknowledged Rada.

"No, but I haven't finished. I looked in the bin, here under the sink, and there was no broken glass there, just a clean bin liner. So I assumed he must have taken the old trash with the broken glass outside to the street bin, something *he's never done before*. But it wasn't there, I checked … and they don't come to collect the trash on a Thursday, you see.

"But the strangest thing of all was that there was quite a strong smell of disinfectant in the kitchen. I asked him why he'd used disinfectant when he hadn't cut himself and nothing had spilled? He said he'd got confused, probably because of a concussion or something from the fall, and originally poured disinfectant before sweeping up the glass. He even joked that it had made tidying up much harder than it should have been. He said he had new respect for me now he realized how hard housework could be. Something didn't add up."

"Mrs. Tenenbaum, you understand that what you're telling me could put a different complexion on our investigation. Can I ask you straight? Do you think Baruch could possibly have killed your son, Zvi?"

A look of resignation and a gentle shaking of the head told its own story.

"I'm very sorry to say that I think he may well have done, or at least he is very much involved, especially now the green coat that has hung in my wardrobe all those years, turns up with my boy in the forest."

"It's something we're going to have to look into as a matter of urgency," said Rada.

The two detectives began to get up from the table.

"Oh, there is one other thing I didn't mention," added Yoheved. "You see the state of this kitchen? Everything's falling apart; every drawer, cupboard, the oven doesn't work properly - I've been cooking with three rings instead of five for at least nine months - and these tiles here on the floor have been broken for years. He refuses to spend any money on our house and things go years before anything is ever fixed. God help me if I were to buy something new."

"I see, but what does this have to do with what you've already told us?"

"Well look behind me. He rang around desperately and eventually found someone - he agreed to pay double the usual fee! The glass in the cabinet was replaced within an hour of that call. Look at the handle of that cutlery drawer, and at my broken floor. Now if that isn't suspicious, I don't know what is!"

"Tzahi, step outside and keep an eye on Mr. Tenenbaum please. Mrs. Tenenbaum, I'm going to have to seal off this kitchen and nothing must be touched. Please step out into the lounge with me.

Thank you very much for your help. I know this must have been very difficult for you."

"Why do I feel so bad for speaking out though? I feel as if I'm betraying him."

"Solomon, he's gone," Tzahi told his boss. "No one's seen him for the last few minutes."

"Contact HQ right now and put out a bulletin for all available units to start scouring Mea Shearim looking for him. Get them to use his ID card image. Do it now!"

This was massive. Rada sent a high security encrypted message direct to Chief Inspector Carmel: "Major development. Appears Baruch Tenenbaum killed his own son. Suspect's wife has given strong circumstantial evidence against him. Will update. Suspect on the run."

***

12.45 P.M., Arbel, Lower Galilee, May 11, 2048

As the van left the Route 6 highway north and headed east toward the Sea of Galilee on road 77 the scenery became more dramatic. You pass the HaMovil interchange, close to the stunning ruins of Tzipori, past the Arab town of Rumet Heib, the Golani Junction, and soon after that, the descent to the Sea of Galilee itself. At 215 meters below sea level, it is the second lowest point on earth, after the Dead Sea, some miles further south on the other side of Jerusalem.

Before the road drops at its steepest after entering the outskirts of the ancient town of Tiberias, Shmulik took a left turn onto a quiet country road passing through olive and avocado groves, then turned right toward Arbel. He'd been stationed not far from here during his military service 45 years earlier. He hadn't been back since. Not a great deal had changed.

Arbel is a small village sitting at the foot of the stunning Arbel Cliff, a location with a special place in the history of the Jewish people. The view is breathtaking, towering more than 700 feet over the land below with views across the Galilee, north to the Golan. On a clear day, even in May, you can see the snow-capped peak of Mount Hermon, sitting at the junction of three countries: Lebanon, Syria and Israel.

Back in the day, whenever he received a few hours off from the army, Shmulik would come to sit at the top of Arbel and gaze in wonder at the beauty of this place. He loved Arbel; he loved the Land of Israel.

Arbel had a sad place in Jewish history, like so many other locations dotted across the land. Around 38AD the Romans closed in on a community of Jews fighting against the rule of King Herod. The Jews retreated to Arbel and held out for some months, living in the caves built into the cliffs. Eventually, like the more famous Masada fortress further south, the community realized they were going to be killed by the Romans and most chose to die by their own hand, rather than be massacred at the hands of their enemy.

The van parked up and Shmulik left his black hat on the front seat. He paid his entrance fee and set off on the 10-minute walk up the stony path to the top. In his day there had been a large tree standing in splendid isolation at the summit, but it was no more. It had been struck by lightning decades earlier and crashed to the ground.

A group of religious Jewish schoolgirls all wearing pink cotton blouses and long blue skirts, were walking down as he drew closer to the top. When he got there another group, secular American and British teenage boys and girls, were being told the story of the Roman capture of Arbel just over 2000 years earlier. He sat and listened; he understood a little English.

It was a warm day. The climb was so much harder now than decades earlier, and he was perspiring; he was at least 100 lbs. heavier than when he served in the army. The aging Haredi cut a curious figure, sitting on his own a few yards behind the teenagers. As the talk ended, their guide insisted they all take a long drink of water; he didn't want anyone getting dehydrated. One boy, around 15-years-old, dressed in a baseball cap, shorts and a basketball vest, appeared next to Shmulik.

"You look like you need a drink, sir. Have some water," the boy said.

"No thank you. I'm fine, but thank you," replied Shmulik. "God bless you."

"You too," shouted the boy as he ran off to join the others walking back down the path.

Within a couple of minutes, they were out of sight. Shmulik hauled himself to his feet and ambled over to take in that view on his own; the mountains in the distance; the Sea of Galilee below to his right; the kibbutzim; the Arab villages, the olive groves. He loved this place and had dreamed of it many times since his army days. He checked again to see there was nobody around and no one was watching, then took a long, deep breath and struggled to haul his considerable bulk over the safety barrier. One more look around to check he was alone, then he glanced up to the clear blue sky and the heavens beyond, whispered a short prayer, paused for a few seconds, then simply stepped forward. He was gone.

Ten minutes later, following the discovery of a severely damaged old man's body at the foot of Arbel cliff, the police found an unlocked butcher's van in the car park. A black hat was on the front passenger seat, and underneath the hat was a hand-written letter:

My name is Shmuel (Shmulik) Glass of Mea Shearim, Jerusalem. As God is my judge, every word here is the truth. I cannot live with what I have done. My niece, Hila Sonfeld, has been wrongly accused of killing her brother, Rabbi Zvi Tenenbaum. She did not do it. She was not there when he died. I was.

Together with my brother-in-law, Baruch Tenenbaum, we met with Rabbi Zvi, Baruch's son, on Thursday lunchtime at the home of Baruch and his wife, my dear sister Yoheved. Yoheved was not home. Baruch had been personally asked by Chief Rabbi Bermann to do all he could to make Zvi stop speaking out any more in favor of the No referendum vote. Chief Rabbi Bermann had told Baruch that the Yes campaign was slipping because of Zvi's performance in the televised debate. Baruch got into a bitter argument with Zvi. They fought, and Baruch threw Zvi across the kitchen table. His head hit a glass panel in a cabinet behind the table and he died almost instantly having been impaled on a piece of the glass. It was terrible.

Shmulik went on to tell how Baruch threatened and blackmailed him into helping get rid of the body, saying he would swear that Shmulik had also been involved in the fight. Shmulik said he deeply regretted agreeing to help his brother-in-law, and that he had taken the body in his butcher's van to the Jerusalem forest where he did as instructed by Baruch, removing the hands and smashing up the dead rabbi's face in an attempt to make any subsequent identification as hard as possible. He had planned to bury his nephew, he said, but was disturbed by the sound of some walkers nearby. He panicked, left the body in some bushes, and covered it in a green coat Baruch had placed over the body before helping him put it into the van a short time earlier.

He concluded:

> *I cannot live with what I have done. I loved my nephew and should never have agreed to assist Baruch. I was weak and allowed myself to be bullied. And even though I haven't seen her since she left our community, I still love Hila and can't bear the thought of her being wrongly convicted of something she didn't do. Baruch Tenenbaum killed his son, not Hila.*
>
> *May Feige, my children, and my grandchildren forgive me. And may God forgive me.*
>
> *Shmuel Glass*

CHAPTER 27

1:00 P.M., Mea Shearim, Jerusalem, May 11, 2048 (three days to the referendum)

Trying to find a specific bearded religious Jew in a black hat, wearing a black suit over a white shirt in Mea Shearim, was only marginally less difficult than trying to find the proverbial needle in a haystack.

Dozens of police flooded the area but were at a massive disadvantage to anyone living in the enclave who knew every back alley, side street, nook and cranny. This was a maze. The police knew perfectly well that the vast majority of residents of the Haredi district not only distrusted and disliked them, but many had long ago been ordered by their spiritual leaders never to help either the security forces or the police services under any circumstances. Haredi loyalty was to their own people and to their leadership, not to civilian authorities who they were constantly warned were hell bent on doing all they could to undermine their ultra-religious lifestyle.

Baruch Tenenbaum had well and truly disappeared. Nobody had seen him. He'd vanished into thin air.

Out on the streets of Mea Shearim, Rada's phone rang.

"Solomon, just listen to this," said Guy Amichai, one of the office-based team working on the case. "We've just had a call from the head of the Tiberias police saying a Haredi guy jumped off the cliff at Arbel a short time ago."

"Well, it wasn't Baruch Tenenbaum, I can tell you that!" said Rada impatiently. "What's the big deal?"

"His name is Shmuel Glass, of Mea Shearim. He's Yoheved Tenenbaum's brother!"

"The fat butcher? What the fuck!"

"I know. And listen up, he left a hand-written, signed statement saying he saw Baruch Tenenbaum kill Zvi Tenenbaum in the kitchen of the family home last Thursday lunchtime. He says he was blackmailed by Baruch Tenenbaum into getting rid of the body. Seems he jumped because he couldn't handle what he'd done. He also said he did it because he wanted to make sure his niece wasn't wrongly charged with her brother's death. The poor guy went and jumped off the cliff more than an hour after we released her. He obviously hadn't heard we let her go!"

"I can hardly believe it. Send me Glass' statement right now. This is massive."

"I sent it a couple of minutes ago. It should already be with you. But listen, sir, Glass said that Baruch Tenenbaum got into the fight with his son after personally being asked by Chief Rabbi Bermann to do all he could to stop his son from speaking out any more against separation."

"What! Bermann deliberately set father against son?"

"That's what Glass says in his suicide note."

"Thanks Guy. I'm heading across to Bermann's office right now."

It was quicker to go on foot than return to the car and fight their way through the narrow, crowded streets that led to the Chief

Rabbi's Office. Rada and Tzahi walked briskly, their civilian clothes standing out like a sore thumb among the sea of black, white and gray - not to mention Rada's black face being such an unfamiliar sight in these parts. Young yeshiva students on their lunchtime break rushed out onto the already crowded streets; fresh faced, some with *peyot* (sidelocks), others without; some clean-shaven, others with fluffy young beards; many wore glasses; all dressed in a white shirt, black trousers and black shoes; some had wide-brimmed hats, others wore a simple black kippah (skullcap).

The detective inspector decided, in advance, to call for two cars and at least eight officers to meet him outside Bermann's office. He knew this wasn't going to be easy.

***

"Chief Rabbi, Baruch Tenenbaum is here in the waiting area insisting he speaks to you immediately," his secretary informed the leader of the Ashkenazi Haredim. "He says it's very important."

"I'm in a meeting. Tell him to wait and I'll be with him within the hour."

"He's very agitated. He's pacing around like a wild animal. He's not going to take no for an answer."

"Fine. Show him into the side office and I'll come through now to speak to him for a few moments."

Bermann excused himself from his meeting, telling his guests he'd be right back. He found Tenenbaum, as described by his secretary, in a highly agitated state.

"Thank you for seeing me, sir," Tenenbaum panted. He was slightly breathless, partly as a result of hurrying through the streets at quicker than his normal walking pace, and partly due to stress.

"Baruch, calm down. What on earth is the problem?"

"You said your door would always be open to me …"

"I did, and it is."

"Yes, well I need your help. Chief Rabbi, I believe my wife has betrayed me to the police and that they will be looking for me."

"Your wife has betrayed you about what? What on earth are you talking about? Wasn't I at your home just a few hours ago offering my condolences to your dear wife on the loss of your son? You're not making any sense."

"Chief Rabbi, I haven't been truthful with you. I must tell you what happened to Zvi. It was an accident. I didn't mean it to happen. Things just got out of hand."

"What things?"

Tenenbaum was both enraged and on the point of tears at the same time. He reached out and grabbed Bermann's hands, taking the chief rabbi completely by surprise.

"I did as you said and arranged to talk to Zvi to persuade him to stop with his campaigning against separation."

"And?"

"And we had an argument and he attacked me. I pushed him away and he fell back and hit his head on a glass panel. He was dead within moments. It was a million to one chance. He died within seconds. It was an accident. I didn't mean to kill him. I promise you; I didn't mean to kill him."

"May God help you, but the body was found out in the hills. Did you take it there?"

"No, my brother-in-law took the body and did what he could to make sure it couldn't be identified. I had to think quickly and thought if Zvi just disappeared and wouldn't be found - at least until the referendum has been done and we've separated - then at least some good would come of this tragedy. I did it to help you."

"You did it to help me? I didn't tell you to kill him! I told you to talk to him and persuade him to stay away from campaigning. I never wished any harm to come to him. Baruch, you've killed your son. There is no worse crime than for a man to kill his child!"

"But it was an accident. It all happened so fast. I was just forcing him away from me." Tenenbaum fell to his knees. "God only knows how such a thing could happen."

Bermann looked dazed. His mind was racing. Metaphorical red flags appeared before his eyes. He had to calm Tenenbaum down then decide what should be done.

"If, as you say, this was an accident then God will forgive you," he assured Tenenbaum in as calm a manner as he could muster. "I will support you and attest to your good character. I am sure your wife will do the same."

"I am not handing myself in to the police and the civilian authorities," said Tenenbaum, his eyes wide, his head shaking. He was back on his feet, frantically pacing around the room.

"They'll do all they can to convict me and to shame the community. You mustn't let that happen. Help me get away from here. I need to get out of Mea Shearim, to a safe place."

"Baruch, I can't make myself an accessory and jeopardize the office of Chief Rabbi by helping you hide from prosecution in such a serious case. I simply can't. But I will support you as much as possible ... and I'm sure you'll get plenty of support from the community too. And with God's help everything will work out if, as you say, what happened was nothing more than an extremely tragic accident. Let me—"

"You *cannot* desert me!" screamed Tenenbaum. "You cannot! You said your door would always be open and you'd help in any way you can. Well now I need your help! None of this would have happened if you hadn't brought me here a few days ago and asked me to stop Zvi campaigning against you. How can you say, 'I can't make myself an accessory.' You encouraged - never mind encouraged - you almost *begged* me to meet my son and change his mind. If you don't help me and I'm arrested, I'll make sure the police know that you put me up to it."

"I've heard enough from you," snapped Bermann. "No one comes into this office and threatens me. I'll speak out on your behalf, but you must hand yourself in and ..."

The ever-present rage, the simmering constant throughout his life that blighted his fifty-year marriage, the childhood of his fourteen offspring, and triggered the events leading to the death of his youngest son a few days earlier, spewed forth once again. This time Bermann was in the firing line.

Before the veteran chief rabbi had finished what he was saying, Tenenbaum lunged at him. Bermann had the presence of mind to throw a glass table lamp against a wall as the enraged Tenenbaum desperately grabbed his spiritual leader knocking him to the ground. The crashing noise startled those outside and within seconds Haredi security guards were on top of Tenenbaum, holding the flailing attacker down on the floor while at the same time administering blows to his head and stomach. Bermann, badly shaken and still down on the ground, seemed winded but unharmed.

Rada and Tzahi appeared at the doorway of the room right on cue to find the chief rabbi on the floor but sitting up, panting heavily while supported by two of his security people. His kippah had been knocked off his head during the melee. Tenenbaum was viciously cursing Bermann while under restraint from three more Haredi guards.

"You bastard," he screamed. "You'll rot in hell before I do. You bastard. It was all your idea!"

The backup that Rada had asked for just minutes earlier arrived at the Chief Rabbi's Office. Now there were 10 policemen and five Haredi security guards in or around the room where the assault by Tenenbaum on the chief rabbi had just taken place.

The sight of police cars in Mea Shearim was rare in itself, but to see two of them outside the office of the Haredi leader quickly drew a crowd. Some were anxious to know why they were there, but others were immediately angered at the thought of civilian police entering the Chief Rabbi's Office, given Bermann's long-standing demand that his followers avoid any contact with the authorities, especially the forces of law and order. How dare they go in there!

"Tenenbaum will be taken into custody right now," Rada told the Haredi security guards. "Hand him over to my officers please and let them take him in for questioning."

The guards didn't move. They looked toward Chief Rabbi Bermann instead.

"Yes, yes, hand him over. In this case we have to let the police take him and do what they have to do."

The three guards roughly dragged Tenenbaum to his feet and handed him over to four policemen. He was immediately hand-cuffed and read his rights.

"Take him right now," Rada told the four officers. "Get him out of here as fast as you can. It sounds like there's a crowd already gathering. Be careful."

As soon as the crowd, now numbering several hundred, saw the handcuffed Baruch Tenenbaum held by four policemen appear at the top of the steps of the Chief Rabbi's Office, cries of "Let him go!" began to ring out. The policemen rushed so fast down the steps to their car that Tenenbaum's feet hardly touched the ground. But they couldn't get him into the vehicle.

Screaming and shouting, raging with hatred toward the officers, the four were set upon by the mob who tried to free Tenenbaum from their grasp. Stones started raining down on the police, the front windshield of the car was smashed, and its front and rear lights also shattered. When an officer was felled by a blow from a stone hitting his head, one of his colleagues decided enough was enough and drew his pistol, firing three warning shots above the heads of the crowd. They backed a few yards away, halted by the noise of the weapon being fired. All this mayhem took place over a period of less than a minute.

The gunshots immediately drew Rada and the other police out to the top of the steps.

"Chief Rabbi, send your security people out there right now to restore order!" screamed Rada. "This has to stop before someone gets killed."

Bermann stayed out of sight of the crowd and appeared uncertain how to react.

"There'll be blood on your hands if they attack the police again," the detective inspector shouted toward the chief rabbi. "Order your security right now to escort the car out of the district or I'm calling in ten times more reinforcements. Do it now!"

"OK, yes. *Haverim* (friends)," said Bermann to his security detail - at least a dozen were now on hand - "keep the crowd back and make sure they're able to get safely out of Mea Shearim. Do it now - and fast."

Without question they hurried out onto the street, firmly ordering their fellow Haredim to get back and let the police accompanying Baruch Tenenbaum leave the district without any further trouble. "This is by order of the chief rabbi himself', they shouted. "Get back!"

"This is just awful', Bermann said, holding his side and shaking his head. "The man seems to have gone crazy."

"Sir, may I have a private word with you?"

"Of course, come through to my study."

They moved away from the reception area of his office, Rada telling Tzahi to keep the other four officers close to the exit, and to keep an eye on what was left of the second car. It too had taken a hammering. The crowd was continuing to build with around a thousand people blocking the street but held back by a cordon of the chief rabbi's Haredi security guards protecting the police car.

"Are you OK, sir?" asked Rada, seeing Bermann still short of breath and apparently in discomfort.

"Actually, I'm a little shaken, but no more, thank God. I'm not as young as I used to be. It could have been a lot worse if my security people hadn't reacted as fast as they did."

"Why did he attack you?"

"I really don't know," said Bermann. "He's obviously been under a great deal of stress as a result of the tragic loss of his son. Grief can do terrible things to a person."

"Why did he come to you then? You were only at his house a few hours ago. Surely, if he had something to say to you, he would have said it then?" said Rada, matching the chief rabbi in this verbal game of cat and mouse.

"OK," said Bermann with a sigh. "I can't defend this man. He came here to confess to me that his son died accidentally as a result of a fight between the two of them. He was very distressed and came to me for advice. He didn't know what to do."

"And what did you tell him, sir."

"I told him that, as you well know detective, we prefer to deal with most criminal matters within the community, but because of the loss of a life, one so high profile at that, he would have to give himself up to the police. There was no other option. That's when he lost his mind and attacked me."

"Prior to this morning, when was the last time you spoke with Baruch Tenenbaum?"

"To be honest, while I've had many dealings with his son, the late Rabbi Zvi (of blessed memory), I had never met Baruch Tenenbaum until my visit this morning to the shiva prayers at his home."

"Are you quite sure of that, sir?"

"Yes, I am."

Solomon Rada knew this was going to be very difficult. Given the very real potential for violence outside the Chief Rabbi's Office, he had to find a way to deal with this situation as sensitively as possible.

"Sir, I'm going to have to warn you that our enquiries into the killing of Rabbi Zvi Tenenbaum are developing very quickly and there are certain aspects of this unfortunate affair that require us to put a number of further questions to you."

"To me? Really?" Bermann appeared shocked at the revelation. "Obviously, you know that the prime minister has pulled that stunt in declaring a state of emergency and canceled all political rallies, gatherings and the like, but I remain incredibly busy at the moment with so little time to go until voting starts on the referendum."

"Chief Rabbi, I'm very well aware of that, and I wouldn't ask you if there weren't issues of some importance that we need you to help us with. I am also very well aware of your edict imploring your followers not to cooperate with the police. Because of the sensibilities surrounding that issue, and, I should add, around this particular case, I appreciate that asking you to come to the police headquarters raises a number of difficulties."

"Come to police headquarters? For what?"

"I also understand that should the media get to know that you are helping us with our enquiries, regardless of what we may or may not discuss, they will jump to all sorts of conclusions."

"Quite."

"So my suggestion is that, given the exceptional circumstances, we come to you at these premises to discuss the matter. We will proceed with the utmost discretion - assuming, of course, that you agree to do the same too."

"Detective, I appreciate what you're saying, but I still don't understand what it is I can tell you that has any relevance to the case?"

"That's a matter we'll discuss in due course. Do you agree to be questioned here? Under oath?"

"God is my witness. No one else," snapped Bermann. "The oath people in this country are asked to swear is - correct me if I'm wrong - a promise to tell the truth or be liable to the laws of the State of Israel."

"That is more or less correct, sir."

"Well I don't recognize the State of Israel. It has no legitimacy as far as the Haredi world is concerned, so swearing such an oath would be problematic. I'm sure you understand."

"That is a problem, but I assume swearing an oath on the Torah wouldn't create such an issue?"

"I'm not sure such a thing is possible," Bermann fired back, rising to his feet. "It may take some prolonged debate between the members of the Council of Rabbis before such an oath may or may not be undertaken. We don't have any council meetings scheduled in the near future. I'm terribly sorry."

"I don't mean to be curt sir, but either we meet here later on today, or I will have to ask you to accompany me and my officers to Jerusalem Central Police Station right away. The choice is yours."

"Detective, are you threatening me? Are you completely aware of who you are talking to? I'm the Chief Rabbi, not some wretched shoplifter or car thief. I have hundreds of thousands, even millions of followers here in Israel and just as many in the Diaspora. By Thursday evening, I believe I will most likely be the president-elect of the independent State of Judea. You cannot speak to me in such a manner."

Rada was getting angry.

"Sir, that may or may not be the case by Thursday evening, but this is not Thursday evening; it's Monday afternoon. As of now you are, whether you like it or not, a citizen of the State of Israel, and, like it or not, you are still subject to our laws. I will ask you one more time; can we reconvene here, let's say at 5 p.m., or do you prefer to accompany my officers and I to the police station right now for further questions?"

"I can't wait to be rid of the likes of you, detective. You make my stomach turn. I'll receive you back here at 5 p.m. You may leave."

"Thank you, sir. And for the record, it's Detective Inspector Rada, not plain detective. We'll continue this conversation later. If, by any chance, you happen not to be here when I return, a warrant for your arrest will be issued without any delay. I don't think that would do your electoral prospects a power of good, would it? I'll see myself out."

CHAPTER 28

Solomon Rada was exhausted. The pressure to tie up the investigation as fast as possible, combined with the non-stop press coverage and the knowledge that the case could have a major impact on the way people might vote in the referendum in a few days' time was taking its toll on him. Back at the police station Tzahi made him a cup of very strong Turkish coffee.

Baruch Tenenbaum was in custody in the cells in the basement. In fact, he'd been given the same cell in which his estranged daughter had spent the night just a matter of hours earlier. Rada jotted down a few thoughts while sipping his coffee, or "botz" as it was generally known in Israel. "Botz' is the Hebrew word for mud, something the thick and pungent Turkish coffee closely resembles.

He was fairly sure that Tenenbaum had killed his own son. Would he be charged with murder? Maybe, but it would likely come down to manslaughter as it would be very hard to prove premeditation. His lawyer would probably argue "diminished responsibility." The combination of the testimony from Yoheved, as well as the suicide note from Shmulik Glass strongly supported the case against Baruch Tenenbaum, but they needed a piece of physical evidence to directly link him to the killing. The forensic people were at the

Tenenbaum home at that very moment. Rada hoped they would come up with something.

He still had a nagging doubt about Hila. She was up to something and had repeatedly lied during questioning. Given that he was fairly sure her father was responsible for Zvi's death - and the relationship between father and daughter was apparently non-existent - the likelihood of her having any role in the death of her brother was slim. He was sure she was trying to protect someone. The question was who? It was a puzzle.

The telephone message from Reverend Larry Turner was a surprise. His public persona was of an affable, cultured man, but his message had been unpleasant, menacing, and suggested a genuine hatred of Zvi Tenenbaum. Wasn't it so often the case that the best of friends can so easily turn into the best of enemies? Maybe he'd also incited Baruch Tenenbaum to do what he did? Maybe, but unlikely.

But Tenenbaum had screamed at Bermann, "It's all your fault" when he was pinned down by the Haredi security guards at the Chief Rabbi's Office an hour earlier. Rada clearly heard him blame Bermann; there was no mistake about it. Tallying that with Shmuel Glass' suicide note that said, *"Baruch had been personally asked by Chief Rabbi Bermann to do all he could to make Zvi stop speaking out any more in favor of the No vote.",* there was no doubt Bermann had lied when they had spoken in his office just a short time ago. He too was hiding something.

Ilana Shwartz's aggressive tweet was another strand that would have to be looked into, if nothing more because it may have contributed toward inciting the violence that took place a few hours later after Zvi Tenenbaum's death had been announced.

Then there was the concerning matter of the leaks to the press. They were really troubling him. If news of his upcoming questioning of the chief rabbi also leaked - which he suspected it would - he would be certain he knew where the leak was coming from.

He called home and told his wife he'd be working late; so what's new. He had no idea when the next time he'd get a proper night's sleep might be. Tzahi called his wife too and told her the same. Rada sipped the Turkish coffee down to the dregs hoping the caffeine would do its job, then received a video message from Rita to come immediately to the investigation room. There'd been a big development.

"Hi Rita. What's up?" he asked, sinking into an easy chair.

She got up and closed the door to her glassed-off section of the office.

"It's a good job you're sitting down. I've just had a call from Washington, from the CIA!"

"Don't get too excited; we've had dealings with them plenty of times before."

"Do you think I don't know that! No, this time it's the big cheese who wants to talk."

"Really! About what?"

"They wouldn't discuss it with me. They asked to speak either to you personally, or to the boss. I told them the boss was out of the office today, but I'd ask you to get back to them right away. Do you want me to call Carmel and get him in here?"

"No, not just yet. You did the right thing."

"Shall I call them back and put it through to your office? It will be a video call. Yours is the only space here with the black-out blinds."

"Perfect. Give me a minute to get my mind together."

***

3:30 P.M., Jerusalem police headquarters, Monday May 11, 2048

"OK, Rita, send the call through."

"Good luck."

The phone rang twice before it was answered, then the well-known figure of CIA Director Lorne Simmons appeared on the screen.

"Detective Inspector Rada, this is Lorne Simmons of the CIA. Thank you very much for getting back to me so soon. I appreciate you've got a lot on your plate at the moment."

"No problem sir. It's nice to meet you, although I'm puzzled to know what it is you want to discuss?"

"OK. This conversation is absolutely off-the-record, and it goes without saying is in the strictest confidence. This link is double encrypted and, at this point in time what I have to tell you is a matter for you alone."

"Excuse me sir, but I understand you also asked to speak to Chief Inspector Carmel. Don't you want me to try and bring him in on this call?"

"That won't be necessary for now. Anyway, your colleague mentioned he's out of the office and this is a matter of some urgency. Look Solomon, we understand that you'll be interviewing Chief Rabbi Bermann under caution in a short while."

"What the … How the hell do you know that? Only a couple of people here know that."

"Well, we are the CIA?" chuckled Simmons. "The thing is, we feel it is important you be made aware of something that is highly pertinent to your investigation into the Tenenbaum case."

"Well, as you seem to know just about everything going on here, you'll doubtless be aware that we are fairly certain we have the man that killed the late Rabbi Tenenbaum."

"That's as maybe. This is much bigger."

That remark took the metaphorical wind out of Rada's sails. Simmons continued.

"I'll come straight to the point. We have it on very good authority that Chief Rabbi Bermann is working for the Iranians. He and his religious foundation have been receiving massive sums of money of late from the Islamic Republic. They've reached an understanding that as and when the Yes vote win the upcoming referendum, he will rely on Iran to "defend" (Simmons signed quotation marks) his new nation after the Israeli army pull out and leave the State of Judea without any significant military force with which to protect itself. Are you with me?"

"I'm listening, sir."

"Clearly, such an arrangement is deeply concerning to us here in Washington, and I'm sure will be of a great deal more concern to folks in Israel once it becomes public knowledge. You'd have the Iranian Republican Guard breathing right down the neck of the Israeli people. It would make Iran's sponsorship and control of the Hezbollah terrorist forces in Lebanon, Syria, and even their influence in the Palestinian part of the West Bank look like child's play.

"The late Rabbi Tenenbaum," continued Simmons, "was horrified at the prospect of the deal that Bermann has cut with the help of the Neturei Karta. He was determined to fight against it. Whether that had anything to do with his unfortunate death is a matter for you to determine through your investigation."

"Indeed it is."

"It is our view here at the CIA that what Chief Rabbi Bermann has done is an act of treason. From a purely selfish perspective we believe any alliance between a Haredi Jewish state and the Islamic Republic of Iran would constitute a massive danger to regional security, never mind the clear and present danger it would pose to the existence of the slimmed-down State of Israel. We thought it important for you to be aware of this given the fact you are questioning the chief rabbi in the next few hours."

"Well, Director Simmons, I'm really very grateful to you for sharing this information with me. Obviously, it's a matter of great concern. Might I ask you a few questions that spring to mind?"

"Sure, fire away."

"Evidence, sir. What evidence do you have to prove what you have just told me?"

"We received a first-hand report from a recent meeting at which the chief rabbi confirmed his intention to ally with Iran should he succeed in the referendum."

"Would I be stepping out of line sir if I suggest it might be somewhat difficult to corroborate that statement as I assume the source of such information was buried on the Mount of Olives yesterday?"

"Solomon, I'm not at liberty to divulge the source of our information. It's classified."

"And what you told me a few moments ago isn't! Well what can you give me? You see sir, let's envisage a scenario where I accuse Chief Rabbi Bermann of collusion with the Iranians. That's a massive accusation. He'd doubtless deny it and ask what evidence I have for such an outrageous claim, or whatever. This is a very powerful man with a fanatical following. Some of his devoted followers would be incensed at the suggestion that he's a traitor, while others, a large percentage of whom are anti-Zionist and don't even recognize the State of Israel, would dance in the streets at the potential for its destruction - even at the hands of Iran - and say "so what." Just a short time ago some of my officers barely escaped what could have developed into a lynch at the hands of the Haredim, outside the Chief Rabbi's Office when we arrested Tenenbaum Senior.

"If I were to drag Bermann in for questioning about his Iranian connections, or press charges, this country would probably go up in flames without Iran having to lift a finger. Many people, even the moderates, I suspect, would not believe it and would say it's a conspiracy to undermine his referendum campaign, while his fanatical followers would say he's just being pragmatic, and at least the Iranians aren't trying to make Jews less religious!"

"Solomon, I understand you have a reputation for being a smart guy. Now I know why."

"Not so sure my wife would agree with you there! Director Simmons, this is an absolute tinder box. It is by no means beyond the bounds of possibility that whichever way the referendum vote goes on Thursday night, we could find ourselves in some form of Israeli civil war on Friday morning. The losing side may go berserk. I know you'll have been briefed on the dynamics here and the possible scenarios that may ensue following the referendum decision, but I promise you, whichever way it goes, all hell could break loose."

"So what are you trying to tell me?"

"I'm just speaking off the top of my head. What you've told me is a surprise, but not something that hasn't been mooted here and there in recent times - although nobody actually believed it would happen. My gut feeling is that if I pursue Bermann at this incredibly delicate time it could cause even more damage than if I don't. I'd have to have an absolutely cast-iron case against him with unequivocal evidence such as witness statements, bank transfer trails, etcetera, and even then the fallout might prove as dangerous as having Iran, as you say, breathing down our necks."

"I see. That's a little disappointing."

"I'm sorry sir, this is my view. Israel has always been capable of defending itself from external threats, be they from Egypt, Iraq, Jordan, Syria, Iran, etcetera over the last hundred years. Many people, myself included, believe that regardless of who is right and who is wrong here - and I'm not sure it's possible to say with any degree of certainty who is right and who is wrong; it's such an enormously complicated issue - the biggest danger to the survival of Israel comes from *within* the Jewish people itself, not from any external threat. I don't want to be responsible for lighting the touch paper that sets Jew against Jew and results in us imploding. Sorry to sound so apocalyptic.

Simmons was listening intently.

"Whatever happens on Thursday, at least there is a small chance we might get out of this, one way or the other, with a relatively small amount of destruction or loss of life. My personal view is that if either side really took a step back and looked down the road at the long term consequences of them winning, they'd come to the conclusion that a compromise needs to be found without carving the country up."

"An interesting take on the situation," said Simmons. "The Judgment of Solomon, you could say, just like in the Bible. The one who loves the baby most wouldn't allow it to be cut in half. You paint quite a picture. I assume you'll be voting No?"

"I didn't say that," said Rada with a half-smile.

"Whatever, but of course we could go over your head and see if Chief Inspector Carmel shares your view."

"Of course you could. You should. But at least you're aware of my view. This might be out of order, but if it hasn't already been passed on to him, my personal view is that it would be problematic to disclose this information to Prime Minister Gal. He'd immediately make it public knowledge in order to boost his side of the campaign. It would also constitute outside interference in Israeli internal affairs, wouldn't it?"

"As we're speaking so candidly," confided Simmons, "suffice it to say we're certain your current prime minister will be charged and convicted in relation to the ongoing corruption cases that are due to brought very soon. We're quite sure of that."

"We'll see. That man's like Teflon; nothing sticks. It's always disappointing though when the highest in the land have *erred* in such fashion. I guess it's a shame you Americans have never been able to lock up *your* top dogs over the years despite all the evidence presented against them."

Simmons burst out laughing.

"You know, there aren't many people that would dare to come up with a crack like that straight to my face. People sometimes say to me, 'Look at the way things are in Israel; corruption this, corruption that. Everyone with their fingers in the cash register, the prisons overflowing with bent politicians and public servants.' I say, 'Well at least the Israelis lock 'em up. Here, people have gotten away with much worse for much longer and end up with international awards, then make a fortune on the lecture circuit instead!"

"Solomon, we'll certainly consider your views on this very troubling issue, but I must ask you to think again, very seriously, about the information I presented you. I'm grateful for your time. Anyway, next time I'm in Israel I'd like to meet you in person to discuss this further … that is assuming your doom and gloom scenario doesn't play out to the full by then."

"Me too. Thank you for the info on Bermann."

"Goodbye."

CHAPTER 29

3:30 P.M., Jerusalem, Monday May 11, 2048 (three days to the referendum)

Hila Sonfeld's release had been big news. In the court of public opinion, she'd already been tried and convicted by many. The woman who fled the Haredi community to escape a forced arranged marriage, whose brother had become a leading light in the Haredi world and led the campaign against separation, whose husband was a prominent figure in the Hofshi campaign in favor of separation, who lived in Tel Aviv and cherished her free and easy lifestyle was the obvious culprit, they said. She had to have done it.

Solomon Rada couldn't be bothered facing the press so had a statement sent out to the media as soon as he returned from the arrest of Baruch Tenenbaum and the furious scenes in Mea Shearim.

"At approximately quarter to two this afternoon there was a major development in the investigation into the death of Rabbi Zvi Tenenbaum. A man was apprehended in the Mea Shearim district of Jerusalem and has been taken into police custody where he is being held on suspicion of killing Rabbi Tenenbaum. The man can be named as seventy-year-old Baruch Tenenbaum, the late-rabbi's father. Further information will be made available in due course."

The impact of the arrest was felt almost immediately. Together with the news of the death of Shmulik Glass, the suspect's brother-in-law, rumors spread like wildfire that Baruch Tenenbaum's wife had informed the police that her husband was the probable killer. The atmosphere in Mea Shearim on the back of the scenes at the Chief Rabbi's Office shortly before could only be described as incredibly tense.

An angry crowd gathered outside the Tenenbaum home where just a few minutes earlier a forensic team had been seen leaving carrying a number of items. Inside, Yoheved and some of her children and grandchildren were trying to come to terms with the triple blow that had befallen their family. First Zvi's shocking death, then the arrest of Baruch for the killing of his son, and now the additional blow that Shmulik had committed suicide at Arbel that lunchtime.

Yoheved suffered another collapse on hearing of her brother's death and there was debate as to whether or not she should be admitted to hospital. Ruth, her eldest daughter, wanted her to go immediately, but the majority view was that they should give her time to recover at home. Her condition wasn't helped when a stone thrown from the crowd outside smashed a lounge window.

"Traitor! Traitor!" cried some, incensed that not only had she allegedly informed on her husband, but that she had done so to the police and not to the enclave's Haredi security. For some Haredim, regardless of the crime, there was never any justification for working with the Israeli authorities. All this as the family was in the midst of the seven-day mourning period for Zvi.

On the rare occasions that people went outside the Haredi world and turned to the police or social services for help it was not uncommon for the injured party to be subsequently driven out of the community. Invariably, they had reached out beyond the usual confines only after failing to receive what they perceived to be a fair hearing, or justice from the rabbinical authorities. It was forbidden for anyone to talk to them. Life would soon become unbearable. Despite being the victim who had suffered at the hands of a criminal from within their own Ultra-Orthodox world, they were the ones who ultimately would be driven away. The guilty party would be dealt with, within the community, by whatever means were deemed appropriate.

Examples of this medieval-style mob justice happened not only in Haredi communities in Israel but had been reported in other Haredi communities in other parts of the world. They were rare, but not unknown.

Inside their apartment the Tenenbaums knew such a fate may be about to befall them. It was almost impossible to comprehend. Just four days earlier they had been hugely respected due to Zvi's meteoric rise. Now, the Tenenbaum family's world had been completely turned upside down.

The grandchildren were moved to a bedroom at the rear of the apartment to protect them from hearing the cries of the mob outside - all male - and the danger of another projectile hitting the front window. They moved away just in time; another brick smashed through, sending glass flying in all directions to the accompaniment of loud cheers and whistles. The situation was on the verge of getting out of hand when Haredi security personnel suddenly appeared in force. They'd never before been known to intervene in such a situation in Mea Shearim.

Around forty men barged their way through the crowd and stood with their backs to the apartment, facing the mob. A senior figure among them bellowed out a statement from the chief rabbi, saying that any form of abuse or violence against members of the Tenenbaum family would not be tolerated. They should all leave immediately. "This is by order of Chief Rabbi Bermann," he shouted. "You must leave now. Go home!"

Such an intervention in the name of the Haredi leader, a man who years earlier deemed it illegal to offer any support or assistance to the police force or military services, was a bolt completely out of the blue. It flew in the face of everything he had spoken of so many times, for so long. A look of collective puzzlement fell across the Haredi crowd, but they did as they were told and beat a retreat, disappearing down the main street and into the alleyways that sprouted off the crowded thoroughfare both left and right.

The Tenenbaums were no less shocked by the unexpected turn of events than those who had just tried to harm them.

***

"Solomon, it's Harry."

Harry Tchernikov was head of the forensic team that had been at the Tenenbaum household.

"What you got?"

"I think it's good news. We should know in just a few minutes. He'd done a good job scrubbing the place down and we were struggling to find anything worthwhile. Then Suzie asked Yoheved a few questions - this was before the old girl had another funny turn when she heard her brother had jumped - and she told Suzie this and that, mentioning that Baruch had put disinfectant down and then swept up afterwards.

"Then, Suzie had a light bulb moment, went back into the kitchen storeroom and, lo and behold, what did we find embedded deep in the bristles of the broom, but an inch- long piece of glass with traces of blood on it. Because the broom had been moistened by him putting disinfectant on the floor, the glass had stuck in there among the bristles and he missed it. Otherwise, that guy did one hell of a job covering his tracks."

"Brilliant!" said Rada. "When do you think you'll have a DNA trace on the blood? I need it as fast as possible. I was just about to go down and talk to Baruch Tenenbaum when you called."

"Really, it shouldn't be long. We'll get the result to you as soon as we have it."

"Thanks Harry. Let's hope."

***

Baruch Tenenbaum looked a pale imitation of his normally bombastic, arrogant self, but he straightened up when Rada entered the interview room with Tzahi and Rita alongside him. Tzahi read him his rights before they went any further.

"Hello Baruch. How are you?" asked Rada.

"I've been better."

"Have you had something to drink?"

"I don't want to drink anything here. It's probably not kosher anyway."

"Everything's kosher, just as it is in all state institutions."

"That's what you say."

Rada heaved a heavy sigh.

"OK, so you killed your son," he began.

"It was an accident."

"That's what you say."

"That's the way it was. I wasn't alone. You can ask my

brother-in-law, Shmulik Glass. He was there. He saw how Zvi lunged at me, how I pushed him away, and how the glass in the cabinet broke and killed him within seconds. He doesn't like me, but one thing about Shmulik is that he's an honest guy. He'll tell you just how it was."

"As a matter of fact, we already have a signed statement from Mr. Glass, pretty much describing the circumstances of Zvi's death in those terms."

"Well there you are. It was a tragic accident, as I said. He's an honest guy."

"Mr. Glass also said that you threatened him and forced him to get rid of the body while you tidied up the kitchen. He said you blackmailed him by saying you would tell that he was also involved in the killing, if he didn't help you. It's true, isn't it? Like you said, 'he's an honest guy.'"

"Did he? Well, no comment."

"Oh, Baruch, by the way, Shmulik Glass died this lunchtime when he jumped off Arbel cliff in the Galilee. He left his account of Zvi's death in his suicide note saying he couldn't live with what he'd done."

"What! Shmulik's dead!"

"I'm afraid so, so whatever occurred in your kitchen on Thursday lunchtime, you are now the sole living suspect."

Tenenbaum's shoulders slumped. He gazed at the table and wouldn't look up. Then he started laughing, quietly to himself at first, then more audibly. Rada, Tzahi and Rita watched on in amazement.

"When we removed you from the Chief Rabbi's Office a few hours ago you accused Bermann of being involved, saying, I quote, 'You'll rot in hell before I do. You bastard. It was all your idea!'

Bermann says he had no part in what happened, only that he asked you to speak to your son and try and stop him from speaking out any more for the No campaign, didn't he? That's why you asked Zvi to meet you on Thursday, wasn't it?"

The laughter had subsided. There was no response.

"Why did you run to the Chief Rabbi's Office while myself and my colleague were speaking to your wife in the kitchen? You heard that we knew Zvi's body had been found in the green coat, didn't you? And you suspected she might have seen that it wasn't hanging in her wardrobe anymore, isn't that right? You realized she'd just put two and two together."

Rada was speaking louder and faster, then he received a phone text message: "Blood on glass was Zvi Tenenbaum's. One hundred percent."

He showed it to both Tzahi and Rita, then continued. They simultaneously raised an eyebrow.

"You suspected that your wife had put the pieces together from Thursday and figured out exactly what had happened," Rada continued. "You suspected she was telling us what she knew, and that's why you ran. And the fact that you ran to Bermann's office only serves to reinforce the likelihood that he was also involved.

"Mr. Tenenbaum, your son is dead. Your brother-in-law is dead. Your wife is unwell—"

"She should *gehen dred* (Yiddish for 'drop dead')."

"You're wishing your own wife would die? Your wife of fifty years or so, mother of your fourteen children, grandmother to your ninety-whatever it is grandchildren. You wish your wife would drop dead!"

"She's a traitor. Shmulik was a traitor. And Zvi was a traitor. Yes," said Tenenbaum, suddenly springing back to life, his chest bombastically puffed out and his chin held high, "Zvi was a traitor. He fought against establishing a Haredi state; what could be more treacherous than that? And now I know it was he who helped my dead daughter leave the community all those years ago."

"You mean Zvi arranged for Hila to get away - that's who you're talking about, isn't it? Hila. Say her name, she's your daughter. She's not dead."

"I've never spoken her name since I said kaddish for her, since she brought such shame on me and the family. She's dead."

"Just a minute, you said Zvi helped her leave Mea Shearim. How do you know that? How long have you known that?"

"I know it to be true. Bermann showed me a file he had on Zvi going back to that day. There were witnesses who saw Zvi go into a synagogue in town and speak privately to those whores who helped her get away. That's how I know Zvi was a traitor. I didn't mean to kill him, but he was a traitor, and it would appear it was God's will that he died the way he did."

"Don't you feel *any* sadness at the loss of such a son, such a highly regarded man?"

"I used to love him - until I found out he was a traitor. It appears, with God's help, he died a traitor's death."

"How can you dare bring God into this? It's perverse. This is hard to listen to, especially after your so-very-heart-rending performance at the cemetery the other day."

Tenenbaum remained unmoved.

"Let's just go back a moment. So Bermann showed you evidence that Zvi (of *blessed* memory) helped his sister leave the community. He told you Zvi's performance on the televised debate had dented the momentum behind the Yes campaign and asked you to have a fatherly chat with your son and make sure he didn't speak out anymore."

"That's more or less the size of it."

"Have you anything else to add?"

"No."

"Are you absolutely sure?"

"Just get on with it!" Tenenbaum demanded.

"OK, Baruch Tenenbaum, I am hereby charging you with the murder of your son, Rabbi Zvi Tenenbaum, at your home in Mea Shearim on Thursday May seventh, 2048. You will be remanded in custody pending trial."

"God is on my side and will protect me," grinned Tenenbaum. "Who's going to look out for you?"

"Mr. Tenenbaum, here's a little food for thought for you before I go," said a rattled Rada. "Your crime was committed in Israel, you will stand trial in Israel, regardless of the result of the referendum. And, if convicted, you will serve your time in Israel, not in any possible State of Judea."

"You mean like Moses; I'll see the Promised Land but never enter it? Then I'm in good company. As I said, God will protect me."

"If there really *is* a God, Mr. Tenenbaum, he'll surely turn his back on the likes of you."

The three detectives left the interview room and stood outside the door.

"That man's lack of remorse is absolutely chilling," said Rita, eyes wide open. "I don't think I've ever seen anything like that."

"The guy's a monster," added Tzahi. "He's a waste of good oxygen. Shame we don't have capital punishment."

"That was the second biblical simile I've had fired at me in the last fifteen minutes," said Rada blankly.

"What was the other?" asked Rita.

"You don't wanna know!"

Tenenbaum was taken down to the cells and Rada left instructions that the press be informed some 15 minutes later that he had now been charged with the murder of his son. It transpired however that they already knew. The statement was therefore reduced to no more than official confirmation.

There was a message waiting for Rada when he wearily returned to his desk. Chief Rabbi Bermann would not be available to meet as planned at 5 p.m. He had been taken to Hadassah Hospital complaining of chest pains, possibly as a consequence of being knocked to the ground a few hours earlier.

Rada sent a plain clothes officer across to the hospital to try and establish if the rabbi's condition was genuine.

CHAPTER 30

8:00 P.M., Israel, Monday May 11, 2048 (sixty hours to the referendum)

As the sun set across Israel on the evening of May 11th tanks rolled onto the streets of the major cities. Other army and police vehicles took up key positions on highways and at major traffic intersections. There were only a few minor disturbances, from those protesting the introduction of the state of emergency, something they saw as a political tool being used by the prime minister to protect the lead the No campaign had seemingly established in the previous days.

Campaigning on the streets and at rallies might have been brought to an abrupt halt but the prime minister was not in a position to shut down the media, be it through TV or social media channels. A number of polls appeared on the eight-o'clock Monday evening news broadcasts all producing similar results. They had been conducted in the previous two hours following the news of Baruch Tenenbaum being charged with the murder of his son.

There had been a swing back toward the Yes campaign. The hypotheses among the TV news pundits suggested that: a) it appeared that many of those who had been persuaded by the conspiracy theorists that Zvi Tenenbaum had been murdered by his sister, with her Hofshi Party links, or someone else determined to silence him and halt the fightback of those against separation, had now swung back the other way: and b) despite the rioting that flared across the country and cost a number of lives, Prime Minister Gal's decision to use the army as a tool to silence rallies and quell protests had seemingly backfired with many of the electorate.

The average across the three main Israeli TV news channels now suggested the Yes campaign was back at 49%, No had fallen to 45.5%, and the 'don't knows' represented 5.5%. The 52.5% winning line had once again appeared on the Yes campaign's horizon but was by no means certain to achieved.

***

"I thought you were out of the office today?" Rada said on seeing Chief Inspector Carmel putting in an unusually late shift.

"You've done a great job, Solomon. Really, well done."

"Well sir, it's been a bit of a shocker, but we got there, didn't we - despite the damage done to us by news of the investigation being leaked at every turn."

"It's problematic, I admit. But at least we got our man."

"Sir," said Rada, "I know it's you. Do you think I'm stupid?"

"What on earth are you talking about?" said Carmel.

"Look, Gal appointed you despite plenty of opposition. You're his man. You probably feel you owe him big time. That's why you put the pressure on for this to be wrapped up fast, gambling that the culprit would come from the Haredi side - more specifically, the Yes side of the Haredi campaign."

"Solomon," said Carmel, his hackles rising. "You should think very carefully about what you're saying."

"Making sure the body was taken away as soon as possible and potentially undermining the investigation. Hurrying things along. Gotta get this wrapped up fast so it can be used by Gal. Was that it? Leaking Hila Sonfeld's name, the wife of a senior Hofshi figure, an opponent of Gal. Leaking Baruch Tenenbaum's name within seconds of us concluding our questioning and charging him. Wow, you must have been pissed when it turned out Hila Sonfeld didn't do it."

"Detective Inspector Rada, you've gone too far. I'll give you one chance and one chance only to apologize. These accusations are both grossly insulting and ridiculous. What has gotten into you? If you don't apologize right now, you'll be suspended with immediate effect!"

"And if I am, the recordings of our conversations, along with my notes on the case where relevant to the two of us, will be made public."

"I don't believe you. You wouldn't record our private case discussions. That's completely unethical!"

"No more unethical than you recording every word said in this office and elsewhere around the building. I suspected you were in Gal's corner from the very start. You should be ashamed of yourself. We're meant to be impartial arbiters of the law, but maybe I'm just old fashioned. Of course, if he wins on Thursday, I suppose you'll be even more 'untouchable' than you are now - and I'll be persona non grata. I suppose Gal has promised to take you into the cabinet as a minister? Makes sense. Then again, if he doesn't win ..."

Rada was out of Carmel's office door before he finished the sentence.

***

Washington, 5:00 P.M. EST, Monday May 11, 2048

Director Lorne Simmons had hoped he could rely on Rada to come down on Chief Rabbi Bermann like a ton of bricks.

They had a friendly conversation, but despite revealing that Bermann was in the pay of the Iranians he hadn't been able to persuade Rada to tackle Bermann now, before it was too late.

He got Rada's argument about the fragility of the situation and the potential for an explosion of violence from the chief rabbi's legions of supporters if he was brought in and charged with treason. Of course, there would be consequences. But the Haredi leader had to be stopped.

The CIA knew that Bermann's agreement with the Iranians was verbal. There was no signed document; neither Bermann, nor Samtalan in Iran were foolish enough to formalize their pact at this point in time and leave any sort of incontrovertible trail. It was too risky. That would come afterwards.

Following the call with Rada, Simmons and his advisors (who had been listening in opposite their boss) understood they were left with only one option. They had to get to Bermann before the referendum result was confirmed, regardless of whether or not his Yes campaign prevailed. They couldn't risk him winning and immediately declaring a new State of Judea, with all the geo-political consequences such a development would have.

The phone rang for nearly half a minute before being answered.

"Hello, Misha."

"Oh, hello."

"Remember the scenario we mapped out some time ago relating to the man at the top?"

"Of course."

"You have to get to him - and get to him in the next forty-eight hours."

"He's in hospital at the moment, although I hear he's probably coming home in the morning. It's all very 'hush hush' though."

"Isn't he scheduled to be at the get together on Wednesday evening at the president's house?" asked Simmons.

"Yes."

"You're invited, aren't you?"

"Yes, I am."

"Well, Misha, it's got to be Wednesday evening. This hospital business is a big help. He was probably more shaken by that incident earlier today than it appeared at first glance."

"He's not in the best of health, although it's never discussed. He's been under a lot of strain of late," Misha noted.

"If he slipped away it would be just one of those things. You understand?"

"Yes, I completely understand sir."

"OK. Goodnight. And good luck."

CHAPTER 31

Israel, Tuesday May 12, 2048

Less than 48 hours to go to the referendum; it felt like a phony war.

Looking around you could easily be lulled into believing that everything in the garden was rosy. The beaches were packed with families enjoying a balmy spring day. There were masses of tourists milling around the promenade running from Tel Aviv port in the north of the city all the way to the ancient port of Jaffa in the south of the metropolis. Restaurants were doing a roaring trade, the food and craft markets in the area around Allenby St. and Shenkin St. was bustling, street cafes were buzzing, shops were busy, and the working people of central Israel were going about their daily routine.

You'd never know the nation was standing on the verge of a momentous decision.

In Israel's third city, Haifa, dominated by the stunning Baha'i Temple that overlooked the sprawling, multicultural Jewish-Arab city, there were similar levels of everyday activity. Looking down from Mount Carmel, the famous backdrop to the port city, you clearly see the white cliffs of Rosh Hanikra on the horizon marking the border with Lebanon. And just before it, on the same horizon, the historic city of Acre (known locally as Akko), at over 5000 years old one of the oldest cities on the planet. Acre also has a mixed Jewish-Arab population.

And Jerusalem, now a bastion of Ultra-Orthodox Judaism, was, as ever, thronged with tourists of all colors, creeds and denominations, pouring in through the Jaffa Gate and the other six gates of the Old City on their way through the ancient *shuks* (markets) to visit the famous sites; the Church of the Holy Sepulcher, the Via Dolorosa, the Western Wall, the subterranean City of David, the Golden Dome Mosque, the Mount of Olives, Gardens of Gethsemane, and the many other stunning locations that make the Holy City such a draw for the masses, regardless of whether or not they were religiously inclined.

All across this ancient land it appeared on the face of it to be business as usual, with the obvious exception of evening activities having been summarily curtailed due to the curfew enforced as part of the state of emergency.

***

There was a time when Jews who committed suicide were denied the dignity of burial in their community cemetery. Suicide is a sin in Judaism. Even in the Haredi world though, for the most part, that rule had changed. Shmuel ("Shmulik") Glass was given a proper burial in the usual manner, despite it being public knowledge that he had taken his own life when jumping from the cliff at Arbel.

His wife, children, and grandchildren prayed for him and paid their respects to a man who had been a central figure in the community, and a popular one too. The members of the extended

Tenenbaum family, in the midst of their own shiva prayers for Zvi, also attended. There was genuine sorrow expressed across the Haredi community at the loss of a good man who, it appeared, had been bullied into doing something so out of character it drove him to a place in his soul where he couldn't live any longer with what he had done.

***

Hila Sonfeld was still in shock at the events of the previous few days. She'd been overwhelmed with emotion when learning that her father had been charged with killing her brother, and that her uncle had taken his own life. She was in torment at not being able to be there to support Yoheved, even though she knew her siblings would do all they could to help their mother and stand by her.

The press frenzy that accompanied Hila's police questioning in Jerusalem and the sordid headlines that prompted every Israeli to have an opinion as to whether she had or hadn't been involved in her brother's killing had died down as fast as it had blown up. The story had moved on. She was yesterday's news - and grateful for it.

Ed had resolutely stuck by her and never doubted her innocence, but they had both been playing the blame game since her return home. She was still furious with him for telling Ilana Shwartz of her Haredi background, and she was livid with Shwartz for publishing that tweet. Schwartz had betrayed her confidence after promising not to make her relationship to Zvi Tenenbaum public. She was happy that Shwartz's treachery backfired spectacularly, and she let Ed know she was pleased Shwartz had been publicly humiliated.

For his part, Ed was angry at having been deceived. His anger hadn't dissipated as Hila refused to explain why she had been secretly visiting Jerusalem, dressing up as a Haredi woman and going behind his back for so long. There was a frosty atmosphere in the Sonfeld household, not helped by Ed's loyalty to Shwartz, despite his boss having been the cause of such trouble between Ed and his wife.

Sivan, Hila's best friend, had been a rock. Among her many good friends in Tel Aviv, Sivan was the only one who truly understood what she had been going through over the previous few days. With Ed back working almost round the clock at Hofshi Party headquarters, Sivan, herself a mother of three, had insisted on coming to stay at Hila's home to keep her company. The two ex-Haredi women who both embraced and appreciated their current existence in such a different world, had long ago become like sisters for one another.

***

Solomon Rada hoped to speak with Chief Rabbi Bermann that morning but had again been told his intended interviewee was not well enough to receive anyone or answer questions. He'd agreed to speak to Bermann "at the first reasonable opportunity."

He told his wife, Oksana, she should take the day off work. She hadn't taken much persuading. They drove forty minutes north from Tel Aviv to the ancient port of Caesarea to have lunch together at a well-known fish restaurant. It was mid-week and he hadn't booked, but initially, when they asked for a table, they were told the restaurant was full. Then the manager recognized Rada and hurried over. He said he'd find a table especially for them, and within a couple of minutes a table for two was found overlooking the crystal-clear blue waters.

Oksana was uncomfortable with people staring at them, but

when the food came, she was sufficiently distracted to enjoy this rare recent opportunity to spend time with her husband. Throughout the meal people came up to chat and shake hands with the detective. He was genuinely taken aback by their reaction. His face had been all over the TV and social media throughout the previous days.

When he asked for the bill the manager came to sit down with them at their table and told Rada the meal was on the house. The detective inspector was flattered, but insisted on paying, eventually getting his way. Not to come off second best, the manager presented Oksana with a good bottle of wine to "take home and enjoy."

***

The clock ticked on through Tuesday into Wednesday. Under Israeli law the publishing of opinion polls was not allowed in the 48 hours prior to any national vote. The media continued with their speculation, and the talking heads did what they do best; talk - a lot.

By sunset on Wednesday, the eve of the referendum, with the security forces once again rolling out onto the streets and highways across the nation, the Israeli population knew the crunch was coming. Each and every voter, more than 11 million in all, would play their part in the destiny of this tiny strip of land that has for so long held such a disproportionate influence on the hearts and minds of people across the globe.

You can ask the man in the street about issues in Benin, Columbia, Croatia, Vietnam or most other places on planet earth, and for the most part they will have little or nothing to say. But Israel ... everyone, everywhere seems to have an opinion on Israel, whether they believe themselves well informed or not. That's just the way it is.

CHAPTER 32

7:30 P.M., President's House, Jerusalem, Wednesday May 13, 2048 (just over 12 hours to the referendum)

For more than two decades tradition dictated that on the eve of an election the main protagonists would meet on neutral ground at the president's residence in the swanky Rehavia district of Jerusalem.

The position of President of Israel is essentially a symbolic role and wields little power, the exception being when tasked with asking the leader of the party polling the greatest number of votes to form a government. On the eve of Israel's first ever referendum, surely its most important and historic vote, a select group was invited to President Levi's official residence to raise a glass.

Prime Minister Doron Gal, leader of the No campaign, was in attendance and raised plenty of eyebrows by bringing the now former Commander-in-Chief of the Israeli military, General Roni Milchek, along for the evening. A clear sign (if ever there was one) that Milchek would be moving into a senior political role in the near future if the No argument prevailed.

Ilana Shwartz, Gal's main secular political rival and leader of the opposing Yes referendum campaign was there, of course, as too was Chief Rabbi Bermann, leader of Israel's Ashkenazi Haredi community. He looked pale and less robust than usual given the events of the previous days but was not going to miss the gathering under any circumstances. The ancient Chief Rabbi Benchimol, leader of Israel's Sephardic Haredi community was there too, as was the respected diplomat Hamudi Halabi, on behalf of Israel's Druze community.

Yusuf Karaman, a senior Arab figure and former politician, represented the nation's significant Arab minority. Rabbi Nusbaum, mentor of Rabbi Zvi Tenenbaum, was invited along as a tribute to his late prodigy, while the guest of honor was none other than Reverend Larry Turner, former US presidential candidate, philanthropist, and respected friend of all at the gathering, who had flown in from America especially for the referendum.

The ten-strong party posed for official photos and joked with one another in front of the cameras before the president stepped forward to say a few words.

"Israel is at a crossroads," said Levi. "The world is changing at an unimaginable pace and Israel is not immune to those changes. We are a unique nation, like no other on earth. No better, no worse than anyone else, but we are unique as the only majority Jewish country in the world. Tomorrow, the Israeli people will decide if there should now be two majority Jewish nations, instead of one, representing different bodies of thought within the Jewish world.

"It is the duty of every citizen to weigh very carefully the pros and cons of both the Yes and the No options. Once made, this decision cannot be undone. The last week has been a difficult time for our people, but I want to thank all those involved on both sides of the debate for their respective contributions. Tomorrow, at 8 a.m., the polling booths will open through until 10 in the evening. I pray for a peaceful day, and for the people of Israel to make a decision that is best for us all."

The leaders were invited by President Levi's chief-of-staff to make their way through for a private reception starting with a glass of wine to bless the success of the next day's historic events.

Away from the cameras there was plenty of tension. Doron Gal was reluctant to engage Ilana Shwartz in any meaningful conversation. Roni Milchek proved good at chit-chat and appeared to be getting along particularly well with Larry Turner, who, as ever, was getting along just great with everyone. His enthusiastic personality helped ease the atmosphere. Rabbi Nusbaum, was in conversation with President Levi, while the two chief rabbis took to a corner of the room and sat together discussing recent events. Halabi and Karaman were also deep in conversation, in Arabic.

"I hope you gentlemen and lady won't mind me saying something before we bless the wine," said President Levi. "It would be wrong for me not to mention the absence in our midst. I met Rabbi Zvi Tenenbaum a number of times and liked him very much. He was a very engaging and persuasive young man. The shock of his untimely death last week has reverberated across the whole nation and, as we are all aware, may have some impact on the way people vote tomorrow.

"Some of you here agreed with Rabbi Tenenbaum, and others disagreed with him. That, of course, is the nature of politics, but I am sure we all truly regret his passing which, it appears, came at the hands of his own father - something that makes his death all the more shocking. Whatever the outcome of tomorrow's referendum, I hope Rabbi Tenenbaum's memory will live on and that we can find a path to tolerance and respect for all Israelis, regardless of where they come from and what they believe."

"I must just add a few words," cut in Rabbi Nusbaum before the opportunity had passed. "Zvi's death has been a huge blow to me. Some of you may know, others may not, that my wife and I were not blessed with children. That is hard for any couple, but especially hard in the Haredi world. It did, however, allow me to completely dedicate my life to study of the Torah and Talmud and for that I am grateful, but I do not exaggerate when I say that over the last two decades or so, Zvi became like a son to my wife Haya and I.

"He had so much to live for and so much to give to our community and to the whole of Israel. It is not for us to question God's will - as I'm sure the two venerable chief rabbis will agree - but it is so hard to fathom just why he was taken from us at this time, in such a way. May his dear soul rest in peace."

Everyone nodded their agreement and Chief Rabbi Bermann, who had known Rabbi Nusbaum for so many decades, placed a steadying hand on his old friend's shoulder. They had their differences when it came to the direction the Haredi world should take, but there was a bond between them.

The wine arrived and the two chief rabbis joked with each other about who should conduct the blessing. Eventually, they willingly agreed to recite the prayer together. The ten glasses were filled, and they all wished "L'chaim" ("to life"), the traditional Jewish toast before drinking wine.

Larry Turner was very much the star of the show. He engaged in animated conversation with everyone in the room, most of whom had seen their respective organizations or charities benefit as a result of the Christian Evangelist's generosity. Only Chief Rabbi Bermann kept his distance from the former presidential candidate. Doron Gal was having a laugh and a joke with President Levi and Yusuf Karaman, while Rabbi Nusbaum and Chief Rabbi Benchimol were engaged in conversation for some time.

Bermann left to go to the bathroom, and a few moments later Larry Turner followed him in. The chief rabbi was standing by a sink, splashing water on his face when Turner saw him.

"Chief Rabbi, we haven't had the chance for a proper chat so far this evening," said Turner. "It's been a while since we spoke; actually, since I stepped down from the presidential race."

"I can't tell you how sorry I was to hear you decided to retire from politics, Larry. It came as a very big shock, in view of our previous discussions."

"Yes, well it came as quite a shock to me too, I can tell you. Let's hope the right result comes our way tomorrow anyway."

Turner thrust his hand out to Bermann who offered his right hand while still holding on to the sink with his left. He seemed unsteady. Turner stepped forward and, defying convention, gently hugged Bermann, holding him close. The chief rabbi was taken aback.

"With God's will, we will prevail, Chief Rabbi," said the reverend.

With that, Turner left the bathroom and returned to the gathering outside in the lounge.

Glancing around the room a minute or two later, Misha noticed Bermann hadn't returned from the bathroom. He toddled off unnoticed to look for him and walked in to find Bermann on his side on the hard-tiled floor. Had someone got to him first? Or was this just a 'lucky coincidence'?

"Bermann, can you hear me?" he whispered.

Bermann was breathing, but his pulse was weak, and he wasn't responding. His skin was a pale shade of gray and he was clearly in critical condition, his life very much in the balance. Misha glanced around, then took a detachable press stud from his cufflink and eased the point into the upper part of Bermann's neck, an area hidden by his bushy gray beard, before laying his head gently back onto the tiled floor. He returned the stud to the cufflink, then calmly walked back out into the lounge as if returning from a morning stroll.

It was a few minutes later that one of the staff of the president's residence entered the bathroom, saw Bermann prostate on the floor and immediately raced back to alert the guests.

"Quickly, quickly, call an ambulance! The chief rabbi has collapsed in the bathroom!"

They rushed in, led by Larry Turner and Ilana Shwartz. Shwartz checked for a pulse. There was a pulse there, but it felt very weak. Turner turned Bermann onto his side and reached into his mouth to check his tongue wasn't blocking his airway. Rabbis Nusbaum and Benchimol prayed together for Bermann to pull through. The paramedics arrived very quickly and took over, simultaneously radioing ahead to Hadassah Hospital to alert them that a high-profile patient was coming in and they should be on standby with all facilities available.

"It looks like a heart attack," one of the paramedics told President Levi and Prime Minister Gal.

"Tell the ambulance he must enter the residence only from the rear and with no lights flashing or siren wailing. That's an order," Levi instructed the paramedic. "There must be no mention of the chief rabbi's collapse to anyone in the media. And that's an order too," said Levi to all in the bathroom. "Let's hope he pulls through."

Within five minutes the ambulance arrived unnoticed at the rear of the president's residence, as instructed. It whizzed away onto the deserted streets where the curfew remained in place, so no need for flashing lights or a siren. Levi instructed his security detail to keep the press back as far as possible and that his guests' cars be brought right up to the entrance. Shaking hands briefly with them all, clearly shaken by what had just occurred, he finally shook hands with Ilana Shwartz, the last to leave.

"I'd stay away from Twitter, Mrs. Shwartz, if I were you," Levi hinted, as he escorted the leader of the opposition into her car.

***

It took no more than 10 minutes for the ambulance to arrive at Hadassah hospital, but by the time the emergency team waiting at its entrance received the chief rabbi, he was no longer breathing.

Given dispensation to break the curfew, Bermann's close family and closest advisors rushed to be with him. There was pandemonium among the ranks of his senior staff.

They worked on the holy man for more than twenty minutes. Three times he received electric shock pads to help stimulate a heartbeat. On the second occasion the monitor began to bleep but stopped again just a few moments later. At 10.48 p.m. on Wednesday 13th May, Israel's Ashkenazi Chief Rabbi, Akiva Bermann, was declared deceased.

Mrs. Bermann and the rabbi's three elder sons received the news with complete shock. Along with his chief advisors there were floods of tears. Then they gathered in a side room along with the doctor who led the ultimately losing battle to save Bermann. The chief rabbi's eldest son, Rabbi Shaul Bermann, took charge.

"No one must know yet that Abba (father) has passed away, do you understand? His legacy depends on us winning the referendum tomorrow. If news breaks that he has gone from us there will be tens, maybe hundreds of thousands who will begin mourning and will not vote. That is not what he would have wanted," he told both family and his father's senior staffers.

"Obviously, it's essential for him to be buried as soon as possible, but I suggest we agree he should be buried at midnight tomorrow, two hours after voting ends. We will make an official announcement, just a few minutes after the polling booths close tomorrow at ten pm."

"I know there are ethics involved in such circumstances," said Shaul turning to the doctor, "but you must take my father's body to a private room and we must continue as though he is still alive - until tomorrow night."

The doctor looked nonplussed by the suggestion.

"But I've already recorded his death as happening a few minutes before," he said, showing the certificate to the chief rabbi's son. Shaul snatched the certificate and tore it up. He saw that the doctor was a religious man, maybe not Haredi, but he was a believer.

"My father was very close to God, you understand. Our community demands that his life's work not be jeopardized by this minor manipulation. Please inform everyone who was in there that the chief rabbi is still alive. You understand?"

A brief statement sent out to the Haredi media at 23.15 that evening read:

> *Chief Rabbi Akiva Bermann was admitted to Hadassah Hospital earlier this evening in a serious condition following a suspected heart attack. He is continuing to receive treatment and we hope and pray for his return to good health. He reminds all Haredim and others who appreciate the golden opportunity that has been presented by the referendum to vote Yes to support separation tomorrow. There will be a further bulletin in due course.*

CHAPTER 33

Israel, May 14, 2048 (referendum day)

This was to be a historic day.

Regardless of the views of the pundits and the opinion polls, no one really knew what lay in store for the State of Israel on this momentous occasion. The only certainty was that whatever the result of the referendum it would have massive ramifications in the country and across the Jewish world.

By 1000 reports were coming in of queues at many polling stations. People seemed determined to take advantage of what had been declared a national holiday, casting their vote early then doing their best to enjoy the rest of the day.

By noon it was estimated that more than 35% of the electorate had already cast their votes, and both the Yes and No campaigns were busy trying to get a feel for the way things were going, conducting their own hour-by-hour exit polls. The queues to vote were longest in the Ultra-Orthodox and Haredi areas, with some people reportedly waiting up to four hours to cast their ballot. Even on the coastal strip and in the center of the country, from Ashkelon in the south all the way up to Acre in the north, people were reportedly standing patiently in line - a trait almost unheard of in Israel - for up to two hours to have their voice heard on the referendum issue.

By five o'clock, the pundits were reporting 67% of those eligible to vote had already visited a polling station. Across all news and media outlets there was consensus that the result was too close to call. Both campaign teams were bombarding the public with text messages and calls urging them to get out and vote, if they hadn't already done so.

At nine o'clock, with just an hour left until the polls closed, it was widely reported that the board overseeing the vote had indicated that the turnout had reached a remarkable 85.4%, and at some polling stations there were still queues. Then, in an unprecedented move, President Levi called both Prime Minister Gal and Ilana Shwartz to ask if they would agree to a one-hour extension in an attempt to give as many people as possible who wanted to vote, the opportunity to exercise their franchise and not be 'timed out'. They both agreed.

At nine fifteen, the president, in a live broadcast, confirmed that polling stations would stay open until 2300 after special dispensation had been given by Israel's electoral commission, a move endorsed by the leaders of both campaigns. When the polls eventually closed, very few, if any people had been denied the right to express their opinion on the choice to separate into two states. Final turnout was put at 91.6%, an astonishingly high figure in a democratic nation.

From ten o'clock, the original time the polls had been due to close, Israeli media along with most of the major international broadcasters, hosted panels of experts giving their views on what had happened over the previous 14 hours. There had been reports of scuffles at some polling stations and a few incidents of possible ballot stuffing, but overall, in the view of independent international observers invited to oversee the vote (as the birth of a potentially new state was at stake), the referendum was declared absolutely free and fair. The result would be announced around midnight.

In Jerusalem, Prime Minister Doron Gal and his team gathered to await the result. Privately, they were expecting to poll less than the Yes campaign but were confident the Yes campaign wouldn't achieve the 52.5% required to win. In Tel Aviv, Ilana Shwartz and her political partners were no less nervous. Hofshi pollsters had come back with figures at around 51.7%, suggesting they would win, but not by enough to achieve their goal. There was a somber atmosphere in Tel Aviv as TV predictions more or less backed up that view.

In Mea Shearim, tens of thousands of Haredim were already out on the streets, dancing and celebrating. They had been assured they would win, and by enough of a margin to have a state of their own before the night was out. How, for once, Ilana Shwartz hoped the Men in Black were right!

Due to the one-hour extension to the referendum, the family of Chief Rabbi Bermann held back the announcement of his passing, but as soon as 2300 came and went, they posted a short message:

> It is with the greatest of sorrow that we have to inform you of the death of our beloved leader, Chief Rabbi Akiva Bermann, who passed away at 22.48 this evening with his family at his side. His funeral will take place at 0100, later this evening, on the Mount of Olives.

The Haredi dancing and celebrations in anticipation of their referendum success came abruptly to a halt. The joyous atmosphere changed to one of complete grief. Thousands swarmed to the Chief Rabbi's Office and to his home. Within minutes of the announcement a sea of black and white began to make its way through Jerusalem towards the Mount of Olives as they rushed to pay their respects to their leader who, it had been reported, had passed away just 12 minutes before the polls eventually closed.

Bermann's death sent the local and international media into a frenzied panic; on one hand awaiting the referendum result with bated breath; and on the other having less than two hours to have teams in place for what would be a massively emotional funeral taking place in the middle of the night for the man that would have been the first president of Judea, if the polls favored his Yes campaign.

At eleven fifty-six in the evening President Levi emerged onto the steps of his official residence, accompanied by the head of Israel's electoral commission, and the head of the international observers. He looked stony faced and gave little away. After thanking all those who had taken part in the campaign and all the volunteers manning the polling stations around the country, he got down to the nitty gritty. More than 15 million Israelis held their breath, along with hundreds of millions more people around the globe:

"Ladies and gentlemen, we have the result of the referendum that has so dominated our politics and our thoughts in recent months. Before I deliver the result, I want to express my heartfelt condolences to the family of Chief Rabbi Akiva Bermann who we learned passed away just a short time ago here in Jerusalem. The loss of this great man, along with the loss last week of Rabbi Zvi Tenenbaum - two titans of the Haredi world who represented different sides of the referendum question - are crushing blows to that community and to Israel as a whole. May they both rest in peace."

Levi paused and took a very long, very deep breath.

"Following ratification of the referendum that took place today on the question of whether Israel should be divided into two states - one religious, one secular - the final result is as follows: In favor of separation - 52.7%, against separation - 47.3%."

It was barely possible to hear Levi announce the figure for those against as a roar erupted around him and across the country. The Yes vote had prevailed by the slimmest of margins, just 0.2% above the victory threshold.

People in their cars who voted Yes began tooting their horns. In Tel Aviv and along the coastal strip fireworks exploded into the air and they partied till dawn. In Mea Shearim their rollercoaster night of emotions suddenly turned back to joy with people seen dancing and giving thanks to God on the way to the Mount of Olives to attend Bermann's funeral.

On the other side of the coin there were many tears, some even shed in sadness by those who voted Yes. The Israel they had known all their lives was about to be carved up. They were going to lose Jerusalem. In the Haredi city of Bnei Brak, near Tel Aviv, there was dismay. Among those living in the corridor between Jerusalem and Beit Shemesh they realized their lives under a Haredi government could very well prove untenable. And across the country in all communities, Jewish, Arab, Druze, Christian, Baha'i and others, the mix of emotions was no less pungent.

The only way of life Israelis had ever known was about to come to an end. It was, for a slim but significant majority, cause for great celebrations, providing, they sincerely believed, the very real prospect of a better balanced economy, an end to religious coercion, and the hope of a society where all people contributed their fair share. But for a massive minority they feared it could prove disastrous, separating families, causing financial hardship, and exposing the whole of the nation to increased danger from foreign aggression.

The map of the Middle East was about to change again with no one knowing whether it would be for the better, or for the worse. There would now be two Jewish nations; the State of Israel, and, on its official inauguration on January 1, 2049, the new State of Judea.

CHAPTER 34

Israel, May 15, 2048

The morning after the night before. The fallout began.

At a lunchtime news conference Prime Minister Doron Gal announced his immediate retirement from frontline politics. He'd gambled his political future on successfully leading the No campaign and had come agonizingly close to foiling those who sought to split the country in two. Close wasn't good enough though.

With three major corruption cases still pending, he said he would now concentrate on clearing his name. He stepped down as Likud leader, urging his party to choose a new leader to take the party forward and help them gain a solid foothold in the soon-to-be new look State of Israel. The slimmed down version.

A snap general election in Israel would take place on June 16 in which Haredi parties would not take part. The jockeying for position between parties like Likud, Hofshi, Labor, the Greens, the Arab parties and the rest, was already beginning. Having led the Yes campaign it was all but certain that Ilana Shwartz and her Hofshi Party would be the biggest party in the new parliament and would form the next government.

Tel Aviv City Hall, on Rabin Square, would temporarily serve as the new Israeli parliament until a dedicated building was erected. No decision had been taken on where that would be so this stopgap venue was expected to be the seat of Israeli power for some years to come.

The stunning Knesset building in Jerusalem, the longtime home of Israel's parliament, would become the new parliament for the State of Judea on January 1.

On the streets of Israel - both in Tel Aviv and Jerusalem - there was calm. People were going about their everyday business, but everyone was wondering just what the future would look like. The enormity of what had occurred the previous day was only now beginning to sink in. Such a historic decision was only the first step to separation; now the logistics of such a task had to be cranked into gear.

Emergency meetings were taking place among those many communities, large and small, who were about to find themselves isolated in a nation that no longer represented their way of life. For the few remaining secular Jews of Jerusalem, so many able to trace their roots back to the great city through countless generations, there was despair. How could they leave this place, despite everything it had become?

Those living on kibbutzim and in the villages and small towns that would form part of the corridor between Jerusalem and Beit Shemesh were faced with the prospect of having to accept living in a new Haredi-governed society or selling up. But who was going to buy a farmstead, or a luxury villa and be governed by the Haredim? Many were convinced they faced financial ruin, even though the Hofshi Party had insisted there would be financial assistance for those who felt forced to leave their homes and businesses in what would become Judea, and move to a new home inside the redrawn Israeli border.

A similar dilemma faced those Haredim who were about to find themselves an unrepresented minority in the State of Israel. They weren't being forced to leave, but if they stayed they would have to serve in the army, have their social security and unemployment payments slashed; they would be surrounded by shops and restaurants that opened seven days a week; their children would be forced to learn English, mathematics and science (among other subjects so long alien to them); public transport would run through their neighborhood on Shabbat, and for them this would be intolerable.

Bnei Brak, with its half a million and more Haredi residents, would become a very different place. Most Haredim rented their homes; only a small minority worked and could afford to get on the property ladder. Sunday, May 17th, saw the start of the Haredi exodus. With Shabbat over and the start of the new working week getting underway, many Haredim from Bnei Brak and other towns and cities across Israel began to pack up their belongings and race to Jerusalem and the West Bank. As tenants, and not property owners, they had more flexibility and most understood that there was only a limited amount of rental stock available in what would become Judea.

"First come, first served" was the motto. The rush east to Jerusalem had started. But with limited housing stock and massive demand, rental prices began rocketing from day one. The task of providing homes for the influx of new citizens of Judea was going to prove a major headache for the new authorities.

On the other side of the coin, while most of the accommodation they were leaving behind in places such as Bnei Brak was dilapidated and sub-standard, those Israelis who had been struggling to find even half-decent, affordable rental accommodation in the center of Israel suddenly saw a golden opportunity. They would move in where the Haredim had moved out. They would repair and refurbish and turn Bnei Brak into a desirable place to live. After all, it was only a short commute into the center of Tel Aviv. Bnei Brak was about to become a boom town.

Haredi and non-Haredi landlords alike with properties in Bnei Brak saw unprecedented demand - and like their counterparts in what would very soon become Judea, the prices immediately began to soar.

There were so many other issues. What about those needing healthcare? Haredim who had been treated in Israeli hospitals were uncertain if plans had been put in place for their care to continue or not? And vice versa for those who had been treated in Jerusalem's hospitals but who were preparing to leave to remain part of Israel. What about schools? Were places available for children who moved from one side of the divide to the other to continue their education? There were similar concerns for those at university. Israeli students at Jerusalem's Hebrew University wondered if they would still be able to continue their degree studies.

Questions of taxation, customs, freedom of movement, and so many more also had to be addressed - and fast. There was so much to do and so little time.

Then there was the key question of the border. If Judea was to be established as a fully functioning independent nation by January 1, what sort of a border would there be between the two Jewish entities? Would it be a hard border with a wall or barriers, or a soft border, similar to that which separates Northern Ireland from the Republic of Ireland, or different states within the EU or USA?

Opinion polls held prior to the referendum suggested that most of those who voted Yes to separation wanted a physical structure to separate them from Judea, for no other reason than security. They feared Judea would struggle to manage its own security and might expose Israel to potential terrorist attack. There was much on both sides to be discussed and decided.

Israel's general election would be on June 16, but a decision on who would lead the State of Judea would be taken much sooner. The Rabbinical Council was set to vote on the appointment of a first head of state on May 31. Following the unexpected loss of Chief Rabbi Akiva Bermann there was no obvious front-runner for this pivotal role.

The jockeying for position was about to begin, but would the Haredi world come easily to a decision on their first ever president, or would this be an issue that set the different factions against each another?

CHAPTER 35

Jerusalem Central Bus Station, Sunday May 24, 2048

The previous few weeks had been the most traumatic in the life of Yoheved Tenenbaum. She'd been through so much turmoil and heartbreak, but the human spirit is not easily broken. Her life had changed beyond recognition. She'd suffered the loss of her son and her brother, and the horror of what her husband had done. Despite it all, she was still standing.

And now she was standing in line, with Ruth, her oldest daughter alongside her as they prepared to board an intercity bus to Modi'in, a half-hour ride from Jerusalem. This was not one of the gender segregated Haredi buses; this was a regular intercity public bus service. She hadn't ever been on such a mode of transportation, but now, approaching seventy years of age, she was about to turn over a new leaf.

They took their seats on the half-filled driverless vehicle and it eased out of the station and onto the main Route 1 highway heading west towards Tel Aviv. Descending the steep Jerusalem hills, then climbing again, they passed the Jewish town of Mevaserret Zion, then the Arab village of Abu Ghosh, long famous for serving what it firmly believed was the best hummus in Israel.

There had been so much building in this once mainly forested area but it was still beautiful, thought Yoheved. Eventually the bus eased off the highway and headed toward Modi'in, a town that had developed fast around the turn of the century and was now home to some 200,000 residents: some religious, some secular. It would sit inside the border of Israel once the two Jewish states came into being at the end of the year.

Pulling in at Modi'in Central, Yoheved and Ruth looked outside as they gathered themselves up at the end of their brief journey. Out they stepped from the comfortable air-conditioning to the blazing heat of the Israeli summer. The bus pulled away, people headed off in different directions and the two Haredi women were left alone by the bus stop.

"Imma!" came a voice. Blonde hair flowing over the shoulders of her cotton summer dress, sunglasses raised on top of her head; Hila Sonfeld ran towards her mother and towards the sister she hadn't seen for more than 16 years. The three of them hugged; they were all crying. Ruth, now almost fifty years old, was shocked and thrilled at the same time with how her youngest sister looked these days. There was so much to say, but they couldn't yet find the words to say anything to each other.

Eventually, Hila led them across to the car park where her vehicle awaited. The three of them squeezed into the back seat together and away they went. It took an hour and a half for them to reach their destination during which time they had a lot of catching up to do. So many questions, so many stories. So much heartbreak to talk through as they relived the events of the past few weeks.

Ruth hadn't had a clue about Hila's secret meetings with their mother; it came as a big surprise when Yoheved decided to come clean. But in the grand scheme of things, given all that had occurred in the days before, Ruth gave her mother her blessing then asked if she too could meet her little sister.

It was much hotter in the Jezreel Valley than at the 800 meters above sea level of Jerusalem. When they stepped out of the car it was like stepping into an open oven at around 41 degrees (106 f). They were at Gilboa Prison just a few miles west of Israel's border crossing with Jordan at the Allenby Bridge. They headed to the main entrance where their bags were searched, and they had to pass through a body scanner. Then they were ushered through to a waiting area.

"Hello ladies," said Solomon Rada. "I hope you're all doing as well as can possibly be expected in the circumstances. And what a lovely sight to see the three of you together. I can't imagine the emotions you're all feeling right now. Shall we get a cup of coffee?"

They headed into a cafeteria area and took a table in the corner of the room. Rada brought four cups of coffee over and a selection of biscuits. Yoheved and Ruth said a prayer together before they took either a sip of the coffee or a bite of the biscuits. Rada and Hila glanced at each other as the other two prayed.

"Detective Inspector," began Hila, "I owe you an apology for lying to you during questioning. I want to put all my cards on the table and clarify things."

"Well, I'm glad to hear that."

"I was with my mother on Thursday May seventh, in Jerusalem." Yoheved nodded in agreement. "For the last four years we've been meeting on the first Thursday of every second month in the same place, just at the edge of Mea Shearim. I couldn't tell you as I feared that if it became public knowledge then - given the way someone like me is viewed within the Haredi community after running away

- it could have made my mother's life unbearable. She had so much to lose if anybody knew."

"I see. And what about your late brother? I assume you also met with him on occasions?"

"Zvi, may he rest in peace, was the one who helped me leave back in 2032. He couldn't bear to see me suffering. I couldn't go through with the arranged marriage. He saw in me a person who just wasn't built to fit in with this aspect of Haredi life. He reached out to Ahutza - I don't want this to go any further, by the way; it's still an incredibly contentious issue and I don't want his memory to be soiled - and the next day I left.

"I didn't see him for ten years, although he always managed to get a message to me on my birthday."

A tear rolled down Yoheved's face as she listened to Hila, but she remained silent.

"Then six years ago he called my home and said he wanted to meet me. I was overjoyed, but I didn't tell Ed. Ed's a great guy but has very strong opinions about how my life panned out in Mea Shearim. We decided long ago to agree to differ. I didn't like keeping it from him, or later on not telling him about the meetings with my mother, but it seemed the best thing to do at the time."

"Well, I suppose I can understand that," said Rada.

"Zvi was a wonderful person. He didn't judge me. You saw in the photo you found at his office just how at ease we were with each other; we were just like kids all over again whenever we met, which was always in the Tel Aviv area when he was visiting on political business."

"Well, family relationships are almost always the most complicated, aren't they," smiled Rada. "Let's just leave it at that. Listen, to today's business. This isn't going to be easy for any of you, but I'm sure you don't need me to tell you that. He's in a dark place these days. He doesn't talk much. My suggestion is that you don't all go in together. Hila, let the other two speak to him first and we'll see how things go."

They got up from the table and followed the detective inspector out of the cafeteria to a visitors room from which a door led to a vestibule through which another room could be found. Baruch Tenenbaum was seated at a table in the center. A prison guard stood conspicuously in the corner. Yoheved was first to go in.

"Hello Baruch." There was no response. She took a seat opposite her husband. He refused to even look up and continued to stare down into his lap.

"Hello Baruch. How are they treating you?" Silence. Yoheved looked across to the guard who showed no reaction.

"You're not going to talk to me? No? Like some little schoolboy." A pause. No reaction.

"Are you ashamed to say anything to me? Fifty years, and this is all I get? Fifty years of bearing fourteen children, looking after you, despite your unpleasant behavior. Fifty years of poverty. Fifty years of fetching and carrying, cooking and cleaning? Fifty years of supporting you, even though there were so many times when I couldn't stand the sight of you. And now you've got nothing to say?"

Baruch remained silent and maintained his downward stare.

"You killed our son! Do you hear me, Baruch? You killed our beautiful son! I've lost my little boy, Nava's lost a wonderful husband, our three grandchildren have lost their father, and you just sit there and say nothing! You won't look at me?"

She slapped her husband hard across the face. He flinched but still said nothing. The guard intervened and told Yoheved she would have to leave if she laid another finger on him.

"How could you?" she continued. "That boy did so much good for us, for our world. But you killed him! You bastard! You killed our boy and you say nothing!"

Yoheved was shaking with anger and anguish in equal measures.

"He was a traitor." Baruch suddenly broke his silence.

"Pardon me. What did you just say?"

"He was a traitor. I didn't plan to kill him; it just happened. He deserved to die. It's God's will."

"God's will! You sick, depraved creature. Don't you dare bring God into this. Don't use Him as a convenient excuse to try and purge yourself of the guilt that you'll have to bear for the rest of your miserable life. You coward! You don't even have the guts to take responsibility for your own actions. You have to sully God's name by bringing Him into it. You are wicked! Evil!"

"He was a traitor, Shmulik was a traitor ..." he raised his head and looked his wife straight in the eye for the first time, "and you, Yoheved, my dear, you are a traitor. You turned me in to the police. Your own husband. *You* are the evil one. You will rot in hell. I hope they drive you out of Mea Shearim and you rot in hell."

"Only one of us will be rotting, Baruch, and that is you. What you did has shocked everyone in the community. You know Bermann sent the Haredi security to protect me and the family when the mob came? Did you know that? No? No one has come near our home, no one has threatened us, they continued coming to shiva for Zvi. Even now that Bermann has gone there has been no trouble. Decent people know right from wrong. Unlike you. You're a monster!"

Ruth came into the room. Baruch's demeanor changed. He looked at her, his firstborn, seeming to cling on to some faint hope that she might be more forgiving.

"Abba, I've come here to pass on a message from myself and my brothers and sisters," said Ruth with barely a hint of emotion. "You made our mother's life a misery and treated her so badly for so long. For what you did to me and the others as children, your time in this place should be punishment for that alone. But what you did to Zvi, and Uncle Shmulik, for that matter, can never be forgiven."

Tears flowed down Ruth's face as she continued.

"We will not come to see you. We don't want to hear from you. You have shamed us beyond belief, and you have shamed God with what you have done."

In her summer, sleeveless dress, Hila entered the room.

"Ah, the whore!" exclaimed Baruch. "What an unpleasant surprise. How *dare* you come to see me! You whore! As far as I'm concerned, you're dead, and have been for 16 years. Look at you! Look at the way you are dressed. Are you looking for business?"

Hila said nothing. She took the hand of both her mother and her sister, stood between the pair of them, then turned around and led them out of the room.

CHAPTER 36

Jerusalem, May 31, 2048

Forty-nine of the most senior Haredi rabbis in Israel, representing both the Ashkenazi and Sephardic traditions were gathered in the capital to determine who would be their new leader and first president of the new State of Judea.

Each and every one of them felt a huge burden of responsibility. It was essential to choose the right man. They had to choose someone who could lead the Haredi world through what was sure to be a difficult period as they established the new nation, accommodating the massive influx of so many Haredim who continued to pour into the Holy City and its surrounds. They faced so many challenges.

Had Chief Rabbi Bermann lived he would have been the automatic choice of the overwhelming majority on the Rabbinical Council. His sudden loss had thrown a huge spanner in the works. His powerful personality had been so dominant that his unexpected departure left a massive void that might prove difficult to fill.

Not unlike the period prior to the College of Cardinals going into conclave to decide a new pope, a host of names were being bandied around but there was no clear front-runner for President of Judea. Rabbi Mintz was a popular choice but made it clear he was reluctant to take the job. He'd never sought publicity or looked for the trappings of power, even though he led the biggest Haredi sect and was widely revered. Sephardic Chief Rabbi Benchimol was mooted as a possible stop-gap choice, but he was in his late-eighties and in poor health, and the majority Ashkenazi Haredim may not take kindly to having a president with such sweeping powers who hailed from the other major strand of Haredi thought.

Rabbi Shaul Bermann, the late chief rabbi's eldest son, was a popular choice to continue his father's legacy. At just 56 years of age he represented a new generation of rabbis, although his views were a carbon copy of those held by his father.

It hadn't been lost on the Haredi world, in fact it had been a major focus of attention in the Haredi media, that the breakdown of polling data from the referendum revealed some interesting statistics. Of most significance to the Haredim were the respective percentages for and against separation. It had been anticipated that despite Rabbi Zvi's Tenenbaum's call not to separate, he would be in a tiny majority of Haredi voters. The figures, however, showed that 76.4% of Haredim voted Yes, but some 23.6% of Haredim voted No.

Given that just about all the leading rabbis had insisted their followers vote Yes, the fact that nearly a quarter of the Haredi electorate had defied the edict showed there was no little disquiet among the ranks. This was a point being widely raised in the Haredi world.

Unlike the Catholic church, the decision to choose a new Haredi leader and first President of Judea was expected to be made within a day, but by late-afternoon and heading into the evening rumors were beginning to spread that it was proving harder than anticipated to come to a decision.

Leaks from within the Rabbinical Council indicated that at least eight candidates had initially been in the ballot and they had been whittled down to four fairly quickly after the first few votes. A simple majority of 25 and above was required to elect a new leader from among the 49 senior rabbis tasked with making the appointment.

At ten o'clock in the evening, a spokesperson for the Rabbinical Council informed the Haredi media that a final decision had not yet been reached. Given the advanced age of a number of those present it had been decided to reconvene the following morning at nine to continue their deliberations.

Back they came the following morning, but by lunchtime there was still no announcement. The breakthrough came mid-afternoon. A major press conference at which the new President of Judea would be announced was open to not only the Haredi press, but also to the Israeli and the international media.

Rabbi David Blau, a much-respected senior figure in the Haredi world, stepped out to face the cameras. Interacting with the mainstream media was a rarity for most Haredi leaders, but the appointee would have to deal with international affairs as well as matters within the new Haredi state. This was something they would have to get used to very quickly.

"After many hours of debate, and after gradually narrowing down the candidates through a series of votes," announced Rabbi Blau, "the Rabbinical Council has chosen both a President and a Vice President to lead the new State of Judea.

"First, the Vice President role has been handed to a man who hails from a great tradition of learned Haredi rabbis, and who the Rabbinical Council feels will continue to represent the path of his late-father, Chief Rabbi Akiva Bermann (may he rest in peace). We are delighted to announce that Rabbi Shaul Bermann will be the new Vice President of Judea."

This came as a bit of a surprise. Shaul Bermann had been most people's idea of the favorite to succeed his father, but it made sense that he had been awarded the vice presidency in a nod to his father's role in leading the separation campaign.

"The first ever President of Judea is a rabbi who has for decades been respected across the Haredi world. Born in New York, in the United States, in 1971, he hails from a long dynasty of revered Haredi rabbis. He emigrated to Israel with his family in the early-1980s when his family made their home in Mea Shearim.

"For many decades an acknowledged Talmudic authority, he represents the generation that helped us deliver the wonderful result of a few weeks ago. His wisdom and tolerance of all views within the many strands of Haredi thought has been cited as one of the key factors in him being chosen to lead our people into a new era. He possesses that rare combination of scholarly prowess and adherence to traditional views, allied to a deep understanding of the world outside of our Haredi community. These talents place him in a special position to lead from a platform of both spiritual strength and worldly knowledge.

"The first President of the State of Judea will be Rabbi Julius Moshe Nusbaum."

Applause broke out at the conference as Nusbaum and Bermann moved out onto the stage together. It was Rabbi Nusbaum, now President Nusbaum of Judea, who addressed the Haredi and other media.

"I thank God for the task with which he has entrusted me, and I look forward to leading the Haredi and Orthodox world to the very best of my ability. I must pay tribute to the late Chief Rabbi Akiva Bermann, *zichrono l'bracha* (of blessed memory). We were friends and colleagues for many years, coming up through the ranks together from our yeshiva days. Had he lived, he would surely be standing here now, but I am proud to have his son, Rabbi Shaul Bermann, here by my side representing a continuation of his father's legacy.

"While I was not allied to all he stood for politically, I must also pay tribute to the late Rabbi Zvi Tenenbaum, *zichrono l'bracha* (of blessed memory), whose passing just a few short weeks ago came as such a great shock to us all. He studied with me from an early age and had a great mind. He was a very fine young man. While I come from a very traditional Haredi standpoint on many issues, I also understand - and this was made clear to the whole Rabbinical Council by the Haredi voting figures at the referendum - that there is a notable minority with more progressive views on a variety of subjects. Under my leadership these views will be very seriously taken into account and have a place in the new State of Judea too.

"There is much to be done before January First. Rabbi Bermann and I have work to do, and we're going to get on with it right away:

יְבָרֶכְךָ ה' וְיִשְׁמְרֶךָּת יָאֵר ה' פָּנָיו אֵלֶיךָ וִיחֻנֶּךָּ
יִשָּׂא ה' פָּנָיו אֵלֶיךָ וְיָשֵׂם לְךָ שָׁלֹם

(May the Lord bless you and keep you; May the Lord make His face shine upon you, and be gracious to you; May the Lord lift up His countenance upon you, and give you peace").''

***

77-year-old Rabbi Julius Moshe Nusbaum, the new President of Judea, found himself suddenly thrust into the international spotlight. Not only the leader of Israel's Haredim, but also the leader of the many Haredi communities across the world, he faced a herculean task to guide his new nation through what were certain to be very choppy waters in the months and years to come.

Shown around his new office in the Knesset - the soon-to-be new Haredi parliament of Judea - Nusbaum, the rabbi who had not been blessed with any children had suddenly become the father of the Judean nation. This had never been something he yearned for, but he took consolation that it must be God's will that he was chosen to take on this task.

At his new office, calls and messages were flooding in from around the world congratulating the aged rabbi on his appointment. He took none of the calls himself, asking his secretary to thank all the leaders who got in touch, and assure them he would call in the near future to have a personal one-to-one conversation. There was one call though that he felt obliged to take.

"Rabbi Nusbaum … I mean President Nusbaum," said Daniel Shaltiel, his longtime secretary, "The President of the United States is on the line. Shall I put him through?"

"Yes please, Daniel. Thank you."

Nusbaum waited for the beep then took the call.

"President Dominguez, how kind of you to call."

"Well, I wanted to be among the first to congratulate you on your appointment on what is a historic day for the people of the new State of Judea. They could not have made a better choice. I speak on behalf of everyone in the United States when I wish you and your nation every success as you make your way as the newest member of the family of nations."

"Why, thank you very much, Mr. President. Your kind wishes are very much appreciated, and I look forward to a mutually beneficial relationship between our tiny nation of Judea, and the United States. There is much we have to discuss."

"There certainly is, Misha. I mean, of course, President Nusbaum."

THE END

Made in the USA
Middletown, DE
18 September 2020

19994910R00196